Also by Ron Schwab

The Lockes
Last Will
Medicine Wheel
Hell's Fire

The Law Wranglers
Deal with the Devil
Mouth of Hell
The Last Hunt
Summer's Child
Adam's First Wife
Escape from El Gato
The Prince of Santa Fe
Peyote Spirits

The Coyote Saga
Night of the Coyote
Return of the Coyote
Twilight of the Coyote

The Blood Hounds
The Blood Hounds
No Man's Land
Looking for Trouble
Snapp vs. Snapp

Lucky Five
Old Dogs
Day of the Dog

Lockwood

The Accidental Sheriff
Beware a Pale Horse
Trouble

Sioux Sunrise
Paint the Hills Red
Grit
Cut Nose
The Long Walk
Coldsmith
Ghost of the Guadalupe
Bushwa
Unbroken

Dismal Trail

Ron Schwab

Uplands Press

OMAHA, NEBRASKA

Uplands Press
512 S 51st Street
Omaha, NE 68106
www.uplandspress.com

Publisher's Note: This is a work of fiction. Names, characters, places, and incidents are a product of the author's imagination. Locales and public names are sometimes used for atmospheric purposes. Any resemblance to actual people, living or dead, or to businesses, companies, events, institutions, or locales is completely coincidental.

Ordering Information:
Quantity sales. Special discounts are available on quantity purchases by corporations, associations, and others. For details, contact the "Special Sales Department" at the address above.

Uplands Press / Ron Schwab -- 1st ed.
ISBN 978-1-943421-78-7

Dismal Trail

Chapter 1

ORGAN FRASER SAT in his favorite rocking chair in front of the fireplace on a late March night, listening to the rain patter against the wood shakes that sheathed the roof of his single-story limestone house. The kerosene lamp offered ample light for reading the book that lay on his lap as he fought sleep.

He had read everything of Mark Twain's and had found a copy of *Travels with a Donkey in the Cevennes*, an account of Robert Louis Stevenson's travels through the mountains of southern France. Morg always finished a book he started, but this one certainly was not going to keep him awake at night and would last a while. He might be forced to interrupt the story and read something else, maybe a dime novel, before he finished the Stevenson tale.

His eyes opened, and he leaned forward in the rocker when he heard the howling outside. It was not the wind, although it whipped so hard against the house right now that the windows shook. Coyote? Maybe, but they generally had the good sense to shelter in a storm like this one. A shiver raced down his spine. The mournful cry sounded eerily like Rambler, the treasured shepherd dog he had buried almost a month ago and still grieved. He had started a family burial plot when he laid his good friend to rest and fenced off space to hold a dozen plots, although he had no expectation that, other than himself, there would ever be other occupants. Of course, if he continued his present life, he would most likely be buzzard and coyote food before he had a chance to join Rambler. But he figured there might be another owner in the future who might claim a plot or two.

There was a faint scratching at his door now, barely discernable midst the rain, wind, and thunder. Out of habit, Morg reached for the Colt six-gun on the lamp table and lifted himself from the rocker. There were too many men standing in line to kill him, and he knew there was a price on his head. He stood, and straightened, trying to work the painful kinks from his back. He had just reached his sixtieth birthday two weeks earlier, but damned if he didn't feel ninety lately.

He limped toward the front door that was located at the end of the parlor where the kitchen began. There were no wasteful hallways in the simple home, a box-like structure with an imaginary line between parlor and kitchen and two bedrooms accessed off the parlor, only one of which was occupied these days. Before opening the door, he edged to the side of the adjacent window and pulled back the curtain just a bit. The windowsill was chest high on his six-foot frame and the openings on all the windows were no more than two feet by two feet, strategically planned for defense against Indian attacks originally but now useful for protection against other enemies.

He peered out into the darkness and saw an object resting on the front porch, huddling against the door. A dog, maybe. Racoons often investigated the porch and were not shy about scratching on the door, but they generally stayed on the move. In any case, a racoon would race away if he opened the door. Morg stepped over and unbolted the lock on the thick oak door and inched it open a bit to identify the visitor.

The dog lay there shivering and lifted its head, looking up at him with mournful eyes that stole his heart. The creature appeared to be injured and did not get to its feet. He laid his gun aside, opened the door wider, and knelt in the doorway beside the dog and reached out, wrapping his arms around its chest and upper back, and half-dragged and half-lifted the dog inside the house.

Only after he maneuvered the dog to the well-worn buffalo hide rug in front of the fireplace did he notice the blood splotches on his hands and fingers. In front of the crackling fire he had lit this wet, chilly night, he stretched the dog out. Its breathing appeared steady but somewhat labored, and it finally moved some, trying to lift its head before lowering it back to the floor.

Morg knelt beside the dog, tracing his fingers through the short, dense fur and seeking out the source of the bleeding. He found a slice between the front shoulders and the top of the neck, but it was scabbed over. He sighed. He would need to roll the dog over. He noted that the dog was female, apparently young because her teats showed no sign of having ever been nursed. A medium-sized dog, he estimated she might not weigh quite forty pounds, especially in her sickly condition.

He recognized her as what some folks called an Australian cattle dog, said to be a mix of collie and wild Australian dingo dogs. It was not a recognized breed as Morg understood it. Generations of breeding the mixed animals would be required for that if it ever happened. This dog was of the red variety, brown and white hair closely intermingled to give her a light reddish look and appearance that looked more like the dingo ancestor. There was a 'blue' version of the cattle dog coated with black, white and brown hair, sometimes coating the dog with patches to give it a different, unique hue, although the origins of the two dogs were similar.

"Well, Dingo," he said, "I've got to move you." He rolled the dog over, feeling his lower back muscles stretch, telling him he would have a hell of a time getting off the floor after a bit.

The dog whimpered, but did not resist, probably too weak to do so. Instantly, he spotted the blood source high in the hip. A bullet wound. Morg knew the signs. He had caused a good many and taken more than his share over the years. There was a story behind each scar on his body. He traced his fingers over the swollen flesh about the slug's entry and could feel the object under skin. It was not a deep wound, and the slug was not imbedded in bone.

There were several men who held themselves out as veterinary surgeons in North Platte, but mostly they dealt with cattle, hogs, and sheep. One was quick to put a cat or dog out of its misery with a bullet in the head. Morg did not hesitate to assign himself the task. He had handled dozens of such wounds on humans over a lifetime. If Dingo did not resist much, he could remove it and maybe get in a few stitches to help the healing, leaving a gap for drainage.

He grabbed his rocking chair to leverage himself to his feet and started to get up. The chair toppled over as he was getting to his feet, and he fell to the floor. "Clumsy son-of-a-bitch," he scolded himself, rubbing the elbow that had struck the floor. Next time, he used the lamp table and made it without mishap. He was fine when on the move, he reminded himself. His body just was not made for sitting. He went into the kitchen area and put a small pot of hot water on the woodstove to boil. Then he retrieved a few clean rags, his sewing kit, a sharp kitchen knife, and tweezers. He hoped the knife would not be needed.

When the water was ready, he took his surgical supplies back to the parlor, this time he let himself down carefully to the floor and tended to his mission. He worked gently as he could, cleaning the wound and probing with the tweezers to latch onto the slug and remove it, glad that the knife was unnecessary. The dog he was now calling "Dingo" did not resist, and he suspected the poor thing was too weak after the apparent loss of so much blood and likely being near starvation, according to the ribs protruding from her side.

When he had finished the stitching and put his crude instruments away, he pumped a panful of water from the little pump at the kitchen sink. He also put some meat scraps from supper that he was going to dispose of anyhow into another pan and took both to the dog. But she was just sleeping now. He placed them near enough that she could reach the pans if she got to her feet.

Morg went into his bedroom and yanked several blankets and a pillow off the bed, dropped them on the floor next to the dog, near enough that he could share part of the buffalo rug. After tending to the bolt lock on the door, he sat down in his rocker and pulled off his boots before he slowly let himself down onto the floor and made up his bed. This was luxury in comparison to sleeping on the ground in the woods someplace, as he had done so many times over the years, especially when it was storming outside. Maybe it was about time to change his way of life. He had a few weeks to decide. He would think about it long and hard. Several minutes later, sleep crept in and claimed him.

Chapter 2

MORG'S EYES OPENED when he felt something cold and wet against his cheek. He brushed his fingers against the spot and felt the whiskery snout that could only be a dog's. At first, he thought it was Rambler, and then he remembered. He turned his head and found himself face to face with the injured cattle dog he had taken in. The dog had crowded up against him but was lying upright now, head raised, and front paws stretched in front of her. Streaks of sunlight streamed through the curtains, so the day looked more promising. The storm had evidently moved on, and somebody else might enjoy the spring rain now. In cattle country, a man never complained about rain for the pastures.

He tossed the blankets off and sat up, reflexively resting his hand on the dog's head. She did not flinch away, so she had accepted him as a friend. The pans he had set out were both empty, so sometime during the night Dingo had consumed badly needed nourishment. He would replenish both when he got to his feet, but first he would see if he could get her outside so they could both relieve bladder and bowels.

He fried extra bacon that morning, and Dingo gulped down one of the biscuits with the bacon treats. While the dog ate, Morg applied a salve to the dog's wounds, the same greasy stuff from a tin labeled 'Doc Wilder's Miracle Salve' that he used for cattle, horses, and himself. At least the medicine seemed to do no harm. Dingo was moving stiffly—that made two of them—but, barring infection, he did not see her being disabled for more than a few days. His guess was that exhaustion and hunger had been the major causes of her pitiful condition the previous night.

She was eating from the pan on the floor—no table privileges, not yet anyhow. "Feeling better, Dingo?" The dog did not respond. He did not expect a reply in English, but a friendly turn of the head and tail wag would have been welcome.

Dingo looked disappointed when he held her back as he was leaving the house to tend to chores. "Sorry, girl. You're not up to that yet. I don't want you to pull those stitches or start to bleed again. You've got to take it easy for a few days. You can rest on the rug while I'm gone. Maybe we can take the rug out on the porch when I get back. We'll sit out there and soak in some sun."

He was talking to the dog just like he used to do with Rambler. The big shepherd always seemed more interested, though, offering a yip or a whine now and then, and always attentive. Maybe that will come later. He chided himself for thinking that he had a new dog. He wasn't up to taking in another just yet, wasn't sure he ever would be. He would always compare the new dog to Rambler, and it would never measure up.

He would not likely outlive a dog as young as Dingo, and it would not be fair to the dog for him to keep her. Hell, he was thinking crazy. She belonged to somebody, and he was pretty sure who. He wanted to know more about the gunshot wounds, though. He would talk to Jaye Boyden. He came over every other day to check the cattle, and this was the day Jaye was due to show up.

Chores did not take long, since he just had to tend to the three horses in the small stable section of the big barn. He grained the critters in their separate stalls and opened the rear stable door that led to thirty acres of fenced-in grass. He forked some hay into the pen from the big stack outside the fence. Some of it would be wet, but the horses would eat it. He did not want them gnawing the grass down to the dirt before it came back, so he offered ample portions of hay.

When he turned the horses out, Buckshot, the dark gray gelding that had been with him for a dozen years, did not join the others immediately as they headed for the hay outside. He waited for some rubbing behind the ears and stroking of his muzzle by his longtime rider before he moved on. He was Morg's special mount, and they shared a bond that only horse owners could understand. The horse had been dubbed with his name for the sprinkling of white on one hip that reminded Morg of the appearance of a shotgun target.

It was midmorning by the time Morg and Dingo were settled on the small, roofed porch. Dingo lay on the buffalo rug, Morg sat in his weathered porch rocker with his feet propped up on the railing. The house was perched solidly on a sandstone flat overlooking the Dismal River, well above any threat of flooding, although the river channel was no more than seventy-five feet distant from the front porch.

The river was easily accessed by a gently sloping path from the house, but he no longer depended upon the river for his water supply with a windmill and water pump located midway between the house and barn that also connected to the house kitchen. Two others were set out in the Sandhills pasturelands on the nearly 1,800 acres he owned adjacent to Jaye's ranch operation.

His eyes were focused on the billowy, white clouds rolling northward with a soft south wind over the seemingly endless sand dunes surrounding the ranch. Spaces between the clouds were a glowing, brilliant blue, not the sort of hue that would be easily captured by an artist's brush, he thought. The sunlight filtering between the clouds was strong and bright, assuring him the rain had likely ended for a few days.

The breeze shook the tiny emerging leaves on the cottonwood, birch, and oak trees and shrubs that covered the bottomlands along the river, and as it caressed his face it was like soothing, healing balm. The Dismal River, so anointed by some mapmaker, he supposed, would be called a creek by some, but however classified, it carried generally clear water from its spring-fed source and snaked its way through less than a hundred miles of west-central Nebraska until it forked and merged with the larger Middle Loup River.

The southerly boundary of the Bar F edged the Dismal's north bank and officially ran to the river's center, presenting legal problems for some when a river cut a new channel. Near the Bar F, the river was more than halfway on its journey to the Middle Loup and ran waist deep and was normally no more than a dozen feet wide. At other places it might be half as deep and twice as wide on stretches where sandstone cliffs and walls did not contain the water.

Beyond each side of the river were seemingly endless sand dunes rolling over the plains. Early explorers had dubbed the area "the Great American Desert," but later it was discovered that the dunes were grass-covered and held intact by the deeply rooted carpet, and water was beyond plentiful. The bison had discovered that years before and thrived here, providing sustenance for the Indians without depleting the herds that were easily replaced until the white hunters came, and later the cattlemen, to reduce and drain their numbers beyond replenishment.

There was something about this morning that cleared Morgan Fraser's mind. He reached over the rocker's arm, and his fingertips found Dingo's head. He scratched the dog's ears and looked down to see the dark eyes staring back at him. "You won't be leaving me, Dingo, unless you choose to, and I've decided it's time for me to stay put. This is where I want to spend the rest of my days."

Dingo just looked at him and then suddenly got to her feet and stared eastward along the river in the direction of what locals called the Dismal Trail, a narrow horse and deer path that sliced through the river woodlands before they gave way to the Sandhills dunes. It served as a short-cut for riders travelling from ranch to ranch but too narrow for a wagon. Buckboards were forced to connect to a series of county roads that passed the north side of the ranch. He just leaned back in the rocker and waited, his fingers patting the grip of the Colt holstered at his waist.

Chapter 3

A RIDER ASTRIDE A big sorrel gelding emerged from the trees, and Dingo offered a few barks but did not seem unduly excited. It was Jaye Boyden, and Morg winced at the pain in his back when he got up to greet his young friend. He waved when Jaye reined his horse up the slope from the Dismal riverbank toward the house. Jaye dismounted as he came up on level ground and led his mount to the hitching rail in front of the house. Horse secured, he ambled to the porch's edge and took the single step onto the planked floor.

"Good morning, Morg. Nice rain last night."

"Yep. Ought to give the grass a good start." He had to look up a bit at the strapping man who stood a few inches over six feet in his stockinged feet, some four inches taller than Morg. Black hair that was not allowed to get past mid-neck or over the ears, and always the tan-colored, clean-shaven face. It had been a couple of days since Morg shaved, and as usual his thick mustache needed a good trim, not to mention the shaggy graying hair that was falling over his ears.

"Appears you've got a guest," Jaye said, nodding at the dog that was staring at him with interest.

"Storm washed her in last night. She'd been shot, twice it appears. But I patched her up. She's doing fine today. I thought she was good as dead when I brought her in. Sit down. We need to talk some before you ride the pastures."

Jaye sat down on the two-seat bench next to the door, and Morg scooted his rocking chair around to face the young man, pushing it nearer because he had finally admitted he wasn't hearing as well as he used to. "About the dog, I'm dang sure where she came from."

Jaye said, "Her name is 'Worthless,' and she came from the Tall T Ranch. She's supposed to be dead. Thomas Towne told Andy that the dog got sick and died while he was at school, and he'd buried her. Even had some ground dug up to show Andy the place. The boy was heartbroken. First time I ever saw tears in his eyes. Of course, Towne shot the dog, and I'm sure Andy had that figured out. The dog was with the boy almost all the time, and he would have been aware if she was coming down with a sickness."

Morg shook his head in disbelief that anyone would do such a thing. And, still, he was not surprised. "The dog's new name is Dingo, by the way. Why did he try to kill her?"

"Because she was living up to her name. Towne decided she was untrainable. She ignored every command, and I suspect he got mad one day and shot her before he thought of how he would explain to Andy. Your son loved that dog, and the feeling was mutual. Towne won't like it if Andy finds out the dog ended up at your place. Obviously, she ran off, with him assuming she died down by the river someplace and became buzzard and coyote food. Nope, he'll have a hell of a time explaining to the boy."

Andy was Andrew Fraser, Morg's twelve-year-old son. His mother, May Towne, was Morg's ex-wife. "Well, the dog's found a home. She will stay with me. I don't want to cause trouble, but I'm not above using Dingo to lure my son down this way once in a while."

"Do you think you can take Worth—Dingo with you on assignments like you did old Rambler?"

"That's what I wanted to talk about, but I want to know about Sheena. How's she doing? I gather you were over to

the Tall T, or you wouldn't have learned about the dog."
Sheena was Morg's twenty-year-old daughter, who hadn't
spoken to him for some years, seemed to hate him for the
atrocity of being divorced by their mother. Of course, he
could not deny that he deserved it.

"Well, she loves her teaching at the school, and I think
she likes boarding with the family near the school better than living at the Towne place. Of course, she's never
lived that much there. Went off to North Platte to high
school on your money—which she doesn't know about—
and now boarding someplace else. In the ten years May
has been married to Towne, Sheena's only lived there four
years fulltime. Otherwise, it's been a month or two summers and some holiday vacations that she's come back
home."

"What about you and her?"

"We just don't see much of each other, with all the distance between us. She's back for a two-week break that
runs into Easter and then she's gone again. I dropped by
for a visit, and that's when I talked to Andy. The school
out here is losing their teacher, and I suggested she try
for that job next school term. She could probably snatch
it in a minute. Then we could see each other regular-like.
She asked who would want to live in this lonely godfor-
saken country. Well, I sure do, and that triggered a big

fuss, and I don't think I'm welcome to visit—for a few days anyhow. Gotta be honest, she flies off the handle every time I talk about you and me being in business together."

"Do you think you could stay married to somebody with a temper like that?"

"I'd like to try."

"I suppose I'm partly the cause of your problems. I haven't even seen her for a few years. She's either not there when I ride to the Towne place, or, if she is, she refuses to see me. It's nearly a half day there and back if I spend any time at all, and I try to ride over every other week when I'm in the Sandhills to visit with Andy. He'll talk to me some, but it is mostly yeses and noes, and he won't come over here to visit for a few days. And what can we do together in a few hours' time? Of course, I've been gone for months at a time over the years. I don't blame May for finding another man and getting rid of me. I wasn't a good dad or a husband. Those are only a few of the demons that chase a man like me."

"Don't be so hard on yourself, Morg. You did what you had to do to support your family."

"I did what I wanted to. I could have found another way to make a living. I was twenty years older than May when we married. I had been doing my work for fifteen years by then, saved about every nickel I earned. I should have known that a man like me wasn't meant to be married, but she was the sweetest, loving gal when we got hitched. Prettiest young woman in Nebraska, and she worshipped me for a spell, but I started trying her patience after a year or two, being gone all the time and my mind somewhere else when I was home."

"You're leading up to something."

"I'm resigning from the service. Within the next few weeks, I'm taking my written resignation to the U.S. Marshal at North Platte and turning in my marshal's badge. I won't take on any new assignments. I'm done. I can't handle any more saddle time, and I'm moving like a danged crippled turtle. It wouldn't be long before some no-good took me down. I can't do the job anymore, and whatever time I've got left I want to spend here if the live demons don't catch up with me."

"What do you mean?"

"I've got a price on my head. Kill me and deliver proof to a certain fella in Denver, and you can collect three thousand cash money. Deliver me to the man alive, and I'm worth twice that."

"I don't understand."

"His name is Oxford. Monte Oxford. He's like an octopus with his tentacles mostly in places like Denver,

Kansas City, Cheyenne, and even Chicago, as well as a lot of small towns in between. Some of his investments are legitimate—mining, hotels and such. Then there are gambling dens and bordellos, openly where legal, secretive where they are not. He doesn't hesitate to bribe appropriate officials where necessary. And then his brother Joe Oxford ramrodded the train and bank robbery division. I tracked Joe for months, and a few years back I intercepted Joe and two of his colleagues robbing a bank in Fort Collins and killed all three."

"You do know how to use that sidearm that I've never seen you without."

"I'm not proud of it these days, but my life could depend on always having my six-gun within reach. Anyway, my assignments after taking Joe Oxford down were mostly focused on the Oxford enterprises, and with the help of a few deputies, we closed a half dozen of Monte Oxford's operations, but the goal was to nail the head man who holds himself out as a respectable businessman. He has not taken this kindly, and as far as he is concerned, I murdered his brother. Someone close to Oxford informed the marshal at North Platte about the price on my head. I don't know why, and that man is dead, allegedly from suicide, which I doubt."

"Does Oxford know where you live?"

"I have no way of knowing, but he eventually will find out. I have some hope he will call off his wolves if I'm no longer on the case, but I won't count on it till the guy is dead or behind bars. Few have seen this mystery man. I don't have a notion of what he looks like. His Denver office has three employees, but the boss is never in when a marshal or deputy stops by with questions. And they know nothing, of course, and are no doubt paid well for that."

"I'd be danged uneasy if I were you. You're carrying a big load on your back."

"Most of us do over a lifetime. I do want you to know that I want to continue our business arrangements. Maybe I can help a little more than I have in the past, but I'm way past my prime when it comes to working cattle. I won't be adding to my herd, and you can still run the same numbers on my land in exchange for looking after my cattle. I won't run more than fifty cows with calves at side."

"I appreciate that."

"All I ask is that if something happens to me, you will take Dingo in."

"Done. But you haven't figured out Dingo's problem yet, have you?"

"What are you talking about?"

"Andy says that Dingo is deaf. She can't hear. That's why she can't respond to voice commands. Andy has tried to convince Towne, but the Aussie doesn't believe it and says it doesn't matter. He is trying to establish these mixed dogs as a legitimate breed. Towne claims he's the only man in the country breeding the dogs. He has at least four bitches and two stud dogs, but while there's a local market for the animals as cow dogs, he's got a problem finding a way to produce more pups without inbreeding which often results in inferior offspring."

Morg looked down at Dingo dozing on the rug, basking in warm sun rays that found their way under the porch roof. "First, I've got to convince myself that Andy is right about Dingo's deafness. If his opinion proves true, Dingo and I are going to learn sign language. And when you come over later in the week and she is well enough, I would like you to look after Dingo for the day, maybe take her with you to check the cattle. She doesn't seem uneasy with you here. I want to ride up to the Tall T to talk to Andy and tell him about his dog. I've got to think about how to handle it."

"I haven't run across her much, but I've known her since she was a pup. She wouldn't be quite two years old. She's always been a friendly dog. We'll get along."

"I'm still skeptical about her deafness. She knew you were on the Dismal Trail long before she could have seen you."

Jaye shrugged. "I don't know. Maybe she hears some kinds of sounds or can just feel it sometimes. I've been around blind animals that move around dang good. They can't see, but they know you're there."

"Well, I guess this will give me something to think on without getting out of the rocking chair."

Chapter 4

A WEEK LATER, MORG took the Dismal Trail along the river on his ten-mile journey to Thomas Towne's Tall T Ranch. Dingo had watched him wistfully as he rode away, held back only by Jaye holding onto the rope leash attached to the collar the dog had inherited from Rambler. He looked back only once, and it nearly brought tears to his eyes, so he did not turn his head again.

The Towne Ranch headquarters was a mile north of the Dismal River, but Towne owned a five thousand acre spread, and his cattle grazed nearly that much of surrounding public lands. Towne did not dirty his own hands more than necessary and lodged a foreman and three year-round cowboys in the ranch's bunkhouse. As near as Morg could tell, Zeke Grammar, the foreman who was about his own age, pretty much ran the cattle operation, although another man named Packer Osborne carried the foreman title. Towne apparently had more money than a man would ordinarily make in the cattle business.

Most ranchers were land and cow poor, always hurting for cash, but not Thomas Towne. Morg had been told that Towne was an Australian immigrant who had brought money with him, which Morg assumed was inherited, but he did not know that much about the stepfather of his children. Hell, he had not been around enough to know that much about Sheena and Andrew.

It was a perfect spring morning, and the wooded areas that edged the narrow trail were quiet with a gentle breeze not strong enough to shake new growth. He could see birds nesting and squirrels scurrying about, all preparing for new families. In his own pasture, he had observed fresh, new calves testing thin legs with their mamas not more than a few steps away.

Yes, it was the time for rebirth following a rugged winter, albeit it had been nothing in comparison to the historic blizzard that had struck a year earlier. Of course, he was relying on what folks had told him because he had been on assignment in Arizona Territory during December and January of 1888—while his children were surviving a storm that killed so many.

Buckshot nickered and his ears came to attention. Morg immediately reined in the gelding. He had learned long ago to pay attention to the horse. He listened, and it irritated him that his hearing was not so reliable these days. The rustling brush behind him suggested a rider on horseback moving up at a slow pace. A rider did not hurry on the Dismal Trail. The turns and twists were too sharp, and he could easily break through the woods and catapult into the river.

The rider could be a cowhand, or anybody for that matter. Morg dismounted, his back popping when he lifted his leg over his mount's back. He pulled his Winchester from its scabbard, and holding onto the saddle's pommel, he leaned against Buckshot and waited. The horse nickered again, but Morg had already heard somebody crashing through the brush farther up the trail. Somebody afoot and coming from the north where a horse was no doubt hitched. This one was a clumsy oaf and certainly was not Sioux.

The two obviously thought they were stalking him and were going to catch him in a vice-like trap. He doubted they had a brain between them, but he had yet to encounter a smart outlaw. Morgan Fraser saw himself down the list a ways when it came to intelligence, but he always figured he had patience and persistence to offset any shortfall. He stepped back and slapped Buckshot on the rump. Buckshot headed on up the trail, but he would stop at fifty yards or so and wait for Morg to whistle or catch up to him. This experience was not new to either horse or rider. That was why Buckshot took the train with him when the mission was too distant for horseback.

Morg stepped back into the wooded area lining the riverbank, seeking cover behind an ancient cottonwood tree. In less than five minutes, a man astride a bay gelding appeared on the trail. He was a skeletal man who looked like he was built of sticks. A scraggly goatee dropped from his chin midst a crop of whiskers that were likely shaved on occasion. He guessed the rider to be in his mid-twenties, too young to throw his life away like this.

A hoarse voice hollered from up the trail. "Dax, the son-of-a-bitch ain't on his horse. Critter just went past me without a rider. Watch yourself."

With a cartridge already levered into the Winchester's chamber, and the rifle held a bit above his waist, Morg stepped out from behind the tree with gun leveled at the young man's chest. "Unbuckle that gun belt and drop it on the ground. Then do the same with your rifle, and you might live a few more days. Now."

He knew the other man could be no more than a few minutes away, and there was no time to waste. The man called Dax had nearly jumped from the saddle when Morg appeared, and the marshal figured he likely pissed his britches, but the fool had his pistol in his hand, ready to squeeze the trigger when Morg fired his rifle, driving a slug into his chest. At the sound of the gun, the horse reared, and the would-be killer tumbled out of the saddle and landed on the trail.

Morg swung around, readying for the other gunman, and found he had already arrived. He fell to the ground just before the man fired his pistol. Morg rolled over, pulling his Colt from its holster at the same time. Back pressed to the ground, he got off two shots at the big, black-bearded man, one slug boring into the shooter's throat and the other into his eye. The man's gun clattered against a stone at the trail's edge, and following a choking, broken scream, his knees folded, and his crumpled body joined that of his partner.

But that was not the end of it. Morg struggled to his feet when he heard more noise in the brush that blended into the dune-like grasslands that rose beyond the river bottom. He picked up the rifle he had dropped on the ground and prepared for another confrontation. Then there was silence and finally the barely discernible sound of a horse racing away. There had been a third man evidently waiting to back the others and then thought better of it after his comrades did not fare so well.

Now, what to do with the bodies and the extra horses? He was certain that the fleeing rider had not taken the horse the bearded man had left at the edge of the woods. The rider would have been forced to retreat to the hills in the absence of a clear trail, and he would have been slowed by trying to lead an extra horse. Dax's horse was lingering no more than thirty feet down the trail and seemed calm enough now. He would strip the horses of saddles and tack and turn them loose. They would not starve this time of year, and some rancher would have a windfall, unless he saw the horses on his return trip. Then he would try to lure them to the Bar F and take them to the U.S. Marshal's office in North Platte when he reported the incident. Horses were easily worth ten head of cows in this part of the country.

He decided to search the men and their saddlebags and salvage anything that might help identify them or be of value. He would hide the gear and weapons in the trees for now, tell Jaye about it and give him permission to claim anything except the guns. Any money would be put in his own saddlebags to be surrendered to the U.S. Marshal's office in due course. He would try to find a gully or wash to stuff the bodies in and then cover them with rocks and sand as best he could. He would mark the spot, so what was left could be found when and if the law wanted to investigate. Nearly eighty miles from any town with an official lawman, he doubted any official would find it necessary.

Chapter 5

MORG'S POCKET TIMEPIECE told him it was nearly one o'clock when he approached the Tall T Ranch. The skirmish on the trail had slowed him by almost two hours. The Tall T headquarters buildings could not be viewed from the river south of the building site, and there was no clear trail because the link to the county road was north of the two-story house. The rolling hills and dunes made it appear that the grasslands went to the horizon.

However, he had entered from the south many times, and he reined Buckshot north across the rolling prairie, and as he neared the place Morg directed the gelding to the top of a hill overlooking the headquarters site. It was an impressive view. The house reminded him of southern mansions he had observed during the war, many of which he watched burning in his thirties as a Union Colonel.

Many demons had attached to his memory during those weeks, and they still haunted, mostly during the nightmares that visited with increasing frequency it seemed.

A collection of buildings was clustered some distance from the house, including a bunkhouse, enormous hay barn, stable, and at least four smaller structures used for workshops and storage. There were several buildings and pens for dog kennels, and the henhouse was dwarfed by the other more imposing buildings, but Morg knew it was larger than most. The cowhands must eat a lot of eggs at chowtime. Corrals and fences were set outside the barn and stable interconnecting at different places, so they looked like a huge maze. No rancher in the Sandhills could match the looks of the place. He had doubts about the efficiency of the operation, but it offered a scenic view from the surrounding hills.

Morg's arrival was announced by the barking of two Australian cattle dogs when he rode into the yard. They were soon joined by a chorus of others from the kennels. He dismounted, and the dogs raced up to him, welcoming him with front paws on his legs and begging him to be petted. He complied. He supposed they could be trained to attack strangers, but that seemed contrary to their nature.

He hitched Buckshot on the rail set a good fifty feet back from the entrance to the house and waited. He had never been invited into the mansion, and when a servant or someone inside identified him, Andy would usually come out, and they would go to the barn and sit on a bench and talk. He had been a hell of a poor father to let their relationship develop this way. He should have found a way to drag the kid back to the Bar F. Of course, that was not possible if he was not home himself. He had virtually surrendered his son and daughter.

He was surprised when his ex-wife, not Andy, emerged from the doorway and walked toward him. He supposed she was going to inform him that Andy refused to see him today. He waited with uneasiness as she approached. He never had difficulty facing down outlaws, but confrontation with May was another matter. Morg admitted he was half afraid of her, and the words between them since their parting had been few.

She was still a pretty thing, though, tall and slim, her chestnut-colored hair pulled back and captured with a ribbon before cascading onto her shoulders. She wore a green dress, a good color for her with those greenish eyes that Sheena shared, and at forty could pass for five or ten years younger. Morg figured he would likely pass for five or ten years older than his sixty. When she reached him at the hitching rail, she looked at him disapprovingly as usual. "Afternoon, May. I came over to see Andy."

"I don't know who else you would be here to see. He'll be out shortly, but I wanted a word with you first."

Morg nodded and waited.

"The boy has become a problem. He and Thomas aren't speaking, and Andy has become very belligerent. He won't do anything he's asked to do. I learned from his teacher a few days ago that he hasn't shown up for school for two weeks. He's a terrible example for his younger brothers—screams at them all the time. Thomas won't put up with this anymore, and he won't pay to send Andy off to boarding school someplace. He'll finish eighth grade next year, and that's the end of his schooling. Thomas said he's already educated beyond his brains, and I'm starting to agree."

The younger brothers were May's children with Thomas Towne, Abraham, age seven, and Simon, age nine. Morg supposed that the stepfather might tend to favor his own blood. Probably killing Andy's favorite dog had helped bring conflicts to a boil.

"I'm sorry. How can I help?"

"You come back with a buckboard tomorrow. We'll have all his things out here, including a bed and chest of drawers, some pillows, sheets and such. I'm guessing you don't have anything to furnish that extra room."

"Somebody cleaned it out." He started to say more and stopped. "I'm resigning from the marshal's service. I'll be around to look after him."

"It's about time. Now, I'll send Andy out."

"Does he know about this?"

"You tell him." She whirled around and marched back toward the house.

Ten minutes later, Andy came out of the house and walked toward Morg with a scowl on his face. Morg watched the boy trying to walk nonchalantly toward his father. The darn kid seemed to grow an inch or two between each visit, and in a few years would likely pass his father's height. He was a bit on the gangly side but had never been inclined to fat. He shared Morg's dark brown eyes. Before the gray started to claim part of his scalp, his own hair had been rust-brown like Andy's. Give him four or five years, and his son would be irresistible to the young ladies. New kinds of trouble.

"Good to see you, Andy," Morg said. He had never been much of a hugger, and he doubted the boy would welcome one in his present mood.

"Hello," Andy said, his eyes narrowing as he looked at Morg suspiciously.

This was going to be difficult. He had no idea how to broach the subject on their agenda. "Shall we go to the barn. I need to water Buckshot at the water tank along the way, maybe steal a little hay."

"I can get him a scoop of grain from the stable. Got a mix of oats and cracked corn."

"That would be nice. I'll get Buckshot a drink and meet you at the barn." He could not recall the last time the kid had volunteered to do something kind. The boy May was telling him about would not have done that, but Andy always did have a good heart when it came to animals.

There was a bench just inside the barn door they usually shared, and after Andy put a pan with a small scoop of grain in it in front of Buckshot and fetched two arms full of hay for the horse Morg had staked outside, the boy joined his dad on the bench.

There had been no need for Morg to fret about broaching the subject he had worried about. Andy asked him abruptly. "What were you and Ma talking about?"

"Your mother said you are having some problems here. She thought maybe you should come stay with me for a spell."

"They're kicking me off the place, ain't they? Thomas hates me. The feeling is mutual. I've been listening to Ma and Thomas yell at each other. I knew this was coming. How can I live with you anyhow? You're never home."

"I am resigning as a U.S. Marshal. I'm settling in at the ranch for good."

"I lived with you once till I was two but I don't remember."

"I wasn't much of a father. I'll try to do better. At least I'll be around. There will be rules. You will have chores. You will show up at school every day. There's a small school held in a house less than three miles from my place. I don't think there's more than a half dozen kids. I've never met the teacher. I understand she's a widow lady and quite nice."

"I hate school."

"Maybe a change will help."

"Not much chance."

"We'll see. I'll talk to the teacher. It's a private school. She doesn't have to take everybody that wants to go there. She charges a monthly fee."

"You got the money for that?"

"Enough. There's something I came to tell you about."

For the first time, Andy raised his eyes from the barn floor and looked directly at Morg. "What?"

"You had an Australian cattle dog here, a female called 'Worthless.'"

"Not by me. I called her 'Dog.'"

"She has a new name. Dingo."

"What the hell are you talking about. That son-of-a-bitch Thomas killed her. Shot her and buried her."

"She was shot, but she didn't die. She's at my place. Jaye recognized her. You can see for yourself tomorrow. I don't think you should say anything to Thomas about this, though. I'm coming with my buckboard tomorrow morning to pick up your things. Your mother said we can even take your bed."

For the first time, Andy smiled. "I'll start packing this afternoon. I don't know what I get to take, but I'll be ready. Your place can't be worse, so I guess I'll find out if you and me can get along. And I sure as hell want to see this dog you call Dingo."

When he rode away from the Tall T, Morg began to wonder what he was getting into with his son. He had been a failure as a father to this point. He had to do this thing. It was a chance to at least partly set things right with this boy he hardly knew. He supposed it was too late for him to have a chance with Sheena, but this was a start. Maybe he could kill a few of the demons that chased him, rectify his failure as a father somehow, but was he bringing the boy into danger? The bounty on his head likely did not disappear with the deaths of the two gunslingers this morning. Others might come for him. He had no way of knowing whether those outlaws worked directly for Monte Oxford, but he needed to learn more about this man regardless of his resignation as a marshal.

Chapter 6

THE NEXT MORNING, Morg drove the buckboard behind a mule team along the county wagon road that bordered his north property line. First stop was Jaye Boyden's ranch house, where he left an unhappy Dingo. She had obviously enjoyed sitting on the wagon seat beside him, but he dared not take her onto the Towne place. If Thomas Towne saw her, there might be too many questions and unneeded unpleasantness. The day did not promise to be a celebratory occasion as it was.

When he slowed the mule team in front of the Towne mansion, he saw an assortment of stuffed sacks and bags on the veranda. The chest of drawers, bed frame, and mattress that May had promised were stacked next to the circular drive that passed near the veranda. The two cattle dogs barked their greetings again, and ran beside the wagon as Morg reined the mules into the driveway and up to the railed veranda.

The door opened, and Andy came out with a small canvas bag of what Morg assumed were personal items. The boy's face was emotionless as he walked across the porch and down the two steps. "I'm ready. Everything I'm taking is out here." The dogs scampered up to him demanding pets and hugs, and he knelt and accepted their sloppy kisses on his face. His stoicism evaporated, and he broke out in sobs, clutching the dogs with both his arms.

Morg fought back his own tears watching the scene. He did not know his son well enough to find the words that might console him upon leaving his friends, so he chose silence.

Soon, Andy got to his feet, wiping the tears from his face with his shirt sleeve. He turned away from the dogs and said, "Where do you want me to start putting stuff?"

"Help me get the chest and bedframe parts on the wagon first, then the mattress. We'll stuff other things around them to hold everything snug. I brought rope to help bind the mattress on."

They worked silently, and Morg thought Andy did more than his share of the lifting. The kid was likely stronger than his old man. There wasn't a threatening cloud in the sky, but they tossed the canvas tarp Morg had brought with him over the load and secured it with rope anchored with multiple diamond hitches like Morg had used on pack horses and mules. Morg enjoyed teaching Andy how to tie several types of knots and hitches and was pleased that his son learned quickly.

When the wagon was loaded and the contents secured, Morg asked, "Do you want to go say good-bye to your ma? Tell her I've got a young gelding you can ride over for a visit anytime." He supposed he should talk to May about staying in contact with Andy, but he was not up to broaching the subject. Things were happening too fast.

Andy said, "Ma's not here. Her and Thomas, along with Packer, left early for Broken Bow to catch a train to Omaha. They'll stay one night at an inn along the trail. Ma likes shopping for stuff, and Thomas has got business of some sort there. I don't know why Packer goes so much. They got a nanny for my little brothers—and a cook and housekeeper, so things don't change much when they're gone. Zeke Grammer runs the ranch anyhow. Thomas ain't here all that much. Suits me fine. Especially now. Thomas has a burr up his ass about something these days. That ain't unusual, though."

It seemed strange that May would not be at the ranch to see her son off, but how could he judge? He was the father who had virtually abandoned his children for his work over the years.

As they rode down the trail, the buckboard bouncing less with a load now, Andy sat beside Morg on the seat. They were silent for a long spell before Morg spoke. "I got a bag with sandwiches and sweet biscuits under the seat if you want to pull it out. They're roasted beef and cheese. The biscuits are my own concoction. Frosted cinnamon biscuits. There's a canteen for each of us there, too. Take your pick."

Andy reached under the seat and found their lunch. "Do you have a cook?"

"Me. I've cooked on the trail for years. Not much variety, I fear, but we won't starve. I've got a boy that comes by once a week selling eggs and sometimes vegetables for his mother, and Jaye Boyden furnishes milk from his milk cow. He even makes cheese when he can grab the time, so that helps with supplies."

"You should have your own laying hens, maybe a milk cow."

"Up till now I haven't been around to look after chickens, but we've got a chicken house. I'd have to think about milking. Can you milk a cow?"

"Yeah, that's about the only thing Ma let me do. The hands didn't like doing it, so Zeke had one of the guys teach me, and I've been milking two cows twice a day for a few years. I don't mind it. The hands will bitch about taking over that job and fuss about who's going to do it."

"We'll think about the milk cow—chickens, too. How are you with horses?"

"I ride a horse to school most days and whenever I get a chance, but I don't get to work cattle or anything like that."

"I don't have much to pick from, but I think you'll like the young gelding. It's a black and white appaloosa. He's got a black patch around one eye. Bought him from a Sioux at the reservation up north. How are you with guns?"

"Packer showed me how to shoot a couple times, but Thomas ordered him to quit. Don't know why. Maybe he thought I'd use it on him someday, but I ain't a killer."

"I've got an old Winchester you can have. I don't know much, but I do know shooting, and we'll start schooling you on that right away."

Andy brightened. "My own rifle?"

"Yep. Once you learn to use it properly." Morg hoped he wasn't unduly bribing his son, but the decision regarding the boy's living arrangements had already been made, and he wanted to give him something to look forward to. Besides, a man in the Sandhills had to learn to shoot and ride a horse for work and pleasure. He would hold off talking about school for a few days.

They pulled the buggy off the main road near a stream to water the mules. They unhitched the critters and led them to drink, Morg showing Andy how the harnesses with various straps, bridles and gear worked and fit together. He was surprised when the boy pitched right in and helped with the harnessing when they readied the mules to work again. He nearly had mastered the task.

Andy pulled his carrying bag from the wagon and reached in and pulled out another small sack. "Can I give them each a few handfuls of grain? I helped myself at the barn when I was getting ready to go."

"Uh, yeah, that would be fine." He watched as the boy brushed the nose of each animal with one hand as he fed the grain with the other. The mules relished the treat, of course.

When the grain was gone, Andy asked, "What are their names?"

"Never named them. I have had them three or four years, but I was never around to handle them that much. Jaye always looked after the horses and mules when I wasn't here."

"They should have names."

"Why don't you think of something?"

Andy nodded, and they both climbed back on the wagon seat. As they rode on, Morg did not say anything because he could see that the boy was preoccupied with something. He understood that. Morg often took journeys in his own head and found that he generally never felt alone in his own company. He supposed that was how he had tolerated the life of a roving marshal.

"Athena and Iris."

Morg furrowed his brow and turned his head toward his son. "What?"

"They are both females. Athena and Iris. Athena is the Greek goddess of wisdom and war. She will be the one on the right. Iris is the goddess of rainbows. I like Greek stuff. Will those names suit you?"

"Uh, yeah, sure. So you know about Greek gods and goddesses?"

"I read about them. I borrow books from Thomas's library. He's got an unbelievable library, but it's just for show. I doubt if he's ever read a book. I sneak them out all the time, and they are never missed because he doesn't even know what's there. There's no current stuff. A lot of Shakespeare and Hawthorne. Those were wrote before the 1870s."

"No Mark Twain?"

"Nope. I've heard of him at school."

"Well, I've got a lot of the modern authors, so I should have some new material for you. And you can just help yourself. If you have been reading the classics, you might not be interested in my dime novels."

"Heard of them. Like to try one."

"I've probably got fifty stacked in my bedroom, so you can pick what looks interesting to you."

"Cowboy stories, ain't they?"

"Yeah. A lot of gunfighting, lawmen chasing outlaws and stuff like that."

"Like what you do."

"It doesn't come as easy to me as the lawmen in the books."

For the first time in their infrequent contacts, father and son talked, and Morg listened, beginning to grasp the hell this boy had gone through, and he cussed himself for assuming things were alright with the kids. He was a professional investigator. He should have found out what was going on in their lives. He could have left his job years back. He was frugal and had saved money. In the early years, the marshals had been allowed to keep rewards paid on outlaw capture, and he had collected plenty, purchased the Sandhills ranch with some of the funds. With the modest ranch income and the money set aside, he was better fixed than ninety percent of his colleagues, most of whom died broke. Why had he run from his children for God's sake? No more.

When they approached Jaye Boyden's homeplace, he caught sight of Dingo sitting in the middle of the road. "Andy, look down the road."

The dog was racing toward the wagon now. Andy yelled, "My dog. I'd know her anytime with that brown splotch across her nose. Pull up, Dad. Please."

Morg complied, and Andy leaped out of the wagon, running to meet the dog, and soon Dingo and her old friend were rolling in the middle of the road. Andy's tears this time were not tears of sorrow.

Jaye had been following the dog at a slower pace, and he walked up to the wagon, shaking his head in disbelief. "Morg, that dog knew you were near fifteen minutes ago. We were down by the barn, and I had her on the leash. I was afraid she'd chase after you. Anyhow, she started barking like crazy, pulling on the rope and about knocking me over. I let her lead me out to the road. I didn't see anything, but she sat down in the middle of the road and fixed her eyes east. I waited with her, and then I saw the dust you were kicking up with the mules and wagon. I figured it couldn't be anybody else, so I turned her loose."

Both men watched boy and dog for a bit before Morg said, "I hate to interrupt the reunion celebration, but we need to get home and get Andy settled in before dark. But this is a special scene we're taking in right now. I'll never forget it."

"That makes two of us. But how did that deaf dog know?"

Chapter 7

SHEENA FRASER SAT at her desk in the single room schoolhouse, checking the schoolwork her dozen students had turned in before they left for the day. She loved teaching, but she was tired. It was a challenge teaching students ranging from first to eighth grade, but never boring.

She was checking little Alice Kleine's arithmetic paper, perfect as usual. The eight-year-old was so bright and always smiling, seemingly unfazed by the loss of one foot, frozen by last year's blizzard. Her older sister, Mazie, had died during that storm when the two girls had started home afoot, and the schoolteacher, Mabel Norman, had died also when she went after the girls to rescue them from the storm's wrath. They had all been found in a haystack, where sister and teacher had lain above Alice to insulate her from the bitter cold.

Sheena thought of the teacher she had replaced often and wondered if she would have the courage to risk her life for her students. She liked to think so, but she had so many doubts about herself and blamed the father who had abandoned her for most of them. She despised him for surrendering her so easily to her mother and Thomas Towne, the man who had sometimes crept into her room at night and touched her forbidden places while she feigned sleep and then, after several years of his sick molestations, crawled in her bed and tried to rape her. She had been fourteen by then and fought back, raking her fingernails across his face till she drew blood.

Her screaming had aborted the attempt, and when her mother ran into her room, Towne accused Sheena of trying to seduce him. Her mother claimed to believe him despite the scratch wounds on his face and scolded her, calling her a liar when she told her of the other times Thomas had visited her room. A fragile relationship between mother and daughter thereafter turned downright hostile.

She was rescued only by a letter delivered by Jaye Boyden, then only an acquaintance and five years her senior. The letter informed her of a scholarship for room, board and tuition to attend high school in North Platte. She was baffled because she had not applied for such a scholarship. She supposed her teacher had contacted the school. But why had Jaye been courier for the message?

Jaye told her he had attended the school under a similar scholarship offered by an anonymous donor from the Sandhills who tried to help young people at remote rural schools attend high school after eighth grade. Jaye's parents had been homesteaders always on the brink of starving out and would have been unable to send him to high school. The parents and two younger daughters remained until after Jaye finished high school, and thereafter they sold Jaye the land, taking his note for payment, and moved to Lincoln where Jaye's mother had family to help them get settled. The father had suffered from a mysterious ailment that forced his wife to assume responsibility for the family's support.

Sheena had wanted to further her schooling, but Thomas refused to pay for it. Her mother pushed her to accept the scholarship administered by a North Platte bank, and she gratefully departed the lavish home, regretting only that her little brother remained behind. She was grateful for where the education had led her. She worked as a clerk in several town stores to earn money to support herself following high school through the one-year normal training program to qualify as an elementary teacher, never asking her mother or Thomas Towne for a penny. A new scholarship from the mysterious donor had paid the school tuition, but she was responsible for her own support.

There was a rapping on the front school door, and it opened. Jaye Boyden stepped in.

She got to her feet and hurried to meet him. He took her in his arms, and they shared a chaste kiss before she stepped back. "Jaye, what are you doing here?"

"I came to visit a lady who doesn't get back our way much. I told Missus Markham she didn't have to prepare supper for you tonight, that we would be eating at the Loup River Tavern. I even borrowed their buggy, and I'm renting a spare room at the Markham house for the night."

"Rather presumptuous, aren't you." George and Clara Markham owned the large house on their homesteaded farm and took in boarders to supplement their income, farm receipts being unreliable. They were kind folks, their children all grown up now, and she would be happy to occupy her room for a long time.

"I suppose. But we've got lots to talk about."

"We do?"

"Yep. But it's almost six o'clock. Let's head over to the tavern."

She sighed. "Okay, give me a minute to grab my jacket and things. I'll need to lock up."

She was a little nervous about the "lots to talk about." She knew Jaye loved her but didn't know why. He shared his life and history generously with her, but she was guarded regarding what she would share with any man. She liked him a lot, but she had never said she loved him, was skeptical about love, and especially marriage.

The Loup River Tavern, as the name suggested, was located along the Loup River at the intersection of two section line roads and the river. It lay about five miles east of the fork where the Dismal River merged with the Middle Loup River to form a larger watercourse. A large trading post that supplied customers for many miles in all directions adjoined the specious tavern-restaurant to provide a symbiotic commercial center for the sparsely populated area.

Sheena and Jaye sat at a table in a corner of the restaurant, a quiet, friendly place where rowdiness was not tolerated by the big, mustachioed bartender who matched the stereotype of the trade created by dime novels. While they waited for their steaks and fried potatoes to be served, Jaye began to explain his presence. "There are things going on back at the Tall T I felt you should know about."

"Such as...?"

"Your brother is now living with your dad. It's been over three weeks now."

"I don't believe it. Why?"

"Your ma and Thomas booted him. He was getting to be a problem with discipline and such, I guess. Your ma told your dad to take him."

"But Dad's always gone."

"Not anymore. He will be resigning from the marshal's service as soon as he can get to North Platte."

"It won't happen."

"They're getting along fine. Your dad's teaching Andy to shoot and work around the ranch. He's got his own rifle and horse. Andy comes over and helps me some already. And they've got this dog, Dingo they call her." He told her about Dingo showing up at Morg's home and the failed attempt of Thomas Towne to kill the dog.

"I'm glad my father is helping Andy, but he is going to let my brother down, and then Andy will be hurt even more."

"I think you are wrong, but time will tell about that, I guess."

"I won't say I hate my father, but I don't like him. He failed Andy and me. If he had stayed home with his family, my mother never would have taken up with Thomas Towne."

"You've got to sort those things out for yourself, but your dad is one of the finest men I've ever known. You're not fair in blaming him for all that's happened in your life."

Their meals were served along with fresh coffee. They ate in silence for a time before Jaye spoke. "I wish this place was closer to my ranch. I'd be taking meals here a lot."

Sheena said, "Why are you always defending my father?"

"Because I've known him since I was a kid. He wasn't around a lot, but when he came back, he always had time for me, taught me how to shoot because my own father was drunk most of the time. Morg might not have been home much, but he was there for me more than my own father, insisted I should get more education and saw that I got it."

"What do you mean?"

"He paid for my so-called scholarship to high school— supported me during those years with deposits in the bank. And he paid for yours, too. He told me I should never tell you, but I never gave a promise back. I've tried to respect his wishes, but, dang it, it's time you were told."

She was stunned. Her father made those arrangements, came up with the funds? "I see. Why was it such a big secret?"

"He said he didn't want you to think he was buying his way into your life. He's a strange man, hard to figure out. But he's a good man. What do you know about his own life as a boy?"

"Very little. He was orphaned when he was eight or nine years old, taken in by an uncle for a few years, then left at an orphanage in St. Louis. But he never told us much beyond that. He had a decent education, but I don't know how much for sure."

"Did you ever ask?"

"No. I guess not."

"He attended college for two years, somewhere in Ohio, thinking he was going to be a college English professor. After his second year, the law called him, and he worked as a deputy sheriff in Kansas, then was elected county sheriff. The war came, and he joined up and was made an officer because of his experience, rose to the rank of Colonel. Got hired on as a deputy U.S Marshal when the war ended and soon was a full U.S. Marshal."

"Why did he become a lawman, for God's sake?"

"His parents were doing business at a bank in Missouri the day they both died. Shot down by bank robbers who were never caught. He decided it was his mission to catch those kinds of people and bring them to justice."

"How did you get all of this information?"

"I asked questions. Sometimes it was like pulling teeth, but he is my best friend, and I thought he needed to talk. He's been going through rough times in his head for several years now. He blames himself for things in his past that he couldn't control or stuff that it's time to forgive himself for. But there are limits to what he'll talk about."

"Are you saying he's crazy?"

"Like a fox. No. Most of us have got problems to work out in our heads. He's just got more years' worth. I'm betting you've got some of your own, especially the notions you've got about your dad."

Maybe she did, but she wasn't going to talk to Jaye about it. Not now anyhow.

When they finished their meal, including slices of apple pie, Jaye said, "School's out mid-May. You've only got a few weeks. Are you going back home for the summer?"

"Home? What home? I'm not going back to the Tall T, that's for certain. No, I'm staying put. I'm taking on a clerk's job at the Loup Trading Post next door."

"I was hoping I would see you more after school's out."

"That would be nice, but I'm done with the Tall T. If I go back for a day or two to see Mother, I'll write ahead of time and let you know, but that wouldn't be often if at all."

"Once we're past calving season, I can get away to see you here once in a while."

"I do appreciate the effort you made today, and it is good to see you."

"Well, I had ulterior motives. I was going to ask you something, but I can see the time's not right. Maybe someday—and maybe not."

She was thankful he was sparing her, and he was right—maybe someday and maybe not. "Why don't we go back to the Markham house? I can change into some britches and comfortable shoes, and we can take a walk into the hills. Nearly a full moon and a balmy night. It's perfect for a long walk."

"That sounds good. After all those hours in the saddle today, I could do without sitting for a spell."

After Jaye settled the bill, they stepped outside, Sheena locking her arm in his as they walked toward the rear of the building where the horse and buggy were hitched. When they turned the corner, a rifle butt slammed into Jaye's head, and he dropped to the earth like a sack of flour. A hand pressed over Sheena's mouth, and an arm wrapped around her bosom dragging her away from where Jaye had fallen. He was still as death, and she thought the blow might have killed him.

A gravelly voice spoke softly in her ear. "You listen close, woman. You let out a scream, and my friend will put two lead slugs in your friend's head. We got nothing to lose. And if you fight going with us, there's two more slugs for you. Understand?"

She nodded. And the man's hand grasped her arm tightly and pulled her with him as he hurried her into a wooded area near the river. There she saw a third man and an extra horse. They obviously intended to take her someplace. "Where's Goober?" asked the third man.

Her captor said, "He's leaving the ransom message where they'll be sure to find it."

Was she going to be held for ransom? Fools. Thomas would not pay a nickel for her release. And when he refused, she was buzzard bait as she had heard cowhands say. She was afraid, but she was surprised she was not hysterical. At this moment, she felt a strange calm. Her main concern was for Jaye. Dear God, let him be alright.

Chapter 8

MORG WAS A bit nervous about taking Andy to Susana Mercer's house for Saturday lunch. He had spoken briefly with the schoolteacher several days earlier about enrolling his son at the private school conducted in her home, and she said she would be inclined to accept him but wanted to meet him first and explain the rules.

Financial terms were more than generous, and he liked the woman. Based upon her qualifications and graduation date from college she had volunteered, he judged Sue, as he had been invited to call her, to be about five years younger than himself, but notwithstanding snow-white hair she appeared even younger. Her gentle voice and azure eyes had entranced him, and after talking for a bit more than an hour, he was struck by a schoolboy's crush on the prospective teacher.

Today, as Andy and Morg, followed by Dingo, rode toward the Mercer house several miles west on the Dismal Trail, Morg had taken care to trim his mustache and shave the rest of his face with the straight edge. He had even taken a bath in the wash tub the night previous, shined his boots, and decided to wear the coat and string tie he wore to testify in courts. He had dusted off his gray Stetson this morning.

"What are you all gussied up for, Dad?" Andy said as they rode side by side on a stretch where the trail widened. "We're just going to see an old schoolteacher. Seems like foolishness to me."

He wasn't sure of the answer to the boy's question. "I'm just trying to be respectful, son. I want this lady to take you on."

"I don't care. As far as I'm concerned, I've had enough schooling."

"Well, not as far as I'm concerned. And she's got what they call a bachelor's degree. She says she can teach you through the first two years of high school, but you would have to test to qualify. I'm not anxious to send you off somewhere to go to school so quickly."

"I ain't interested in high school anyhow. Hardly anybody out this way goes after eighth grade."

"We'll see."

When they arrived at the two-story house, they rode around it to the north side, since the house was set a good distance back from the river and faced the county wagon road to the north. They hitched Buckshot and Palouse, Andy's appaloosa gelding, to the hitching posts in front of the house. Dingo started to follow her companions to the front porch of the house, and Morg stopped and turned toward her, holding up his hand in a halt sign. She sat down to wait but looked at him with the sad eyes that always pushed his guilt button.

Susana stepped out of the doorway with a welcoming smile before they reached the porch. "It's alright. Your dog can come in. You mentioned her when you were here, so I saved some beef trimmings."

"You're sure?" Morg said.

"Absolutely."

Andy had already waved the cattle dog to join them.

Morg said, "I don't think I mentioned that the dog is deaf. But Andy works with her every day, and she's getting a good vocabulary of signals. She seems to be an intelligent creature."

"How interesting. I hope she likes me."

"She will as soon as you place a tin of beef scraps in front of her."

"Well, all of you come in."

The aroma of fresh cornbread and a succulent stew permeated the downstairs which included a large kitchen and a huge parlor crammed with school desks and chairs. A mammoth oak table that would sit at least ten people rested in the open area between the kitchen and parlor. A hallway off the parlor provided access to two other rooms, possibly a bedroom and study, he speculated. A stairway at the end of the hallway apparently led to the second floor.

Susana put a plate of meat scraps on the floor on the kitchen side of the table for Dingo, telling her guests to be seated. She soon placed a pan of cornbread and a jar of honey on the table. "The cornbread's sliced, but you will need the spatula to dig out the pieces. Eat all you want but save room for apple cake." She then added three bowls of beef stew to the feast. After retrieving a pot of coffee for Morg and herself, she put a cup of hot chocolate near Andy's plate.

"I hope this is alright, Andy. I can get a glass of cold water, if you prefer."

"Oh, no, ma'am. Thank you. I love hot chocolate. Ain't had it for a long time."

Morg was struck by Andy's good manners. He had not seen that at his house. On the other hand, he was probably raised with more refinement than his father offered.

Sue sat down. "Shall we bow our heads while I say the blessing?"

Andy tossed a glance at his father and followed his lead in bowing his head.

She said, "Father, we thank you for this food and for this beautiful day. Thank you especially for the special guests, Morg, Andy, and Dingo, who have joined me for this meal. May we all see the opportunities before us and take advantage of them in such a manner as you would approve. Amen."

Morg said, "Amen." And Andy followed.

As they ate, Sue asked Andy questions and talked about school rules. "Andy, I would love to have you as a student here, but you have missed some school since moving to your father's home. We only have two more weeks of classes here. I think it would be best for you to start by coming here two days each week for special tutoring after school is out, so I can determine if you need to do some work to be ready for at least seventh grade level in the fall. We will stop the sessions when I am satisfied that you are prepared. Would you be willing to do that?"

Andy gave a reluctant, "I guess so, ma'am."

"I don't tolerate truancy. If you miss school without a written excuse from your father, you will be dismissed. Do you understand that?"

He was silent for several moments before he replied. "Yes, ma'am, I understand."

"You will likely change several times, but if you could choose a way to earn a living now, when you grow up, what would like to do?"

He did not hesitate. "I would like to be a veterinary surgeon. I love animals." He nodded at Dingo. "All animals. I love helping Dad and Jaye with birthing cows, Dingo's always been special to me, and Dad helped her. I would like to be able to do that."

"There aren't many veterinary colleges in the country, but there is a new one being established at Kansas State Agricultural College in Manhattan, Kansas. You would need to finish high school to get admitted, but if you are willing to work, I know you could do it."

"Most of the vets around here never went to high school, let alone college."

"But someday soon there will be licensing requirements, and if you want to be the best, you should set your sights higher."

The three talked for an hour after lunch while Dingo dozed on a rug. Morg was amazed at the woman's skill at getting the boy engaged in conversation. She would be not only a great teacher but a good friend as well.

Finally, Susana adjourned the session. "Well, gentlemen. This has been a delightful conversation. As I indicated, Morg, my rates will be daily during whatever summer meetings are required—and I suspect there will not be many. The weekly rate applies during the regular school term. If it is still your wish for Andy to attend my school, I would be pleased to have him."

Morg said, "You have a new pupil. Maybe I can stop by when school is out to see when you wish to start Andy's sessions."

"That would be nice. I look forward to seeing you."

Morg and Andy stood to leave. Morg said, "Thanks for the delicious lunch, Sue."

Andy said, "Yes, thank you, ma'am. I ain't had food that good ever. And I sure ain't going to get it at Dad's—not that his cooking is awful, but it's nice to eat something besides beans and biscuits sometimes."

"Well, I enjoyed your company. We will try to do this again."

Dingo sat on the rug looking anxiously at Andy and Morg. Andy gave her the wave to follow, and they headed out the door.

Morg started to follow but stopped and turned around when Susana said, "Wait, Morg." She moved nearer to him, so near he could have reached out and touched her. Sue's eyes fastened on his. "Morg, you're doing fine with the boy. You told me how it's been over the years. It's going to get better. You may have some rough spots, but you and Andy will be fine. I think you're lucky to have each other."

"Thanks. That little boost helps more than you could know."

"Oh, but I do know. And I promise you that before summer is out 'ain't' will be a forgotten word to that boy."

Chapter 9

"I LIKED MISSUS Mercer. I think school might not be so bad with her as a teacher," Andy said as they rode down the trail toward home.

"She seems like a real nice lady." Morg was thinking about that parting moment when Sue stepped so close to him. It had been a long time since he wanted to take a woman in his arms and hold her and share a lingering kiss. Danged if Sue hadn't chased away half of those aches and pains he had been grumbling about, and his back had not even complained when he swung into the saddle as they were leaving.

When they rode off the trail into the ranch yard, Morg saw Jaye's sorrel gelding tied to the hitching rail before he saw his friend sitting on the porch bench. When they dismounted at the rail, he noticed the edge of a white headwrap dropping out from beneath Jaye's black low-crowned hat. He did not like the grim look on his young friend's face.

He said, "Jaye, what in blazes are you doing here?"

Jaye held up a white envelope. "Bringing your mail. I didn't open it, but I was sure as the devil tempted. It has to do with Sheena."

Morg stepped onto the porch and took the envelope before dropping into his rocker. It was sealed with wax, and the only words in heavy, black ink were 'MORGAN FRASER.' He tore it open while Jaye related the story of his evening with Sheena.

"All I know is that we came out of the tavern and were headed for the buggy when something drove into the side of my head like a sledgehammer and flattened me. I woke up after midnight in a bed at the Markham house—that's where Sheena boards. The side of my head had been split, and Missus Markham stitched it and patched me up."

"How did you get there?"

"We had their horse and buggy, and George got concerned when we weren't back at their place by ten o'clock and came looking for us. He figured there was only one place we could have gone for supper. I had rented a room there for the night and told Missus Markham we should be back by nine. Hell, there's no place to go up in that country other than where we went. This envelope was tucked inside my shirt. Beyond that, all I know is that Sheena has disappeared."

"How much time has passed?"

"It was the night before last. I kept dropping off to sleep yesterday morning and tried to head out last night but passed out saddling my horse. I was still dizzy this morning, but Markham helped me get saddled. Then I started home with the envelope. Had to rest my horse and nap a few hours, several times along the way, but we came right here. Poor old Red is about tuckered out, but he did a good job of getting me here."

Morg said, "Here's what the message says. 'Marshal Fraser: Your daughter is held for trade. You for her. Go to Mad Rock on the Snake River. Somebody will meet you there to make the deal. Be there by noon on April 26. She's coyote food if you don't show up'."

Jaye said, "I figured somebody wanted money."

"This is likely how they're getting it. I told you there's a bounty on my head. We've got a little time. Today's the twenty-third. If I can leave before noon tomorrow, I can make Mad Rock in plenty of time."

"I'm riding with you, and I've got somebody else on the way. I thought we might be doing some tracking, and I hired a boy to take a message to my friend at the K Bar K about twenty miles south of the Loup River Tavern intersection. I thought we might need a tracker to find Sheena, and I asked him to take a look-see at the area around the tavern before he came on to my place. I guess we don't need his tracking, but there's no better man to have at your side out in this country."

"Just who are you talking about?"

"My friend, Jim Hunter. He's Santee Sioux—Indian name's Coyote Hunter. He's a ranch hand at the K Bar K— chose not to be a reservation Indian. He'd be a reliable backup with a gun."

"I don't expect any gunplay, but I'd welcome his company since you're not coming."

"I said I was going with you."

"You're not in any condition to ride that distance. Besides, I need you to stay with Andy while I'm gone."

"I've got Avery Holland looking after my stock right now, and he'll take care of your mules and any horses you leave behind."

"And what about Andy?"

"I'm going with you, too," Andy said.

"No. You're staying here. It's decided."

Jaye said, "You've met Susana Mercer now. I've known her a spell. I'll bet she'd take Andy in. That would free me up."

Andy protested. "Sheena's my sister. I need to go."

Jaye said, "And she's my betrothed—or I'm working on it anyhow. And I was with her when she was taken. I owe it to her to get her out of this fix."

"There's nothing for you to do. Does your friend Hunter speak decent English?"

"Hell, I doubt if he even speaks Sioux anymore. He went to a Quaker school near the reservation and decided to take the white man's path."

"Maybe he can help negotiate the way the trade takes place."

"You're not really going to just take her place?"

"I don't see any choice right now. She's my daughter. I'll trade places with her."

"That's a death sentence."

Morg shrugged.

Chapter 10

MORG LIKED JIM Hunter, who rode a coal-black gelding alongside Buckshot and himself. He did not fit the Indian stereotype established by dime novels with black hair cropped shorter than his own and usual cowhand attire with faded denim britches, a dusty low-crowned hat, and scuffed boots. No moccasins and not a feather to be seen. The only giveaway was his bronzed skin and slightly aquiline nose.

Morg guessed the young man would be a year or two short of thirty. He was a handsome devil, but Morg envied Hunter most for his lean, sinewy frame that carried him with the agility of a mountain cat. The two were about the same height and weight, he supposed, but he moved like an old, arthritic hound in comparison to Hunter and carried his pounds in less useful places.

They reined in their mounts near an ash- and cotton-wood-edged stream after a less than twenty-mile ride. There was not much natural cover, but a clear sky above them signaled they would not require shelter from rain. Nebraska weather was known to be fast-changing, but Hunter assured him there would be no rainstorms for at least several days. Many folks granted Indians mythical powers when it came to such things as weather forecasting, but Morg was skeptical.

The mounts and pack mule staked in a patch of grass nearby, the two men sat with cups of steaming coffee by the dying embers of a fire where they had earlier roasted a rabbit shot by Hunter. Stale biscuits collected by Morg in a rushed harvest from his own kitchen had supplemented the meat. They had not talked much about the mission, and Morg decided Hunter was entitled to know just what was planned.

"Jim, I don't think Jaye had much chance to fill you in on just what this ride we're on is all about."

"I know your daughter was kidnapped, and I see a United States Marshal's badge pinned on your vest. That's enough for me, but I might be more help if I knew something more about what you've got in mind. You have said we are headed for Mad Rock. I've passed the place many times. That point on the Snake River is not many miles from the Great Sioux Reservation to the north. Of course, last month Congress broke that up into five separate reservations. Mad Rock is nearest to what will be the Pine Ridge Reservation for the Oglala Sioux."

"You keep up on these things better than I do. I know Dakota Territory likely will be broken up into two states before the year is out. North Dakota and South Dakota are on their way to being the next states admitted to the union."

"I've got family spread out on the reservations. Even though I chose not to make my life there, I want to know what's going on. My people will all be South Dakota residents along Nebraska's north border."

Morg said, "I've never been to Mad Rock. Tell me about it."

"It is a sandstone formation on the north side of the Snake River. It takes a bit of imagination, but it stands on high ground and protrudes from the sandstone shelf below it like a man's neck and then widens into a rough egg shape to look something like a human head. The so-called head is probably a good ten feet high. I don't know if it was carved by humans or nature, but there is a crack in the stone that appears to be a frowning mouth and above that are two slits that look like unfriendly eyes. The face overlooks the river and is a local landmark."

Morg said, "I'm supposed to meet somebody involved in the scheme to abduct my daughter at Mad Rock. We are to work out the logistics of a trade. Her for me. She will return with you. I stay with the men."

Hunter stared across the fire at Morg, his face revealing nothing. "Are they going to kill you?"

"Not likely right away. An outlaw leader has put a bounty on my head. The reward is doubled if they take me to him alive. My first concern is to get Sheena to safety. After that, I'll worry about how to finagle my way out of the mess."

"This assumes they keep their part of the bargain and let your daughter go."

"They'll die if they don't."

"Mad Rock sits about thirty feet above the Snake, and the river narrows there and rushes along the sandstone wall below. There's not a high bank on the south side, and they can see for miles if they are on the hilltop with Mad Rock. The ground behind Mad Rock slopes down gradually and meets with the prairie dunes and grasslands below, where they would likely have set up camp. One man is probably posted as lookout all the time near the rock."

"I suppose the lookout will tell us what we do after we get there. I'll propose that one man meet me where you can keep an eye on me to talk terms."

"I'm wondering if I shouldn't be the man to talk terms. They might have a plan to make off with both of you if they can get you separated from your backup."

"I couldn't let you take that risk."

"We're both at risk anywhere within rifle range, but you don't get your daughter back without risks."

"I'll sleep on this. We've got a full day to figure things out tomorrow."

Both men laid out their bedrolls within hearing distance of the horses. Morg did not hear so well anymore, but he figured it wouldn't take much disturbance to bring Jim Hunter out of his slumber. The ride had sapped Morg's energy, and he dropped off instantly to sleep. It was almost sunrise when he was awakened by a slobbery kiss on his lips. He must be dreaming, but he hoped Sue offered a better kiss than that. He sat up and found Dingo next to his bedroll. He rubbed the cattle dog's ears and petted her for a few minutes, noting that Hunter had vacated his own blankets.

"Dingo, what in blazes are you doing here?" He supposed she had followed them from the ranch, but that seemed like a lot of miles for a dog. Still, she was bred to be a cattle dog, and such creatures were expected to cover a lot of miles in a day, racing back and forth to contain a herd on the move. She didn't seem exhausted, so she must have rested occasionally on her journey.

He got to his feet and signaled Dingo to stay, while he went into the trees to relieve himself. Mission accomplished, he looked around the campsite and still saw no sign of Hunter. The black gelding was still staked nearby, so he had not deserted. He stirred the coals in the fire ashes and found a few still had life and soon had a small fire going and a pot of coffee heating.

Soon, he heard Hunter's voice coming from downstream. He was obviously speaking to someone else. When Hunter stepped into the clearing, he was joined by a companion leading an appaloosa horse.

Morg expressed his anger with a withering glare at first, taking time to rein in his temper. Andy's eyes shifted to his boot toes.

"Explain yourself, boy. What are you doing here?"

Andy's reply was half-mumbled. "I came to help my sister—and my father. I brought my Winchester, and it's in the scabbard."

"I told you to stay with Jaye. Did he give you permission to leave?"

"No, sir. I just went. He and Avery were tending to a cow calving, and I said I would ride over to our place and get my bedroll and things together, since I was going to be sleeping at Jaye's house till you got home. I just didn't go back to the J Bar B."

"You realize Jaye's worried sick about your taking off like that. If I know him, he'll be coming after you as soon as he makes sure Avery can look after livestock at our places." Avery Holland was a grizzled cowhand who worked at different ranches as a handyman these days and lived rent-free in Jaye's bunkhouse in exchange for helping with chores when needed. He was paid a wage when he worked during roundups in spring and fall. Morg had a feeling that Jaye was not going to be especially upset that Andy had taken off and given him an excuse to join the party.

"I don't want to upset Jaye, but me and Dingo felt the need to come."

"Well, you're here, and we don't have time to take you back. You will be punished when this is over." That would give him time to think about punishing the kid. He was not experienced at child punishment. He knew how to render it with a gun facing down an outlaw, but he was not capable of using a razor strap as his uncle and supervisors at the orphanage had done so many times during his childhood. He could be a violent man but not with a child.

Dingo looked up at him and whined as if pleading Andy's case.

"You're in trouble, too, Dingo, for leading him here." Then he remembered the dog could not hear a word and just sighed. "Let's get some breakfast together, so we can be on our way."

Midmorning, they stopped at a spring to water the horses. They had ridden in near silence, allowing Hunter to take the lead. When they dismounted, Hunter said, "When I rode up on that dune a few minutes ago, I saw dust south of us, rider coming faster than he should. I'd say he's got a spare horse and has been switching now and then. I'd look for Jaye to join us in less than a half hour."

Chapter 11

S HEENA FRASER SAT on the rocky ground at the base of a lone cedar tree not more than a mile north of the Snake River and Mad Rock. A bright, spring sun was already dropping a warm blanket on the Sandhills, and the shade from her lonely tree was casting its shadow on the side opposite where she was bound with hands behind her back.

The three abductors were gone for the moment, and her only company consisted of two or three crows perched on the tree. She was not certain whether the birds were eyeing her as a supper prospect or had just found a comfortable place to rest given the dearth of trees on the rolling mounds of grass-cloaked sand. Other than an occasional 'caw,' the prairie was enveloped in dead silence, and to her surprise she found she was savoring the quiet and the beauty of the surrounding hills. It occurred to her that she had never taken the time to see the treasure that surrounded her. Now she was beginning to grasp Jaye's love of this sparsely populated land.

Her captors had not treated her cruelly, and it appeared she was truly being held for ransom. Still, she could identify the men if they released her. She reminded herself repeatedly that folks disappeared all the time in the country, and ransom money would no doubt enable the three to do just that—if the ransom was paid. She feared that her stepfather, Thomas Towne, might not meet whatever demands were being made.

She knew the three men only by single names. Goober, a paunchy young man, with reddish hair and shaggy mustache, seemed to be lowest in the pecking order, assigned most of the errand-boy work by Fincher, a tall, lean, beardless man, who spoke only to issue orders. He was tallest of the three, lean and dark, with eyes that made her nervous when he stared at her. She could see in those dusky eyes that he was undressing her, and she knew what he wanted. He was clearly in charge of the crew, and she was convinced that he was responsible to some nameless person who was not present. He often referred to what they were "supposed" to do, suggesting he must answer to someone else.

Willy was an average-sized man with a dirty, black beard that dropped to his chest. He evidently fancied himself a gunfighter, because his gun belt carried a holstered pistol on each hip. He was a storyteller who liked to brag about the men he had shot down. None of these men had served in the war, however, and Will would have been prime age for service during the War of the Rebellion. He likely evaded the draft by disappearing in the West. She wondered how many of the men shot down had taken a lead slug in the back.

Sheena saw the dust of a rider coming her way and watched as he approached. Goober. That likely meant a message. The ransom was to be paid today, and supposedly she would be released to someone. Her heart raced when Goober rode up and dismounted. He had a broken-toothed grin on his face when he spoke. "Y'all are headed home today, missy. Fincher had his spyglass up by Mad Rock. Two men coming for the trade."

He knelt and untied the knots in the rope that bound her hands to the tree. Her fingers were numb, and she flexed them for relief. She said, "Trade?"

"I guess I can say now. We're trading you for a U.S. Marshal."

"I don't understand."

"Your pa, Morgan Fraser. Somebody wants him bad. Willing to pay six thousand dollars if we take him and get him to where he's going alive. Three thousand if we got to kill him. He's your ransom."

Sheena was stunned. Her father? This made no sense.

"Wait here, Missy. I'll get your mount. Fincher says we got to show the merchandise, and then there's still some dickering to be done. Don't do nothing stupid. Y'all is about free."

She stood up and brushed off the baggy britches that had replaced her dress. At least the men had had the foresight to bring denim trousers, shirt, and moccasins for her to wear. She had never ridden sidesaddle, and a dress just did not adapt well astride a horse's back. She had figured out, though, that a woman wearing a dress might attract undue attention from persons they might encounter on their journey. She understood that when Fincher ordered her to tie her long hair up and then jammed a hat on her head that covered most of her forehead. A rope had been cut for a belt to hold up trousers that were far too wide in the waist, and she thought she could easily pass for a scarecrow.

Goober led her dun mare that had been staked in grass near a spring to the cedar tree. "Saddle up, Missy. We ain't got no time to waste."

"I've got to pee. You've had me tied up all morning."

"Well, get it done then. We got to be moving, or I'll catch hell from Fincher."

She stepped behind the tree, knowing that the spindly thing would not hide much, and that Goober would be enjoying a good view of her butt. She didn't care. Modesty had disappeared the second day out. Several minutes later, they rode away to join the others.

When they arrived at Mad Rock, Fincher was standing next to the big stone with his eyes focused beyond the river to the south. Willy was crouched off to the side about ten feet, half hidden in a fissure in the sandstone base, his rifle cradled in his arm. Fincher said, "Goober, tie the horses downslope with the others, and you stay put until I holler for you. Woman, I want you up here with me for now."

She climbed the slope to Mad Rock, and he handed her the telescope. "They'll be here soon, and then the game starts. Tell me who you're seeing."

She pressed the spyglass to her eye and focused on the riders. It would likely do more harm than good to lie. "One is Jim Hunter. He's a hand from the K Bar K."

"He's got an Injun look."

Sheena shrugged. "I've only met him once when I stopped by the K Bar K on a visit to Broken Bow." She did not add that Jaye Boyden had accompanied her and that they had stayed the night at the headquarters ranch home, or that Jaye and Jim were good friends.

"And the other?"

"My father, Marshal Morgan Fraser."

"Alright, you go back down there with Goober."

Chapter 12

"THAT IS MAD Rock," Hunter said, pointing toward the huge sandstone face that rose above the cliff top on the north side of the river.

"Yeah, and it's not yet eleven o'clock, so we are ahead of the deadline. I guess the next move is theirs. You're still willing to be the go-between?"

"Yes, but I don't like the idea of you going with those men."

"I'm not excited by the prospect, but we've got to get Sheena out of there and with Jaye and Andy before I make any other move. I'll keep my eyes open for opportunities to escape. We're at least a day and a half from any town. I'm curious about where we're headed, and I'd like to meet Monte Oxford. Bringing him down would be a perfect ending to my marshal service."

"If you meet Monte Oxford, your ending is more likely six feet under, and I'm betting he doesn't plan on it being quick."

"Yeah, I'm just talking tough. I've got a son I'd like to see grown-up and a daughter I hope to make peace with. I'm thinking I'd like to take at least one of these men alive and find out if he knows enough to get me to this Oxford."

Hunter said, "After I get your daughter to Jaye, I could double back and set up an ambush."

"You've done more than I ever expected. No, this isn't your job. I want you to see my kids home safely."

Hunter knew there was no arguing with the man and his eyes were now fastened on an object across the river. "Somebody's waving a white flag on the end of a rifle barrel. Time for me to go. I'll see what kind of a bargain I can make."

"Make the deal. Whatever it takes so long as we're assured Sheena will be safe. I don't need to tell you that the word of men like these is worthless."

Hunter nodded and nudged his black gelding toward the river some fifty yards away. When he reached the riverbank, he looked upward at the man who stood on a wide ledge below Mad Rock on much higher ground on the opposite side. The outlaw was a tall, lean man with a smirk on his face.

"Who are you?" the man said.

"My name is Hunter. Jim Hunter. Who are you?"

"Don't know if an Injun's got a right to know, but I go by Fincher. How did you come to be here?"

"Marshal Fraser asked me to."

"You a lawman of some kind?"

"I'm a cowhand helping a neighbor out."

"You don't sound like no Injun I ever heard talk."

"Maybe you haven't met enough of the Indian people. Now, I think we have business to attend to."

"I see you got Marshal Fraser out there. Don't know why he didn't come up and talk for hisself."

"You can talk with him soon enough if we make a deal. Now, I want to see Miss Fraser before we talk further."

Fincher tossed his head back and hollered. "Willy, bring her out."

A heavy, black-bearded man stepped out from behind Mad Rock, pulling Sheena Fraser roughly by one arm. At first glance, dressed in baggy blue jeans and hat brim falling just above her eyes, Hunter did not recognize her, but, yes, it was Sheena. Her pretty face appeared tired and drawn, but her identity was unmistakable.

Fincher said, "Terms are simple. You get the marshal up here. There's a shallow crossing about twenty yards upstream where the high ground drops off. He rides his critter across. Then we send the young lady. After that we head our separate ways. Ain't nothing to it."

"No, we won't buy that. They'll enter at the same time, pass each other midstream. I will be standing on the bank's edge near the crossing, and you'll do the same on the north side. We'll be within easy gunshot range of each other in case somebody causes trouble."

"I got two men with rifles at the ready just over the backside of the cliff."

"And I got a man settled with a Sharps on the first dune after the river bottom to the southeast. He's a crack shot—old buffalo hunter—and you will go down if any harm comes to Miss Fraser, the marshal or me." He was lying, but the grim look on Fincher's face said that whatever suspicions he had, the man was taking his words seriously.

Fincher said, "Go get your marshal, and bring him up here."

"I'll fetch him. In the meantime, I want to see you and the lady on the north riverbank before we ride up to the river's edge."

Hunter reined his mount around and rode back toward Morgan Fraser at an easy gallop. As he approached, he noted that Morg had unsaddled Buckshot and saddled the spare mount, a dun gelding he had owned for only a few years. When he reached Morg, he dismounted and relayed his conversation with the outlaw called Fincher.

Morg said, "It sounds like you made a decent bargain. Do you think he believed your story about the sniper with the Sharps?"

"I think he had doubts, but if all he wants is you, why would he risk it?"

"That's true enough. Well, let's get to it and get my little girl started on her way home." He handed Buckshot's lead rope to Hunter. "Just in case things don't go right, see that Buckshot goes to Andy."

When they neared the river, Hunter saw that Fincher was already at the riverside with Sheena mounted on the dun mare. The river was wider here but still not more than thirty feet he estimated, and its depth should not be more than a few feet. Spring rains might double the depth and widen the river some, but creeks and rivers tended to rise fast in the Sandhills and drop quickly. Anyway, this day the river should be no obstacle, and riders should stay dry.

As they rode up to the bank, Fincher yelled, "Marshal, take off the gun belt and give it to your friend or toss it in the river. That rifle in the saddle holster, too."

Morg handed his weapons to Hunter. "Figured that was coming."

"Alright, Marshal, you start, and your daughter will be right along."

Without a word, Morg reined his horse into the river. Sheena's mare immediately entered from the opposite side. Almost at the river's midpoint, the two paused, and Hunter saw that their gazes were fixed on each other. 'Talking with their eyes,' Hunter always called such looks between people. When Sheena's mount stepped from the water onto the riverbank, he saw the tears glistening in her eyes but said nothing. He turned his horse away, leading Buckshot, and Sheena fell in behind him.

Finally, Sheena spoke. "They're going to kill him, aren't they?"

"Somebody wants to kill him, but I have heard about your father for years. He does not kill easily, and this game isn't over."

"What do you mean you have heard of my father? He's not famous."

"More than you think. The Sioux respect him for the work he has done ferreting out corrupt Indian agents and other government criminals. He has saved many lives with his work. Dime novels have been written about him, not true entirely, but reflecting the admiration many feel for him."

"I've never heard these things. I'm sure Andy hasn't either."

"I suggest you not underestimate your father. Now I have a few questions."

"Of course."

"How many men were with you near Mad Rock?"

"Three. There were four, but one left yesterday. He didn't join us until a day or so after I was abducted."

"What did he look like?"

"Average height and skinny. Young. Blonde with a scraggly goatee. The thing that stood out though was his left eye that looked like it was half shut."

"Okay. We'll talk about him later. We are about two hours from your brother and Jaye Boyden."

"I don't understand. What are they doing here?"

"I'll let them explain."

Chapter 13

DINGO STARTED HER warning barking before Jaye and Andy saw the riders emerge from behind one of the seemingly endless grass-covered dunes to the north. Jaye still could not figure out how the deaf cattle dog could sense the approach of riders, but the handicap had not significantly impaired her value as a watchdog.

Suddenly, Dingo raced away toward the riders. "Dingo, stay," he hollered before he remembered that the dog could not hear him.

"She can't obey unless she sees her signals," Andy said.

"Yeah, I forgot, but I guess it doesn't matter this time. She's joined up with Buckshot and trotting along beside your pa's horse."

"She loves Dad. She's my pal, too, but Dingo always tends to Dad first. Jim's leading Buckshot, but there's a stranger riding beside him. Where's Sheena?"

"That stranger is Sheena. She's just outfitted like a scruffy cowhand."

Andy's face turned somber, and he looked at Jaye with tears glazing his eyes. "They made the trade. I ain't ever going to see my dad again, am I?"

Jaye had his doubts but replied, "It's not over yet. I'm betting your dad's been in a hundred tight spots like this over the years and squeezed through them. He's probably already got his escape figured out."

"I don't think you know, Jaye. You're just trying to make me feel better. I just want to see Dad again, keep on getting to know him better. He's different than I always thought, ain't a bad person like I'd grown up believing. I like being with him and don't want to go back to the Tall T even if they'd take me."

"Morg would be the first to tell you that most of us are a mix of good and bad, but we should try to be more good than bad. Of course, there are a few rotten apples where it's dang near impossible to find the good. Those are the kind your pa has spent most of his life chasing down and bringing to justice, cold-blooded killers and the like." He was not going to add that Marshal Morgan Fraser had a reputation for rendering his own notion of justice before his quarry ever made it to a courtroom.

When Hunter and Sheena rode into the campsite, Andy hurried to greet his sister, and when she dismounted, he wrapped his arms around her.

Sheena, obviously surprised, held onto him for a moment and then stepped back and smiled. "Andy, I swear this is the first time you've ever hugged me, and you always slunk away like a scorned dog whenever I tried to hug you. And my heavens, you're almost as tall as I am now, and I'm not exactly a tiny thing."

Andy shrugged and surrendered a sheepish grin. "Like Dad always says, 'times are changing.' So those men took Dad, huh?"

The few minutes of lightheartedness vanished, and Sheena's face turned grim. "They did, and I feel guilty about it. I don't know what in the devil got into him."

Jaye stepped up and interrupted. "It's simple, Sheena. Your father loves you. He blamed himself for your dilemma. The only thing that mattered to him was getting you away from those men."

"But he had to think I hated him. I avoided him, and if I got trapped, I barely spoke to him. He was like a stranger to me. When I was small, I came to think he was a bad person because it seemed like he was always gone on one of his assignments and didn't care about us."

Andy said, "He's more good than bad, Sheena. Are you always a good person?"

She looked at him but did not reply.

Hunter dismounted. "I'm sorry. You can talk more later, but I must interrupt. We all have things to get done. I am going to be riding out again soon."

Jaye said, "I thought you were riding back with us. That's what Morg directed."

"I am aware of that, but I intend to track these men and see if I can find a way to break Morg free of those no-goods."

"That's not what Morg said he wanted."

"Nope, but I'm not on Morg's payroll. I'm my own boss."

"Well, then I'm going with you."

Hunter shook his head negatively. "And who looks after Sheena and Andy? Do you think Morg would approve of your deserting them out here in the middle of the Sandhills? Besides, I've got another concern. Sheena said that a fourth man joined up with them for a spell, but after they got to Mad Rock, he disappeared. Now he may have gone on ahead to report to somebody else. Another possibility is that he had instructions to kill Sheena after she was released and that he intended to intercept her and any escort and make certain she never got back. She can identify them all, and it's a good bet that there is paper out on at least one of these men in a lawman's office—possibly all. She will be shuffling through wanted posters, that's for certain."

Jaye said, "Then why are you leaving?"

"You can't handle one man?"

Jaye just glared at him.

Half an hour later, after selecting a meager portion of the food supplies, Hunter disappeared. Jaye thought of breaking camp, packing their supplies on the packhorse and starting the return trip but decided that by the time they finished their tasks, they likely would not have more than an hour's riding time before dusk. Considering the risk of a stalker, it would be best to proceed with a bit of caution. He surveyed the site he and Andy had set up after Morg and Jim Hunter had separated from them.

The plan had always been to hole up here overnight. The location was protected by a sandstone cliff on one side. The wall offered a concave surface at the base that sank some four feet into the stone, providing some protection from the wind and any rainstorm. From the growth lining the nearby creek, they had harvested some dead ash and oak limbs for the firepit they had dug out in front of the shelter. The trees along the creek screened the campers somewhat from discovery, but he was aware that anyone searching for them would have no problem locating the place.

Sheena's voice abruptly invaded his contemplation. "While you were daydreaming, Andy and I unsaddled and staked out the two horses I've added to your remuda. Don't expect me to do all the cooking. I like to build fires. I'll do that. We can build a fire, can't we? Or are we going to pretend that smoke might betray our location?"

Jaye turned to where Sheena and Andy were standing not ten feet distant. "Yeah, we can build a fire." He stared at her incredulously. She had Morg's rifle in one hand and his gun belt with a holstered pistol slung over the opposite shoulder. "Can you shoot those things?"

"And why do you think I cannot?"

"I've never seen you fire a gun. I figured you didn't know how to handle one, certainly not a six-gun."

"There are a lot of things you've never learned about me."

"Well, how did you learn to fire a gun?"

"A boyfriend."

"What boyfriend? I never knew you to see any man but me."

"A young man named Charles Vaughn. You didn't see me that much when I was away at high school and normal training in North Platte. You knew me and saw me the brief times I was back, but we weren't more than acquaintances. I was quite serious about Charles then. He was two years older, and he competed in marksmanship competitions and such. We would go out in the countryside and fire his guns. I am a good marksman if I say so myself, maybe better than you."

She was starting to annoy him. First, the boyfriend, and now bragging about her marksmanship. "You fired a rifle, I assume. What about pistols?"

"Mostly a Winchester, but I can handle a pistol and hit a target up close."

"What became of Charles?"

"He worked in the family business for a year after high school, but they sent him back east to school—to Yale—to study law. He should be finished in another year, I suppose."

He had a hundred questions he wanted to ask her about this Charles, but he knew it wasn't any of his business. And he was not an innocent when it came to other female company. Still, he could not deny a bit of jealousy. He had always assumed she had experienced no male romantic relationships before. He wondered just how romantic. Was Charles still a prospective suitor?

Jaye said, "I'll see what I can put together for supper if you want to get a fire going. I think we can count on Dingo to warn us if a stranger comes near the camp."

Sheena said, "You are going to rely on a deaf dog to guard the camp?"

Andy interrupted to defend Dingo. "You can count on Dingo. She's the smartest dog in the whole country. How many can obey hand signals? I'd trust her with my life any day. Dad would, too. He saved her life, and Dingo knows it."

Jaye said, "I'll be standing guard, too."

"You and I will take shifts," Sheena said.

"Include me," Andy said.

"We'll talk about this after supper." Jaye had assumed he was in command of the little party, but now he was having his doubts. He was seeing a side of Sheena that had been hidden till now. Somehow, however aggravating, it made her even more alluring.

Chapter 14

JAYE SAT IN the shadows of the sandstone cliff, resting his back against the wall with a rifle cradled in his arms. Sheena slept not fifteen feet away in the bedroll they had brought for her, and Dingo dozed between her and Andy, who had surrendered part of his blanket to the dog. A full moon cast its soft beam on the faces of his sleeping comrades and somehow made their slumber contagious. He nodded off for a few minutes but woke suddenly when Dingo's cool, wet nose brushed his cheek.

His hand instinctively reached out and ran his fingers over the short, coarse hair on the dog's neck and then scratched behind her ears. Usually, she would bask in this attention, but her ears stiffened and her head turned toward the trees along the creek. Jaye was fully alert when the dog's soft whine told him something was worrying her. He gently grasped her muzzle so she would look at his face, then pressed a finger to his lips to signal silence. Dingo, still obviously tense and nervous, obeyed but turned her head again to the trees.

Jaye readied the rifle but did not move. Together, he and Dingo watched and waited. Finally, a shadowy figure emerged from the trees. Jaye got to his feet and yelled, "Don't move, mister, or you are a dead man."

The visitor already had a pistol in his hand and swung toward Jaye, who dived for the ground just as the man's gun cracked twice sending two slugs his way. Jaye rolled over, came to his knees with the Winchester held chest high and got off two shots of his own. The man dropped his pistol and crumpled to his knees before falling face forward onto the ground.

Dingo was barking wildly now, as Jaye went to confirm that the stalker would cause no more trouble this night. He started to bend over to look at the man he had taken down when the dog's barking turned to near a roar and growling. Someone screamed, and he whipped around, fumbling to position his rifle as he saw Dingo off to his left farther up the creek. A man was stumbling and trying to maintain his balance as he tried to get his pistol pointed at the vicious creature that had anchored its teeth in the calf of his leg.

A single rifle shot echoed in the darkness, and Dingo's would-be killer collapsed. Jaye turned and saw Sheena lowering her own Winchester. Andy stood near her with his rifle at the ready. Dingo had paused her attack but stood beside her victim, daring him to move.

A quick look at the outlaw near his feet told Jaye that the stocky man was dead. One slug had hit an artery at the juncture of his neck and shoulder, and the wound was bleeding him out. The other appeared to be a lung shot and likely would have taken his life but at a slower pace. Jaye judged him to be middle-aged. His hat lay on the ground beside him, revealing a balding scalp. A brushy black mustache decorated his face that was otherwise covered with a good week's growth of whiskers.

He caught up with Sheena and Andy who were headed to the downed man being guarded by Dingo. The moonlight did not reveal his fate until they were near. Jaye knelt and rolled the man over on his back. He was a slim man, fair-haired with chin fuzz, probably not much past twenty years. The slug had driven into the center of his chest. Not much blood; Jaye thought it had likely killed before the recipient hit the ground.

"This is Manny," Sheena said. "The fella who rode with us a spell and then left. I killed a kid who had so much of his life ahead."

"Not likely that much given his chosen occupation. Your dad told me once that life is about making choices and living with consequences. This guy chose the owl hoot trail. That's generally the route to an early death. A consequence."

"And my father chose to abandon his wife and children."

"It's more complicated than that, but you're too dang stubborn to see anything else right now." She seemed not to hear him.

"I've never fired a gun at a person before. The first time I do, I kill a kid."

Jaye did not know what to say that would not lead to a fuss. It was time, perhaps, for Sheena to start sorting some things out on her own. "Consider maybe that I would likely be a dead man if you had not pulled the trigger. I thank you for saving my life if that counts for something. At sunrise, Andy and I will see to the burying of these men. We'll need to go through their things and find their horses before we pull out. I don't know that we need a watch, but I'm the knothead who assumed there was only one gunman. I'll take watch duty the rest of the night."

Sheena declared firmly, "No, it's my turn. I will take a few hours. That will take us to sunrise. You didn't wake me when you were supposed to, and that pisses me some. I'm getting damn tired of your treating me like I'm a helpless ninny."

"Jaye, Sheena." It was Andy hollering. He and Dingo had gone to inspect the other gunman while Jaye and his sister were squabbling.

They hurried over to respond to Andy's summons, keeping some distance between them. "What is it, Andy?" Jaye asked.

Andy pointed at the body. "I know this feller. He came to work at Tall T, maybe a month before I got sent off to Dad's. His name was Arthur. I never knew his last name. Crabby devil, so I steered clear of him."

Chapter 15

THE NIGHT BEFORE they would arrive home, wherever that was, Sheena thought, she sat silently in front of the cookfire, still trying to sort out all that had happened the past week. On the opposite side of the smoke curtain that rose from the dying embers, Andy and Jaye chattered about some nonsense that she had no interest in while Dingo dozed with her head on Andy's lap.

She knew that Jaye was trying to distract Andy from worrying about his father. She regretted the way she had snapped at Jaye so often on this journey. He had been more than a good friend, patient and understanding to a fault. Maybe that was part of the problem. She was itching for a fight with someone, and it was his misfortune that he was the only candidate.

Her father was at the root of her turmoil. She was haunted by the warmth and love she saw in his eyes when they passed in the middle of the Snake River and the whisper that she barely heard: "I love you, Sheena." She had nearly broken out in sobs. Yet she had not responded in kind even though he had quickly offered his life for hers. Jaye had told her there was not a moment's hesitation when he delivered the ransom note to her father. Plans for the exchange had been implemented instantly. He had not considered recruiting a posse to chase down the abductors, knowing that it would put her life at risk.

Sheena stood. "Jaye, I would like to speak with you—alone." She did not flinch at the dirty look that Andy cast at her. Her brother had witnessed too many of their conversations. He was a boy, and decisions were for his elders to make. Jaye got up and followed her to the remuda where they now had seven horses staked out, including their mounts, the packhorse, and the acquisitions from the dead gunslingers.

They paused not far from the tiny stream near the new lush grass where the horses were staked. Jaye said nothing, obviously waiting for her to initiate the conversation. Sheena said, "I have made some decisions, but I have questions and promise I will listen to anything you want to say."

"Alright."

"I am going to stay at my father's house with Andy until my father returns." She hesitated. "If he dies, I will decide after that what to do."

"He would be welcome to stay with me. You would be, too. I have a big house with extra rooms. It may be run-down, and I'm not the best housekeeper, but it might be safest to have an extra gun available until everything is settled. I have no ulterior motives. I promise."

She wondered how she would respond if his motives were derailed. He was a ruggedly handsome rascal, every bit of Charles's match and more. She was not a virgin, and Charles had thoroughly ignited her lust, too long since unsatisfied. Maybe that was part of her annoyance with Jaye sometimes. He was too much of a gentleman. Still, she was far from ready to commit to him or any other man. Best to keep a respectable distance from Jaye for now. She had a brother to care for and a father to worry about.

"Thank you, but I will be staying at my father's house. It will take me a day there to get settled in and then I intend to call on my mother. I still have clothes and other items to retrieve at the Tall T, brothers to say goodbye, too, for now. I also intend to ask her about the man named Arthur who worked there. There is too much co-incidence for me to shake off."

"I agree, but I wonder if we shouldn't be more discreet in learning about Arthur. I am acquainted with one of the Tall T hands, Colt Louden. I've been thinking about trying to hire him on since your dad is considering letting me lease his land and expand my herd. I think I can make a few extra dollars with a hired hand. Besides, there are two quarter sections nearby homesteaders are wanting to sell after fall harvest. That land is for cattle, not corn or wheat, and they have come to realize that and don't want to spend another winter here."

Colt Louden was another eligible bachelor who could steal a woman's heart, and it occurred to Sheena that the Sandhills produced a surplus of such young men. They needed more females in this country. "I know Colt. He's sort of a lone wolf among the Tall T hands, takes on all the dirtiest jobs without complaint. It might be good if you could talk to him, but I still intend to talk to my mother."

"Consider this. I could take you and Andy in my buckboard to the Tall T and see if Colt is nearby. If he is, I'll have a talk with him. If I offer him a job first, it might loosen his tongue some."

"You are bribing him."

"No, I'm not. He's got the job whether he's got anything to say or not."

"You should have been a lawyer the way you use weasel words."

"What do you say? We'll get back tomorrow late. Next day we go to the Tall T."

"I need to go to the Loup Trading Post and let the folks there know I won't be able to work there this summer. The school year's about finished at Willow School, and I'm sure somebody has been found to finish out the year there. I can't promise I would be back in the fall, and I should let the board know they are free to employ somebody else. And I must pick up my things at the Markham boarding house, pay rent for an extra month and inform them of my situation and that I may not return."

"You are making a permanent move to your dad's?"

"Only if he doesn't come back." She could not bring herself to say that he was likely dead. "If he does, I will check back with Willow School, and if they have made other arrangements, I will start hunting for a new teaching job, maybe something in a town that civilization has touched like Lincoln or Omaha—New York City."

Chapter 16

SHEENA RODE NEXT to Jaye on the wagon seat, and Andy and Dingo were curled up together on blankets in the wagon bed as they neared the Tall T ranch headquarters. Jaye had been at the Fraser house before sunrise, and boy and dog had been awakened to eat a quick breakfast. Sheena had slept on the couch, inexplicably uncomfortable with the notion of sleeping in her father's bed.

"Are you acquainted with someone named Susana Mercer?" Sheena asked.

"I've met her a few times. Nice lady. She's a widow lady, owns a small ranch several miles west of your father's place on the Dismal Trail. She rents out all the ground and carries on a private school out of her house. Morg talked to her about taking on Andy at the school, and she told him she could take Andy through the first two years of high school, but he would have to test to that level at the school where he chose to finish at. Your father was real enthused about the notion. Andy was going to take some schooling this summer to decide if he was at the level he should be."

"Why wouldn't he be?"

"It seems he didn't show up for school much."

"My mother should have known and done something about it. My little brothers attended the same school."

"I don't know anything about that, but I do know that Andy is a clever kid who doesn't always channel his brain to noble deeds."

"I don't see how that would improve under my father's care."

"Maybe you can be wrong about something once in a while."

She held back her retort. "I just wanted to know about this Mercer woman. She left a note for my father. It was jammed under the front door when we arrived yesterday afternoon. I tore open the envelope and read the note because of the uncertainty of my father's future."

"Of course."

"I hope your sarcasm doesn't suggest I was being nosey." She told herself she was just curious. That was not the same as nosey, was it?

"Well, your father isn't available to respond to any message, so it seems reasonable to find out if the note was something urgent."

"She invited him over for lunch again and said he should bring Andy and Dingo."

"That sounds neighborly."

"She sounds like a woman on the prowl. They were to go over the day after tomorrow. We should be back from Willow School errands by tomorrow evening. Unless my father is back, I thought I might ride over with Andy and tell her about what has happened."

"A substitute for the lunch guest."

"If she invites us. I hate cooking."

"I have noticed. Probably not much opportunity growing up in a place like the Tall T. Anyway, I think that's a great idea. She does need to be informed."

When the wagon rolled up in front of the house, the two barking dog alarms ran out to greet them, and Jaye reined in the mule team, climbed down from the wagon and went around to the other side to assist Sheena, who was already on the ground by the time he got there. Jaye said, "I'll wander about and see if I can locate Colt Louden after I water the mules. Andy used to treat the critters to a bit of grain and hay from the barn, but I don't think we'll be doing that today."

Sheena looked in the wagon bed. Dingo was up, tail wagging and ready to go. Unfortunately, she would need to stay in the wagon. The dog would not be a welcome guest here if Thomas Towne saw her. Andy was feigning sleep yet, but he was not going to get by with it. "Andrew Fraser, get your fanny out here. You are wide awake, and you are going to pay your respects to your mother."

Andy rolled over and glared at his sister. "Don't want to."

"I don't give a darn. You are going to. Now, get moving."

After Andy signaled Dingo to stay, they walked up to the mansion where their mother now stood on the veranda, arms folded across her chest and a sour look on her face. When they approached, she said, "What are you two doing here?"

Sheena said, "It's so nice to see you, too, Mother."

May sighed, "I don't mean to be rude. It's just that Thomas says that neither of you is welcome here."

The three stood awkwardly on the veranda, but her mother did not invite them into the house. Sheena said, "You heard about my abduction, I assume."

"I did, and I was very worried. I was glad to hear that your father had the decency to surrender himself for the exchange. I was surprised, frankly."

"Why?"

"I just never saw him as a man who would risk his own life for anybody."

"But that's what he did every day in his work." It seemed strange defending her father. She doubted she had ever done that in her life.

"I suspect he took few risks. If he shot an outlaw, he probably did it while the man slept."

Sheena decided that this would be a futile debate. "Mother, I came to remove any remaining belongings of mine from the house. Andy says he has a few things, too."

Andy, previously silent, finally spoke, "Mom, you're wrong about Dad. He ain't a coward. He never hesitated for a second about giving himself up for Sheena, and the work he did all those years saved a lot of lives, got a lot of no-goods locked up or dead if it came to that. And he's been a good pa since I went with him, not the feller I always heard about."

"You poor, ignorant child. I thought such things about him until I came to know him. I was too young, and he wore that shiny badge and swept me off my feet for a spell. You will have to find out the truth for yourself."

Sheena said, "Mother, our clothes and personal things."

"They're gone. Some of the clothes were given to the help. The rest were burned or buried in the dump pit. You have nothing here."

Sheena could not believe what she was hearing. It was as if she had divorced her children. She had never been a woman of great warmth, and defense of Thomas Towne always came first, even when he had molested her and eventually tried to rape her. Was it fear or blind love of the man that drove her to be like this?

"I guess we'll be on our way then, Mother. One question."

"Yes?"

"Did you have a man named Arthur working here at the Tall T recently?"

She was caught by surprise and was obviously struggling with her answer. "Arthur. I don't recall anyone with that name. Of course, I don't mix with the hands much. But no, I'm sure there was no Arthur here. I would have at least heard his name mentioned."

Her mother was an accomplished liar, but it was not working this time. She did know there had been such a man at the ranch and likely had met him. Besides, Andy had already confirmed the man's presence there. "A man named Arthur who worked at the Tall T for a time tried to kill Andy and me. Jaye killed the man, and I shot down the killer that was with him."

Her mother's eyes widened with a look of horror. "I just can't believe that. A man from this ranch tried to murder you? And you killed another man? This is just too farfetched. You have been dreaming."

Andy said, "She's telling the truth, Mom. And I saw this Arthur at the ranch when I was still here. I recognized him."

Sheena turned away from her mother. "Let's go, Andy. I can see Dingo's getting impatient, and Jaye should be along soon."

Chapter 17

J AYE CAUGHT SIGHT of Colt Louden astride a resisting bay gelding at the corral where he and an older cowhand were apparently breaking horses. By the time Jaye reached the corral, the horse appeared under control and Colt was dismounting. He looked Jaye's way and waved, leading the horse over to the board fence where Jaye waited.

The fence boards barred a handshake, but Colt offered his crooked grin and nodded. He was a fair-haired young man who had attended country school with Jaye. After eighth grade, Jaye headed to North Platte to high school, and Colt moved on to whatever ranch jobs he could find. His parents were homesteaders to the northeast with six younger children, and there was no place for Colt on the small farm.

Jaye said, "I brought Sheena over to fetch her things and thought I'd see if I could hunt you up while I was here."

"You going to marry that pretty filly?"

"I only wish."

"Well, you found me at my favorite hangout. I just wish we had more horses on the place. I like cattle good enough, but I love horses."

"I would like to expand my ranching into the horse business. Maybe we could work something out. Well, hell, I'll just come right out and say it. Colt, I'd like to have you come work for me at the J Bar B. It would be year-round, I could pay a hundred dollars a month and let you run some horses of your own, maybe partner on some if you want. I'm probably not matching what you're paid here, but that's the best I can offer."

"You got yourself a hand, Jaye. It's past time for me to move on. I don't fit here. When do I start?"

"As soon as you can."

"I'll be there day after tomorrow."

"You'll have to share the bunkhouse with Avery. He lives there in exchange for some handyman work. He's at neighboring ranches and farms a lot of the time."

"I've known Avery since you and me wasn't much more than tykes. And I don't mind storytelling."

"Show up when you're able to start. Before I go, I've got a question."

"Okay."

"Did you have a man working here by the name of Arthur?"

"Yep. Wasn't here more than a month or two. Mean son-of-a-bitch. Never done a lick of work. I think he fancied himself a gunslinger. Him and Towne was cozy, and Arthur and Packer Osborne, got along good enough. Osborne's sort of a manager, I guess, above Zeke, who's the real foreman of the outfit. Everybody else kept their distance pretty much. He never said as much as a word to me. I steered clear, and he looked at me like I was a pile of cow shit." Louden paused, his eyes fixed on something behind Jaye. "Uh, oh. Trouble coming this way."

Jaye turned and saw the master of Tall T strutting their way, his pendulous belly in front. Thomas Towne was a big, burly man with reddish hair and handlebar mustache with a light complexion that revealed cheeks that turned bright as a red rose when his temper flared. Today, they almost glowed. "He likely wants to welcome me," Jaye said. "Go ahead and get back to your work. I'll chat with the gentleman."

"Next chat I have will be to tell him I'm pulling out. I ain't so sure I won't be bunking at your place tonight."

"Your bunk is waiting." He stepped out to intercept Towne.

"Howdy, Thomas." He extended his hand which was ignored.

"I didn't invite you to my place, and you got no business taking up the time of my cowhands. I want you the hell off the Tall T now."

"Don't get yourself excited, Thomas. I just brought Sheena and Andy over to pick up their belongings."

"They're at your wagon, waiting to leave. Good riddance as far as those worthless kids carrying the Fraser brand are concerned. Those kidnappers are damn lucky they didn't get stuck with that bitch Sheena."

It was all Jaye could do not to drive his fist into the pompous bastard's mouth. Not now, though. Someday, maybe.

Jaye wheeled away without another word and hurried to the buckboard. When he got there, Sheena and Andy were waiting. He noted that the wagon bed was still empty. "You didn't get your things," he said.

Andy said, "They got rid of any stuff Sheena and me had here. I don't understand what's going on. Mom wasn't always like this. I always felt she liked Abe and Simon best, but I didn't think she hated me."

"She doesn't hate you, Andy. I'm thinking she is dealing with some difficult times right now. Things will get better. I'd bet on it."

The anger simmering in Sheena's eyes told Jaye it was best not to pursue the matter further. "I guess we will head on to Willow School and the Loup Trading Post. We will hopefully be able to get lodging with Mister and Missus Markham for the night."

Chapter 18

A CAPTURED UNITED STATES Marshal was somewhere in an isolated village in Dakota Territory that Jim Hunter had never heard of. Badlands City, according to the crude sign at the outskirts, was currently populated by thirteen people. The sign's scratched-out numbers indicated residents had ranged from ten to eighteen since the sign's stake had been driven into the rock-strewn ground. Apparently, someone periodically posted the current score.

The party who named the village must have been someone with a sense of humor, Hunter figured, to have anointed the collection of structures a city considering that the buildings consisted of no more than eight stone or log houses, two taverns, a trading post and what appeared to be a jail. As near as he could guess, the village lay somewhere between the west edge of the Lakota Sioux reservation and the eastern part of the vast area known as the Badlands. The latter word had been translated from the Sioux words *mako sicca* meaning 'bad lands,' referring to the rugged terrain and rock formations with steep canyons and slippery clay soil. With frigid winters and baking summers and little water, few were enticed to settle in the area.

He had followed the men for nearly a week to a place they could have reached in three days from Mad Rock. They were either lost or worried about being tracked. It made no sense that they had crossed the Niobrara River, first heading north to Dakota Territory, then crossing again to the south and after some time, once more to the north. They had camped for several days in a small canyon. A long rest? Watching for someone following?

He wondered if they were waiting for the man to catch up with them after he completed what Hunter assumed was his task of disposing of Sheena and himself. If so, he took the man's absence as a positive sign that his mission had not been accomplished. It worried him that he had sent the others on with the knowledge they could be in danger. Still, he trusted Jaye Boyden to look out for Sheena and Andy, and he suspected Sheena Fraser was as good as any man, likely better than most. Anyhow, he could not reverse his decision now. His job was to locate

Marshal Fraser and then help him escape. He had circled the town, and there was no sign that they had stopped and moved on. Morgan Fraser was here someplace.

It was late afternoon of the day following Hunter's discovery of the village of Badlands City. He had learned the previous night how the occupants of the village survived, perhaps even thrived. He had found a knoll south of town behind which he could stake his mount near a stream where there was enough sickly grass to graze a single critter. He tossed his bedroll within twenty feet of the horse, resigning himself to a cold camp absent hot coffee.

Last night, it was nearly dusk before he could go to the knoll's top and focus his spyglass on the town. There had been a parade of people into the little village, the majority Sioux but a good number of whites as well. The taverns were across the road from each other, and it was obvious the Indians and whites were entering separate establishments. Other than that, the town's visitors appeared to intermingle with ease. It was obvious Badlands City had taken root just outside of reservation boundaries to profit off the red man's curse, demon alcohol. The white men were probably a mix of government people who worked at the reservation and outlaws who were known to hide out in the Badlands from time to time.

Two of the small houses had white men standing in line outside with the doors opening every half hour or so with one man exiting and another entering. He assumed that these were bordellos, and from the ragged appearances of the waiting line, Hunter doubted many could afford more than a half hour with one of the ladies.

The marshal's captors were the only people in the town who might recognize him, but he thought he could resolve that by wearing moccasins and his buckskin shirt into the crowd, perhaps tie a bandana about his head. There weren't many Sioux wearing breechclouts these days, and the majority of men, except for ceremonial occasions, were wearing denims and a variety of shirts. Most whites he had encountered thought all Indians looked alike anyway. Tonight, he would venture into the big city and see if he could find Morg Fraser.

As dusk dropped its shadow over the rocky, rugged earth that surrounded Badlands City, Hunter walked toward the village. He felt naked without his rifle, but Indians were prohibited from carrying such things near reservation land. His Colt was slipped into his belt and covered by the buckskin shirt that fell to his hips, and he did not intend to be near enough to others for anyone to notice any bulge.

As he walked into the village, he saw that the social evening had already started. The hitching posts were all claimed for the moment, and other horses were staked along the edge of the village. Obviously, the town had not been formally platted and mapped. The houses and business buildings were not lined up along defined streets but were set haphazardly and at random it appeared. The passageways must have been opened by wagon and horse travel between the structures.

He walked past the buildings along the convoluted trail that snaked between them—no boardwalks or sidewalks in this village. He made two rounds, keeping his eyes on the jail, steering clear of the two bordellos which were obviously exclusively engaged in white trade. The trading post, however, was doing a brisk business, and only a sprinkling of whites appeared among the Sioux. He stopped suddenly when he saw a familiar face exiting the jailhouse. Fincher, the man Sheena said was bossman of the kidnappers. He stepped back into the shadows of a small stable behind one of the bordellos and watched, as the man unhitched the only horse at the rail and mounted the animal. After confirming that the man was headed for the tavern, he turned his eyes onto the little jail.

It was a box-like structure constructed of native limestone. A small porch protruded from the doorway extending no more than five feet in length and width. It rested on the ground, and no steps were required to access the platform. The hitching post was just in front of the porch. No other structures fronted the jail, and it was set off from the village proper, like it had been built as an afterthought—or for the sake of privacy.

He figured the jail could consist of no more than one or two cells, and he had already determined there were two barred windows at the rear of the building and no back entrance. His only logical move was to get behind the jail unseen and try to determine if there were any occupants.

Fraser had to be there, but he could not understand. A United States Marshal locked up in a local jail? What fool lawman would do that? He thought about it. Any village marshal in this place was likely appointed by the people who owned the town property. The cluster of businesses and houses was likely not even a legal town organized under territory laws. He could not make sense of it, but before he made a move, he must verify that Marshal Fraser was being held there.

The village activity tonight was in the commercial area, and the jail, set off by itself, was lit dimly. He could see the shadowy form of a man at a desk through the window, and the way his head drooped forward Hunter suspected that the man was dozing. Hunter decided that searching through barred windows would take too long and that the door would be quickest. He moved from his cover at the stable and walked deliberately across the rutted, dusty trail that passed in front of the jail. He stepped onto the sagging porch, noted the sign that simply said 'Town Marshal,' and crept up to the doorway.

Very slowly, Hunter opened the door a crack and saw a young, red-haired man with arms folded on a desk, his head cradled in the nest they formed. He stepped in, pressed the door shut softly and waited for the man to awaken. When he did not, Hunter looked about the room, almost breaking the quiet when he saw Morg standing on the other side of a barred cell door. Morg nodded at him and then pointed to the wall just behind the marshal's desk.

Hunter saw the spike sticking out from the wall with the ring of keys. Glad he had worn moccasins this night, he slipped behind the sleeper and removed the keys from their perch. In that same instant, the guard raised his head and started to turn around. Before he completed the turn, the butt of Hunter's pistol drove into the side of his skull, and he fell forward, dropping his head back on the desk.

Hunter took the keys over to the cell door. "You ready to go, Morg?"

"Yep. I'm not many days away from a necktie party, and I'd just as soon miss this one."

Hunter unlocked the door, and Morg stepped out of the jailhouse's single cell. Morg said, "I don't know what the hell you're doing here, but I'm dang glad to see you. We'd best be moving before Fincher gets back. Goober here's not a bad feller, but Fincher is pure mean. You didn't kill Goober, did you?"

"Not likely, but he'll be sleeping for a spell and won't know his name for a while after he wakes up."

Morg walked over to the unconscious man and unbuckled his gun belt, trying it on for size, finding that it would take another half of him to fill it. He buckled the belt and tossed it over his shoulder with the holstered Colt, then went to the gun rack and selected a Winchester much like his own. He levered a cartridge out of the chamber. "Looks like a .44-40. Same as the sidearm it appears."

"I'll check the desk drawer, but they're the same as mine, and I've got two boxes in my saddlebags." Hunter stepped over to the desk pushing Goober's limp form aside. The man slipped off the desk and crumpled onto the floor. Hunter riffled through the desk drawers and came up with another box of cartridges.

Morg said, "Just to be safe we'd better drag old Goober into the cell and lock him up. I don't want to chance his waking up and going for help any sooner than possible."

After they got the unconscious man onto the cell cot, Morg said, "So what's your plan?"

"My only plan was to find you. I got my horse staked at a cold camp behind a hill just outside of town. We should head there."

"Do you have an extra horse?"

"Nope, not yet. I'll get you pointed in the right direction and then I'll circle back and find a mount and saddle and tack."

"The bastards took all my money. Can you afford that? I'll pay you back, of course."

"I can handle it."

Chapter 19

MORG FOUND HUNTER'S mount and nearly naked campsite without any difficulty, and now he waited. His luck was holding. He figured it had about run out till Hunter showed up. He had squeezed out of dozens of close calls over his years as a lawman, but this had looked like the end. They weren't out of danger by a long shot, but there was a fighting chance of making it back to his Dismal River home.

He saw a rider leading a horse moving in his direction, and he assumed it was Jim Hunter, but he reached for his rifle and prepared to use it if necessary. He relaxed when Hunter appeared from the darkness. Hunter dismounted and led the horses over to Morg.

Morg said, "You didn't take much time. You must have made a fast deal."

"You could say that."

Morg stepped over to the horse and began brushing his hand over its neck and running his fingers over its flank and rump, probing the muscular flesh. "Sturdy critter. A gelding. No waste on him. He's covered some miles I'd say." He checked the saddle and saw there was a scabbard with a rifle stock sticking from it. "And this horse. It's a bay with a single white stripe running from between his eyes to the muzzle. This is Fincher's horse. You stole this animal."

"Borrowed. He can have it back when you're done with it. Figured he would be riding nothing but the best."

"He'll be enraged."

"He won't know who took the horse."

"He'll figure it out soon enough. Jim, we're not up against just three men. From talk I heard at the jail, I'm betting half the men in town work for the people that own the place, a fair number of Oglala, too. They will have fifty people trying to track us down, and your Sioux brothers aren't likely to have trouble tracking us."

"We'll head into the Badlands. That will slow down the whites after us. They won't be able to move without an Oglala tracking. The Oglala are a sub-tribe to the Lakota branch of the Sioux nation. They think they are the best trackers. I am of the Santee from the Dakota branch—Wahpekute, which means 'shooters among the leaves.'

We have our own tricks. We can set up an ambush if they are able to find us. They will likely break up into several groups and spread out looking for us. It's not like they will have an army trailing us. There will be many opportunities in the Badlands. It is like a maze puzzle that we played with in school."

"Have you been in the Badlands?"

"Twice."

"Can you find the way out? I would like to head for Fort Robinson on the Nebraska side of the border. I don't think they would expect us to go there. They'd be more likely to head southeast instead of west."

"After we leave the Badlands, it would be at least a three-day ride, but I don't think anyone will pursue a U.S. Marshal into the fort."

Morg said, "I happen to know the commanding officer at Robinson. When I explain what we encountered at Badlands City, he might be interested in sending a small contingent to investigate the place, since it's on the edge of the reservation. I'd just like to stir things up a bit. I'm sure the marshal's service will eventually send folks in to check the law enforcement situation in the town. I wouldn't mind doing that if I had a few deputy backups, but it can take months to obtain approvals, and I'm retiring."

"But how do you know that the man who wants to kill you won't try again?"

"I don't. He likely will. Since he kidnapped my daughter to get to me, he made this very personal. My children are in danger. I do not have to be a marshal to protect my family. That son-of-a-bitch has declared war, and I don't intend to wait for him to strike again. I just want to get home and get things organized there. I've got to see that Andy's protected. Danged if I know what to do about Sheena. I'm just hoping she will talk to me."

Hunter said, "We're headed west. That won't get us nearer home."

"Fort Robinson is about thirty miles from Crawford, Nebraska where there is a railroad connection that will take us and the critters to Broken Bow, a day's ride to your K Bar K Ranch country, two days for me. We'll have to switch trains a time or two, but it will be faster and safer than horseback."

"No argument from me. My boss is likely wondering why my 'few days' are taking so long."

"Now, I think we'd best be moving, or we won't make it to that train. As soon as you collect your things, let's mount up and head out. You lead the way."

A half hour later, Morg and Hunter were leading their horses down a narrow trail that took them into the depths of the Badlands' twisting canyons. In the darkness, Morg could see only faded buttes and pinnacles with chasms winding between them, but he knew he had never passed through more rugged terrain. He was not confident that even in daylight he could find his way out of this eerie land without Hunter as his guide.

Morg asked, "Are we still on reservation lands here?"

"Yes, but not for long. In 1868, the Second Treaty of Fort Laramie provided that the Badlands would forever be the property of Oglala Sioux. Action is now pending in Congress to break the treaty and declare the entire area returned to ownership of the United States. I suspect that the task will be accomplished by the end of this year. Obviously, this doesn't set well with the Sioux, and I worry that it will trigger a futile uprising. This is Sioux Holy Ground. Many Ghost Dances are held within the Badlands."

Morg had heard of the Ghost Dance, apparently started by the Indian prophet Wovoka as the result of a vision. He claimed that by wearing Ghost shirts and performing the dance, Indians would be impervious to bullets. He predicted recapture of the ancient hunting grounds and disappearance of the white man from Indian lands. This vision had become a religion of sorts, and many Indians were becoming Wovoka followers. The Army was concerned that new Indian wars might erupt.

Another hour passed before Morg could make out the canyon floor below. "We're going to hit the canyon floor soon. I'd like to find a place where we can grab some shuteye. I don't suppose there is any grass for grazing the horses down here?"

"On the contrary, there is excellent grazing at places and decent water, too. You just must look for the signs and search it out. That will be difficult till morning. We aren't likely to have anybody even starting to track us down here till daylight. We'll find a place to nap as soon as we get off this trail."

Chapter 20

FINCHER WAS FURIOUS when he emerged from the tavern and found that his horse was missing. He went back into the tavern and yelled at Willy, who sat at a poker table near the back, obviously tipsy from his drinking and gambling away his wages. The dimwit wasn't smart enough to play the game when sober. "Willy," Fincher yelled. "Come on. I need your help."

Willy looked up from his cards. "Soon as I finish this hand, Finch. I'm holding great cards. Ain't going to walk away from this one."

"If you don't get your ass over here, I guarantee, you ain't walking away. You'll die right where you're sitting."

The other three men at the table froze, preparing to dive for cover if bullets started flying.

Willy stood up. "Oh, shit, I'm coming. First decent hand I've had all night." He tossed his cards on the table and stood up.

Fincher prepared to draw his Colt in case Willy in his drunken stupor decided to reach for his own gun. He knew that the man hated him. Sooner or later, he would need to kill the oaf. Not tonight, though, since Willy was staggering his way.

Willy came up to him, smelling like a still, and slurring his speech. "What the hell you want?"

"Somebody stole my horse, tack and all, and my rifle."

"Well, that ain't my worry. You're a damn fool for keeping your rifle with the critter. He'll show up. Some sozzled fool probably just took the wrong horse and will bring it back."

"If you believe that you're even dumber than I thought. Come on back to the marshal's office with me, and we'll talk to Goober and see if we can organize a search."

"Damn, I don't know if I can walk that far tonight, and my critter's at the stable."

"Well, I'm headed for the office. Crawl if you got to, and we'll get some coffee in your gut and see if we can clear your head."

"Dang it, Finch, I was figuring on a stop at Lillie's House tonight."

"You're not wasting time with a dang whore until we find my horse. Pickled as you are, you don't have more than a limp worm hanging between your thighs anyhow. Now, get your ass moving."

Fincher turned and stomped through the batwing doors and onto the dusty trail that passed by the saloon. When he arrived at the jail, he was surprised to see that there was no lamplight coming through the windows, and it appeared pitch-black inside. Why in the hell would Goober turn the kerosene lamp off? When he reached the door, he slipped his Colt from its holster, pushed on the lever door handle and opened it a crack.

"Goober, are you in there?"

He thought he heard a moan, but he wasn't certain. He pushed the door open wider and stepped in, waiting a few minutes for moonlight to reveal more of the room. There was no one at the desk. He moved quickly to light the lamp there, still clutching his pistol, wary of what he might find. After digging out a match from the desk drawer, he lit the lamp, and as the light illuminated the small room, he looked about and saw a figure lying on the cot in the cell. Damn that Goober. Where did he take off to?

Then his heart raced. That was not Morgan Fraser in the cell. It was Goober. He hollered, "Goober, what's going on? Where's the marshal?"

He got a louder moan in response. He went over to open the barred cell door. Locked. He headed for the key peg and froze. The keys were missing. Casting his eyes about the room, he saw no sign of the keys. There was an extra set—in his horse's saddle bags. He went back to the cell door. "Goober, wake up. Do you hear me? We've got to talk."

The body on the cot moved, and Goober rolled over to face Fincher, his eyes were glazed and confused. The side of his head and neck was a mass of blood like a steer that had been shot for slaughter. "You ain't Fraser."

"You idiot. You let Fraser go. What in the hell happened here? Sit up and talk to me." His panic was growing now. Oxford would be here in three days to face the marshal before the hanging. They were to conduct the trial the day before, which would only take an hour, maybe less if they could not keep the addled former judge awake that long. The old fart wasn't good for much but sleeping these days.

Goober struggled to sit upright on the cot, pushing one leg at a time over the cot's edge until he was seated upright and with arms stretched out beside him, his hands pressing into the straw mattress for support. "I'm dizzy. My head's got a hammer hitting it. Don't know how long I can sit like this. Wanna lay down and die."

"Die if it suits you. But first tell me what happened here."

"Don't know."

"How in the hell can you not know?"

"I was at the desk. Then you woke me up, and I come to find out I'm in the jail cell."

"That makes no sense. Something happened to get you in here. Think, you fool. Think."

There was a long silence before Goober spoke. "I don't remember nothing. Just what I told you."

Fincher started and wheeled around with six-gun ready to fire when Willy stumbled in the door. Before Fincher could say a word, the man was bent over and puking his guts out on the floor. How had he ended up with these two morons? He remembered now that Arthur had dug them up someplace. Well, Arthur was going to answer for that when he showed up, which reminded him that Arthur should have arrived by now. He had expected Arthur to arrive before he did. He had not asked for all the responsibility for this job.

Willy was at the dry heaves stage now. Maybe he got rid of some of the booze. "You're going to clean up that mess," Fincher said.

"Ain't cleaning up nothing. Too sick right now." He shuffled over to the straight-back chair in front of the desk and dropped on the seat. He looked around the room. "Where's Goob?"

"He's in the cell."

"What did he do?"

"He let the prisoner get away."

"What good does it do to lock him up for that?"

Fincher sighed. "I didn't lock him up. It appears the prisoner did."

"Ain't you going to let Goob out?"

"The prisoner seems to have all the keys."

"I gotta piss," Goober said. "Bad."

"Use the bucket."

"Ain't here. I forgot to put it back after I emptied it last. It's outside by the water pump. I was going to rinse it, but a feller come by and we got to talking. Then I forgot."

"We can't squeeze the bucket through the bars. You're on your own."

Fincher turned to Willy. "Feeling better?"

"Nope."

"Can you go find Four Fingers?"

"I suppose. He'd be at that teepee he's got set up behind the tavern selling pokes to whites with the two Injun women he's got there. Some fellers like something different once in a while. Got two in the teepee with a blanket for a wall between the two."

"Tell him to get his butt over here now. He's got a partner that can run his business. I'm headed for the stable to find a horse and tack for tomorrow morning. I'll see if Oscar can use his smithing skills to get the damn cell door open. I won't be long."

Before he left, Fincher turned back to the cell where Goober still sat on the cot, hunched over with hands clutching his head. His misery was obvious, but Fincher figured the fool had brought it on himself. He went over to the cup rack near the woodstove and plucked Goober's tin cup from the protruding nail. He reached between the steel bars and flipped the cup towards the cot, and it bounced on the floor near Goober's feet. "Piss in that of you want."

Goober looked up. "What if I fill it up?"

"Drink it. Likely better than your coffee."

An hour later, Oscar, the livery headman and blacksmith, was hammering and prying on the jail lock. The burly, graying man was cussing a blue streak as he worked. "You can forget about using a key on this dang door again. Getcha a chain and padlock maybe."

"Not my worry."

"You're the town marshal, ain't you?"

"Without a badge or even a town council to appoint me. I've got a hunch we won't bring the feller that escaped back alive, or if we do, we'll have a trial and string him up before he needs the jail."

"He must be a bad one. What the hell did he do?"

"Murder and horse thieving for a start."

The jail door sprang open just as Willy walked in with Four Fingers.

Chapter 21

FOUR FINGERS WAS taller than most Indians Fincher had encountered, standing several inches over six feet. He was missing his left hand's thumb, thus his name. Two long braids, bronze-colored skin, and aquiline features attested to his ancestry, but his attire aside from ankle-high moccasins was more cowboy than Sioux, including a black Stetson hat. He spoke passable English and pursued profit with the vigor that matched that of any white capitalist. Most of his efforts were legitimate, a few not so much.

Fincher explained to the warrior what little he knew about the prisoner's escape. "Goober can leave the cell anytime now, but he's dropped off to sleep again. He might be dying—I don't know. No doctors around here, so he's on his own."

"I take him to Oglala medicine man you want."

"Nah, we don't have time for that."

"Why you want me?"

"I want you to find the prisoner that escaped. Soon."

"This prisoner, what he do?"

"He murdered somebody, and now he's a horse thief. Willy and I will go with you, but we need you to pick up his trail and help us track him."

"How much?"

With this greedy bastard, it always came down to money. "Fifty dollars when we catch him."

"Fifty dollar now. Fifty dollar if catch."

"Don't say 'if.' We got to catch this guy and bring him in dead or alive."

"Circle town when sun come. See what can find."

"I guess we got no choice. I hate to give him that head start. I'll be here at sunrise waiting for you. We'll have our horses saddled and ready to ride."

Four Fingers nodded. "Fifty dollar."

Of course, the dang redskin wouldn't forget his money. Fortunately, he had been provided money up front for such things, and he pulled a roll of bills from his front pocket and counted out the money, handing the warrior two twenties and a ten, confident that if the Sioux could read anything, it would be numbers on the bills.

Willy stood near the door amid his pools of vomit, as Four Fingers stepped around the mess and departed. "What do I do now?" Willy asked.

"You get the bucket, pump some water, and clean up that puke. Then go ahead and get that poke for all I care, but you damn well better be here ready to ride at sunrise."

"Don't feel much like poking now."

"Then don't. I'm going to the boarding house to catch a few hours' shuteye. You just show up sober."

The next morning, Willy walked in sober as ordered, and Fincher shared cinnamon biscuits and a pot of coffee he had picked up at the restaurant. He had brought enough for Goober who was sitting up and awake now but in no condition to ride. Fincher had been in a generous mood and even rinsed out Goober's cup at the pump. He had examined Goober's head more closely and could see that the gaping wound needed stitches. "Goober, why don't you check with one of the whores and see if they can sew up that wound? You might have to pay the cost of a poke or two, but it would likely be worth it."

"I think I could walk that far after I eat and have my coffee. I still don't know what happened."

"I think that you got hammered with the butt-end of a pistol grip. Somebody snuck up behind you. But I don't see how Fraser did it unless you gave him the pistol and jail keys."

"Not that much of a fool."

Fincher wasn't sure but said nothing. A few minutes later, the door opened, and Four Fingers stepped in. His stoic face revealed nothing. "Well?" Fincher said.

"One man hide behind hill with horse. Walk here. Moccasins show in sand and dirt."

"An Indian?"

Four Fingers did not reply to the question. "He walk in town like looks for something. Comes here. Goes away with man in boots. They walk together, then man come back to town. Horse leave town and moccasins not go back."

"You're saying the Indian stole my horse and rode it to the hiding place."

Four Fingers shrugged. "Think so. Good guess."

"But the two are gone from the hill hideaway?"

"Gone, yes. Ride to Badlands maybe. Tracks say that, but they might pass by."

"What would you do if you thought someone might be chasing you?"

"Go to Badlands if Sioux."

"And you know the Badlands, how to get in and out?"

"I know."

"Then let's saddle up and get after those two."

"More money to go in Badlands."

"We made a deal."

"Badlands not part."

Four Fingers had him by the balls. He just might end up with a bullet in his back. "How much?"

"Fifty dollar. Half now. Other half if catch."

"Quit saying 'if.'" He peeled off more bills and handed them to the Sioux. Fincher had expected to pocket most of the expense money for himself, but at this rate it would dwindle to a pittance. He could not afford to face Oxford, however, and tell the man that the quarry had escaped.

Chapter 22

SHEENA AND ANDY rode their horses west on the Dismal Trail and soon arrived at Susana Mercer's house. It was not the small home she had anticipated. It was nothing on the scale of the Tall T plantation-style mansion, of course, but it was a two-story spacious home, unpretentious and simple in design but well-kept with a nice front porch and a smaller one at the back that overlooked the river. The corrals and a large combination barn and stable were set a good distance west of the house.

At least three swings and two seesaws were set on the far east side of the house, signaling that the big house also functioned as a school. She was anxious about meeting this woman and worried she was not attired properly for a first meeting, wearing riding britches and boots she had purchased at the General Store. Still she looked forward to talking to a fellow schoolteacher and another woman for a spell.

They dismounted in front of the house and hitched their mounts to the rail. Dingo was already on the porch wagging her tail before they had the horses secured, and a pretty, white-haired lady in a green gingham dress knelt beside the dog, stroking Dingo's head and rubbing her behind the ears. The willowy woman stood as the visitors stepped onto the porch, offering a welcoming smile but her eyes betraying confusion at the unexpected guest.

Sheena extended her hand and said, "I am Sheena Fraser, Morgan's daughter. My father isn't presently home, and I read your invitation for reasons I will explain."

"I see. Morg's not ill or anything, is he?"

"It's all very complicated. If we could sit down for a bit..."

"We'll sit down at the dinner table. I have fried chicken and mashed potatoes and gravy along with beans, biscuits, and apple dumplings—coffee's about always brewing. Come in, please."

They started to enter the house and then Sheena stopped. "Uh, Dingo. You probably don't want her in here."

"Oh, by all means. She's visited before. Dingo's a sweetheart. I already have her bowl prepared. I'm sure she loves chicken." Susana smiled. "She won't eat at the table, of course."

The redolent aroma captured Sheena the moment she entered the house. She could not remember smelling anything so enticing, and somehow it made her feel more at home than she had for years.

Susana offered a short blessing at the table before they ate, and as if Susana knew Sheena was not delivering good tidings, her final words were, "And bless and protect Morgan Fraser, wherever he may be. Amen."

Susana sat at one end of the dining table, and Sheena and Andy each sat at a setting on each side of the hostess. Susana said, "I have taken what would have been Morg's place. Let's just start passing the bowls, and, perhaps, Sheena, you would be so kind as to tell me about your father while we eat. I fear I can't defer that discussion until after dinner."

Sheena said, "I don't know where my father is right now or what has happened to him." She started from the beginning and, between pauses to eat, told Susana the entire story.

"My heavens, you must have been terrified," Susana said.

"Yes and confused when I learned that my father had come for the exchange."

"Why?"

"I hardly know him. My parents were divorced when I was young, and he was a traveling marshal who was rarely home before that. I loathed him."

"Someone you didn't know?"

"Yes. And now I'm starting to learn more about him from Jaye Boyden, who became almost another son to my father. I'm a schoolteacher, and I try to understand children and what challenges they might have endured. Jaye said I should take time to try to understand my father."

Andy paused eating long enough to interject, "I didn't like my dad till my mom sent me away to be with him. But he saved Dingo's life and helped me learn all kinds of things. I like him lots now, and I miss him and want him back home with me." Tears glazed the boy's eyes as he turned back to his food.

Susana said, "Sheena, I will always be here to talk, if you wish, but Jaye seems like a very wise young man. Perhaps you should take time to know your father. You must make your own decisions about your judgment of him, but I have met and spoken with him at length only once, and I daresay no man has ever impressed me more than Morgan Fraser. I am slow to judge people at first meeting, but I immediately saw him as a good, strong man. He tends to be quiet and unassuming, but he carries a conscience that is both his greatest virtue and heaviest burden. I hope I can come to know him better."

"Neither of us may have the opportunities we are seeking. I suspect he is dead by now."

Andy burst out, "How can you say that? You don't know. You don't know anything. My dad's alive, and he is coming home soon. You'll see."

Susana interceded. "Andy, I agree with you. I believe we will see him again. I don't think his time has ended. But whatever the outcome of this horrible experience, he would want us to go on and make the best of whatever life throws at us. In the meantime, I will be praying for him, and I am so thankful that you both have visited and informed me of what is happening."

Susana served apple dumplings for dessert, and Andy seemed somewhat consoled by the scrumptious dish. Sheena found herself almost jealous of her hostess's culinary skills, but it did not subdue her appetite. After she had eaten more than she had consumed at a single meal for years, if ever, Sheena said, "I'll help with cleanup. I'm not much of a cook, but I am an accomplished dishwasher."

"Very well, I have a kettle of hot water on the cookstove. I would welcome some help."

Andy said, "Would it be alright if I took Dingo outside?"

Sheena said, "That's an excellent idea. Go right ahead, but don't wander out of sight of the house."

After Andy left with Dingo, Sheena said. "Andy and Dingo will likely inspect your barn and outbuildings and then sit along the Dismal riverbank and stare at the water flowing by. He has always been a loner of sorts, lost in his thoughts, speaking only when he feels strongly about something—like when he defended his dad. Most of the time, he seems to live in a world of silence like the dog. Of course, I was away at high school and normal training in North Platte and then teaching, so I really haven't had time to know him. When I was home briefly, he was just a little nuisance to me. I had problems of my own and paid no attention to him."

As they stood at the kitchen sink scrubbing and drying pans and dishes, Susana said, "So do you enjoy teaching?"

"I love it. I truly do. And I have been offered my job back at the Willow School for next term, but I must notify them by the first of June, and I may not know yet what my responsibility for Andy will be by that time. If my father returns, I will not stay with him."

"Why not?"

"For one thing, there is not enough room. Also, I barely know him, and I still have trouble feeling much for him. I don't want him to die, and it bothers me that he might give up his life for mine. Still, I would not have been taken hostage if not for him in the first place."

"This is all very strange. If someone wanted your father dead, why didn't that person just hire a man to ambush him?"

"Jaye said my father killed a gang leader's brother, and the man wants to meet him personally and watch him die. It makes no sense to me."

"The twisted minds of such people cannot be comprehended by most of us. But regarding your job, I will have another teaching position available here in the fall. A local school district has contracted with me to educate six more students. The school board cannot find a teacher to come to their isolated school, and the parents are arranging lodging for the children with residents nearer to my home. I have allowed for employing another teacher in my budget. I would be paid privately by parents wishing to have their children complete the equivalent of the first two years of high school here."

"What would I teach?"

"Grades one through six. I would take those from seventh through tenth. You would have a few more students. There should be thirteen or fourteen in all."

"I teach one through eight now. I do best with the younger ones. I am paid seventy dollars monthly plus room and board."

"I will pay eighty dollars plus room and board if your father returns, and you choose not to live with him. Otherwise, if you stay with your brother at your father's house, I will pay a hundred dollars monthly."

"You have hired a teacher."

"I'm confident we can work very well together."

"You obviously enjoy teaching children. Tell me, do you have children of your own somewhere?"

"Three. They are buried with their father in the little cemetery we established here on the ranch. Stephen, John, and Miranda, ages nine, six, and four. Diphtheria took them all over several weeks' time."

Sheena determined to learn more about this remarkable woman who had fought through unimaginable tragedies without wallowing in self-pity, even maintaining an obvious zest for life. She felt like her own education was just beginning.

Chapter 23

JAYE AND COLT Louden turned out the last of the calves that had been corralled for branding, including young bulls that were now steers after meeting the castration blade. They had spent the past three days rounding up and corralling calves that needed attention, and now the task had been completed in a third of the usual time thanks to Louden. He was a tireless worker and a good fit for the J Bar B.

He had taken on Avery Holland full-time now as a cook and handyman. The old man had grabbed the opportunity because he was tired of moving from ranch to ranch to take on odd jobs. His cooking skills left something to be desired, but most of what he cooked was edible if you didn't mind scraping the char off the biscuits and could tolerate the meat a bit beyond well-done. Jaye and Colt contributed cakes and cobblers on occasion, and nobody starved.

Subject to approval of a loan from the bank in North Platte, Jaye hoped to add fifty cows to the herd to bring the J Bar B and Fraser pastures to full capacity. It would require almost two thousand dollars to accomplish this, but he had ambitions and could not support two full-time hands for long without expanding the herd. He needed to be prepared because his neighbor to the north had mentioned selling his thousand plus acres and cow herd after pasture season in the fall, and it was a rare opportunity he did not want to let pass by. He figured he was like most ranchers. He was not a greedy land hog; he just wanted the land next to his.

Jaye and Colt leaned against the corral fence watching the suckling calves race out to join the bawling mothers in the pasture outside that had been protesting the abuse of their babies. They found sympathy there, and after a nosing and few consoling face licks from mom were quickly consoled by nursing at a friendly teat.

Jaye said, "This is the best part of it—having the job done. You've been a big help, Colt. I'm glad you joined up with us."

"Me too. I'm thinking we might be a good fit. You said I might be able to put a few breeding horses on the place.

I'd like to go see Jim Hunter soon and maybe buy a few bred mares. He's building a small herd of his own over at the K Bar K, and he's the best horseman I know."

"Take a few days when it suits you. I know he's not around right now, though. He's following the men who took Morg Fraser."

"You ain't heard nothing yet?"

"Nope, and I don't know if that's good or bad. It worries me sick. Morg's my best friend, sort of like a second dad, and Jim's been a good friend, too, the past few years."

"I never asked about how you got Sheena back here. Figured it wasn't my business, but Arthur had something to do with that, didn't he?"

"Yes, he intended to kill her after the exchange was made. Arthur and another man. They're both dead. I killed Arthur, and Sheena shot the other fella."

Colt said nothing while he rolled and lit a cigarette. He savored a few long draws before he spoke. "What do you suppose Arthur was doing at the Tall T? Him and Thomas Towne was sure cozy. No other hand ever got that close to Towne, well, except for the manager, Packer Osborne, who let Zeke as crew foreman run the operation. Sometimes, Arthur and Osborne would meet up with Towne and talk. Never made sense. Arthur never did any real work. He was more like a guest. Never ate at the chuck cabin with the rest of the hands. Him and Packer ate with the family."

"Really? That does seem strange. What do you know about Packer Osborne's background?"

"Not a dang thing. I think he's been with Towne since the ranch started some ten years ago or so. Of course, I was just a kid then, and I was only at the Tall T for not quite a year. I picked up a little gossip, that's all. I'm guessing Towne and Packer are old friends, but Osborne's somewhat younger, early forties. Packer Osborne wasn't so bad to work for, a hell of a lot better than when Towne stuck his nose in. But he didn't know a lot about the cow business and left most of the day to day stuff to Zeke. I don't know if Towne ever saw a cow before he came to the Sandhills. He seemed to work okay with dogs, but mostly because they was afraid of him, I think."

"He was cruel to the dogs?"

"I never saw, but others said he would kick them or beat them with a stick if they didn't do what he said. I don't think that's the way most trainers do it."

"I'm under the impression Towne traveled a lot."

"Yep. I doubt if he was at the ranch half the time. Sometimes Missus Towne went with him. They always had a lady that looked after the kids. Osborne went along a lot, especially when the wife went, which seemed sort of strange."

"Did you ever hear anything about how Towne got along with the Fraser children?"

"Oh, yeah. It wasn't no secret he hated those two, the boy maybe more than Sheena. Of course, she got out of there first chance she got and hardly ever come back to visit her ma. That's what the old hands said. I wasn't on the place all them years. Some folks don't take kids with somebody else's blood, I've heard. Now, my stepdad is my pa as far as I'm concerned. I got two half-sisters and two half-brothers that got his blood, but he never treated me or my two younger brothers different. There's all kinds of parents out there, and some of us get lucky."

"What would happen if I tried to ask Packer Osborne some questions?"

"Don't. He'd make a beeline direct to Thomas Towne. You'd just as well talk to Towne himself. But I don't like that neither, because I'd likely end up without a job."

"Why do you say that?"

"Because you'd likely end up a dead man if he didn't like your questions. They say not many years back, one of the hands made off with a couple of cows. Somebody tipped off Towne, and the feller was found hanging from a cottonwood tree a few days later. Not likely an accident,

I'd say. No hand at the Tall T cuts out a cow or two now and then. I can guarantee that."

Chapter 24

THE MORNING AFTER his conversation with Colt Louden, Jaye decided to visit Sheena and Andy at the Bar F. He rode his mount at a slow trot, taking in the countryside, his eyes always searching, confident he would always see something interesting and different. Today it was a bald eagle soaring almost directly above him, its majestic form cast against a cloudless, azure sky, likely its keen eyes seeking out unsuspecting prey.

It was a balmy May morning with the sun casting its warming rays over the seemingly endless Sandhills dunes. Cattle grazed lazily on the hillsides, his favorite portrait of the hill country. He could sit for hours and observe this scene while his thoughts traveled leisurely to other places. It somehow drained all tension from his body, deferred his worries for a time. He loved this country. He would live out his life here, die here, and become a part of it.

He heard Dingo barking before he rode into the ranch yard, probably signaling that company was coming. To truly know that creature was to love her. Only Thomas Towne could shoot such an animal. As he caught sight of the buildings, he saw Andy coming from the stable, no doubt responding to Dingo's summons. Andy waved and hurried toward him. Jaye reined in and dismounted leading his horse to close the gap.

"Good morning, Andy," Jaye said. "Still doing chores?"

"Nah, I just turned the horses out in the stable grass. There's good eating there now. At least that's what they say."

"Are you doing sign language with horses now, too?"

Andy chuckled. "Wish I could, but they say a lot if you pay attention. Look at them going after the grass. Ain't that telling you something?"

"Yeah, you're right. Our animals do talk to us. We just need to listen."

"You're here to see my sis, ain't you?"

"Well, I wanted to check on you both, but I would like to talk to her. Are you two getting along alright?"

"Sometimes. Others, not so much. She gets up in the morning, and she's smiling and singing while she tries to burn up a breakfast. Two hours later, she turns into a grump, and me and Dingo get out of her way. I'll tell you this, dad's house is getting a cleaning. I thought she wouldn't be so crabby when she got that job."

"Job? What job?"

"She's going teach school over at Missus Mercer's. If you look up at the porch, you'll see Sheena's watching us, and she's got her arms folded. She's saying she's pissed about something. If you pay attention, you can understand people without them speaking a word, just like dogs and horses. You can go talk to her. Me and Dingo are going to make ourselves scarce."

Jaye led his horse toward the house. "Good morning, Sheena," he said, as he hitched his mount to the rail in front of the porch.

"Hello," Sheena said not so warmly. "What's your business today?"

"Just a neighborly visit. I haven't seen you and Andy for a few days. I wondered if there is anything I can help with."

"We're doing very well, thank you."

"Okay if I join you on the porch for a bit?"

She sighed. "Oh, come on in the house. I've got coffee brewed and hot."

Her voice was not welcoming, but he followed her into the house. He was not just making a neighborly call. They sat down facing each other at the small kitchen table after Sheena poured each a cup of coffee. "You seem upset about something," Jaye said.

"My father has disappeared. I don't know if he's dead or alive. Am I supposed to be bright and cheery about that?"

"No, of course not. The not knowing would make it extra hard."

"You keep telling me wonderful things about my father. You almost worship him. Why?"

"He's always had my back when I needed him, helped me without expectation of anything in return. Sure, like the rest of us he's probably got more than a few flaws, but beneath that tough hide he is the most unselfish, kindest man I've ever known. There isn't anything he wouldn't do for me—or Andy or you. I don't see why you can't understand that after the exchange he made at Mad Rock."

"I'm trying to come to terms with this, and it's a struggle. I've always blamed him for anything that went wrong in my life. In my mind, he still ran out on Andy and me."

"My father was a drunk, sometimes a mean one, but Ma always excused him even when he hit her or any of the kids. She was kind but weak. Morg helped me acquire the little ranch here when my folks abandoned the place. Yet, I blamed them as the cause of any struggle I had. Then one day he told me something that changed my way of thinking—some words an old timer gave him when he was a young man."

"What did he say?"

"While we're young, our lives are shaped by environment and heredity and all kinds of things in the world around us that we can't control. But there comes a time in our lives when we have the ability to take charge and mold our own life into what we want it to be. Only the weak blame parents, their race, sex, or plain bad luck. We all have the power and ability to recognize what we are today and then to determine what we will be tomorrow."

"You sound like a philosopher."

"His words stuck. From that day on I recognized that I am responsible for my own life, and I quit blaming anybody else for things that didn't go the way I wanted. I want Morg back alive in the worst way, but if it doesn't happen, I will pick up and go on, remembering always the things he taught me."

"I don't think I really know you at all."

"I'd like it if we could start to get acquainted again. I have come to realize the same about you. You're no longer just the prettiest gal in the Sandhills to me."

She blushed, rolled her eyes, and couldn't hold back traces of a smile. "That's the Jaye Boyden I thought I knew."

"By the way, there's a rumor out there that you've got a new job."

"You probably picked up the rumor out by the stable. Yes, Susana Mercer is expanding her school and is taking me on as a teacher. If my father comes home, I intend to move in with her. If he doesn't, assuming Andy and I can stay on this place, I will ride over to her house with Andy for school every day."

He said nothing, but he knew that she and Andy were assured of being able to remain. They would inherit the ranch under terms of a will prepared for Morg by a North Platte lawyer, although Jaye would be executor of the will and trustee over the ranchland for ten years. The will was secured in his own safe because of the risk that Morg might not return from a mission.

At least she was staying in the Sandhills, and he realized today that they were a good distance from serious romance and that prospects of marriage were increasingly remote. "There is something else I came to speak with you about."

"So this is more than a neighborly visit. I suspected."

"How much do you know about Thomas Towne?"

"More than I want. I can tell you I hate the man. He's sick."

There was a story behind her words, but this was not the time to pursue it. "I'm referring to his business and his frequent trips."

"Mother divorced my father because he was gone so much. She didn't do much better at her second effort. Of course, almost half the time she travels with Thomas, so I guess that is an improvement—if she loves him."

"You question that she loves him?"

"I truly don't know. She loves his money. Enjoys helping him spend it."

"Do you know anything about his businesses, what he does?"

"Nothing. Remember, I was fourteen years old when I last spent significant time at the Tall T house. I had no interest in his business activities. I was just glad when he was gone. Why are you so interested in his business ventures?"

He guessed she was entitled to know what he was thinking. "I suspect Thomas Towne of being involved in your kidnapping and the effort to kill your father."

She stared at him in disbelief. "What makes you think that?"

"Andy told us about the man named Arthur being at the Tall T. I asked Colt Louden more about the man and learned that Arthur performed virtually no ranch duties and often met Towne and Osborne."

"Packer? He was always friendly enough, but he was certainly Thomas's right arm. He ate meals with the family most of the time. I suppose I could visit mother and see if she might spill some information."

"Let's wait for that. It's likely that she knows nothing that would help. Certainly she would not be a party to your kidnapping. If you even hint my suspicion to her, there is a risk she will tell Towne, and that could put all our lives at risk. The time might be right for such a question at some point but not now. I'll think about this, but I do want to find out if Thomas Towne works for Monte Oxford. This might have to wait till Morg returns home."

"You are convinced that my father will return, aren't you?"

"Between Morg and Jim Hunter, I sure wouldn't count him dead yet. Your father has spent a lifetime dealing with danger, and I'm very hopeful he will dodge a bullet one last time before he turns in his badge. Now, I'd best be getting up to leave. I've got business at the ranch to tend to." He slid back the chair and stood. "Thanks for the coffee. A lot better brew than I get at my place."

She stood to walk him out to the porch. He was surprised when she took his hand. "Jaye, thanks for dropping by. We've talked about some serious things, but you've brightened my mood and given me some things to think about. You're welcome here anytime, and I'll try not to be such a grump."

He was surprised when she stopped, still holding onto his hand, and looked up at him with those sparkling, green eyes. He swore he saw an invitation there and released her hand and placed his arms gently and tentatively around her, lowering his head to meet her lips. They kissed very softly, but their lips lingered beyond a casual peck, before she stepped back. It didn't matter. She had lit a fire and he wanted more, but he was not going to ruin this moment. He just offered an approving nod and headed for the safety of his horse.

Chapter 25

MORG UNDERSTOOD NOW what Hunter meant when he referred to the Badlands as a maze. They had not ventured far into the twisting arroyos and canyons, but he was not confident that he could find his way back to their entry place and certainly would never locate the exit they were seeking without Jim Hunter's guidance.

They had ridden into a gap between two buttes that opened into a tiny canyon offering spring water and a carpet of lush, mixed grasses for the horses, a sharp contrast to the dirt and clay eroding slopes outside. They had grabbed three or four hours of precious sleep here, but a glow above the walls above told him sunrise was no more than a half hour away, and they should be moving. It seemed strange to him to wear the hat of a pursued now. He had always been the pursuer.

Morg was finishing his portion of the dried fruit and hardtack Hunter had purchased at the general store in Badlands City. He had also acquired a decent supply of beef jerky, a can of beans, and another of peaches. They could not risk a fire, so hunting would not bolster the food supply, but Hunter assured him that there were ample edible plants along the way to ward off starvation.

Hunter had left him, taking off afoot after informing Morg that he intended to find out if anyone was following before he scaled the canyon wall, which at no more than fifty feet high was not a serious challenge for a young man of his experience and skills. Morg had no idea where Hunter went after he disappeared over the rim, but he went about saddling the horses so they would be ready to ride when he returned.

It was shortly after sunrise when Hunter walked through the cleft that had led them into the canyon. The sober-faced Sioux came up to him, and said, "I didn't need to go far on high ground to see the trail where we entered the Badlands. We're being followed. I could barely make them out, but there are three. From the way he moves ahead of the others and stops to check the trail, one is Sioux. We expected this, but it means we aren't likely to lose them."

"How much of a lead do we have?"

"Not much as the eagle flies, but four or five hours with all the twists and turns they must deal with. You saw how it was last night. Some places require that you lead the mounts and walk. We lost time descending in darkness. They have the advantage of daylight and will move much faster to this point than we did. Tell me, do you wish to find a place to make a stand now or try to outrun them?"

"If we leave now, can we maintain the four or five hours between us?"

"Not indefinitely, because I will need time to seek out our routes through the ravines and canyons. As we move, we will be carving a map in the earth for the warrior to follow. By day's end, I suspect most of the gap will be closed."

"I can see that. Let's go on and see if we can find a good place to make our stand along the way. I would prefer an ambush."

"You wish to shoot them down without warning?"

"No. I've never been comfortable taking a man down that way. We'd give them a chance to drop their weapons and surrender, but I won't hesitate to squeeze the trigger if it comes to that."

A few hours later, Morg and Hunter were back on their feet leading their mounts on a narrow winding trail that

Ron Schwab

snaked its way through naked eroding walls of clay and shale interspersed with sandstone. Other stones that he could not identify added green and reddish hues. There were formations of all sorts, many crumbling, but the sandstone towers and spires that surrounded them appeared most successfully to ward off the ravages wrought by nature's attacks.

They had abandoned a wider, more often used trail that allowed them to ride, but Hunter had suggested they were more likely to find opportunity to set up a surprise confrontation on this rarely traveled path. When they came upon a fissure in the steep cliff wall that edged one side of the trail, Hunter signaled a halt, handed his horse's reins to Morg and slipped into the crevice. A few minutes later, he emerged. "This would be a good place for us. There is a hollow inside the bluff, room enough for the horses. One of us can climb the inner wall and get positioned at the top. The other can hide in the crevice and step up and fire from there if necessary."

The crevice walls brushed the horses' ribs, but it was no more than a ten-foot journey into the hollow, and when they were all within the enclosure, Morg studied the walls surrounding them. The side adjacent to the trail was a bit over twenty feet high, but potential hand and footholds were scant. There was a time when he might

{194}

have scampered to the top, but those days were past. "I'll take the crevice. You can claim the high ground. When they come, why don't you fire a warning shot to get their attention and warn me, and then I'll step out to inform them they're under arrest?"

"I will do that. Right now, I will seek higher ground and see if I can get sight of them. We don't want to wait longer than we must, or if they have given up the chase, we can move on."

Morg nodded agreement, and Hunter quickly scaled the wall and disappeared. While Hunter was gone, Morg surveyed his surroundings and found himself uncomfortable there. He and the two horses were sharing no more than 150 square feet of space, and he felt like he occupied a tomb. If one of the stalkers found him first from the clifftop, there was no place to find cover, and the horses were vulnerable, too. They could not afford to lose a horse.

A shadow appeared over him from above. Hunter was back quickly. That must mean that the search party was nearing. But when he looked up, he did not see Hunter, but, instead a different Indian, a huskier, grim-faced warrior. The warrior stared down at him with his rifle pointed at Morg's chest.

"White man unbuckle gun belt and drop. You die if you try shoot me."

The warrior wasn't lying about that. For the moment, Morg decided he had no choice, and he moved his hands slowly to obey.

"You drop your gun, Four Fingers. Now." It was Hunter's voice.

The warrior turned away from Morg, who re-cinched his belt. The intruder froze but did not drop the weapon. "Coyote Hunter?" he said. "Why you be here?"

"I am helping this man. He is a United States Marshal. You are breaking the white man's law if you kill him. You will hang."

Morg's horse whinnied and looked toward the crevice. Morg drew his Colt and wheeled. Someone was slinking through the fissure. Morg recognized him instantly when he stepped from the darkness with his own pistol ready. "Drop it, Willy."

Willy started. "Like hell." He turned toward Morg, his gun ready to fire just as Morg squeezed the trigger twice and sent two slugs burrowing into the gunman's chest. Willy's eyes widened in disbelief as he pitched forward and landed face down in the dirt.

Morg saw movement where the fissure met the trail, signaling that someone was retreating, and he rushed into the gap, hesitating a moment before he stepped out onto the trail. He heard a man's voice cussing a horse that was evidently spooked, and he stepped out cautiously before he saw Fincher only about twenty feet up the trail.

Fincher saw him at the same time and released the reins on his mount, diving behind some stones that had caved off the slope and getting off a shot that chipped away some rock and stung Morg's cheek. The marshal went to his knees, bracing the wrist of his shooting hand to steady the Colt as he aimed at the pile of stones. The horses had moved back up the trail away from the gunfire, and Fincher no longer had the option of making a run for his mount.

The two men waited in silence for what seemed like an eternity before Fincher's patience gave out, and he raised his head just enough above his stone fortress to peer out and receive Morg's slug precisely between his eyes. Morg holstered his Colt but reached for it again when he sensed movement behind him.

"Just me, Morg. Looks like you did fine without my help."

He relaxed when he heard Hunter's voice and turned around. "Well, I wouldn't have been here to take care of it if you hadn't showed up when you did."

"I turned around when I realized Four Fingers was circling around behind us. Somehow, they closed the gap faster than I guessed. He knows the Badlands like the back of his hand and must have taken some shortcuts."

"I didn't hear gunfire. You obviously know the fella. What happened?"

"He's my cousin. Our mothers are sisters, both Oglala. My father is Santee, and we never saw much of Four Fingers's family over the years, not more often than every other year when I was growing up. But I did get to know him some. Anyhow, when I told him you are a U.S. Marshal, he backed away fast, but he wanted the money he was owed by those two gunslingers. I said if he saw the two buried, he could lay claim to the horses and tack and any money or valuables they might have. I've got a feeling that he's going to strike a bonanza off this venture. I hope I didn't exceed my authority."

"Nope. You got me out of this mess. You aren't near to the limits of your authority. Let's get the dang horses and be on our way. Do you really think this cousin of yours will bury these men?"

"Probably, but he won't do any digging. He will likely drag them to one of the nearby ravines and cave off some dirt and shale over them. He'll clean their pockets good first, though. Four Fingers plans on becoming the richest

Sioux on the reservations, and I'm guessing he is well on his way. He had no interest in getting killed or arrested over causing trouble for a U.S. Marshal."

"It's good to know somebody's not after my hide. I guess we should move on to Fort Robinson. That's what good sense says to do, but I'm sure itching to go back to Badlands City and poke around some more."

"You're serious."

"Only halfway. We've got folks back in the Sandhills wondering what became of us, and I suppose I shouldn't be pushing my luck. No, we'd better head back. I need a bit of thinking time anyhow."

Chapter 26

J AYE WAS AT the Bar F calving pens helping a cow that was stretched out on the ground with calf delivery problems. Andy, to his credit, had caught sight of the cow in the homeplace pasture when he was doing early morning chores. With Dingo taking charge, they had driven the cow from the pasture to the calving pen. After informing Sheena of the problem, he had ridden to summon Jaye at the J Bar B.

The cow was now hitched to a fencepost in case she refused to cooperate, but Jaye figured she was too tired out to resist. Andy was holding the cow's tail out of the way, and Jaye had a bucket of soapy water within reach to lubricate the calf and the would-be mother's vulva and birth canal to ease the calf's journey. He was stripped naked to the waist and his arm stretched halfway into the birth canal trying to locate the issue.

He stepped back a moment, withdrawing his bloody arm. "The calf's coming headfirst, which is fine, but the front leg is doubled back blocking the way out."

Sheena, attired in britches and a man's cotton shirt today, said, "They're going to die—the calf and mother?"

"Not if I can help it. I'm going to try to push the calf back into the birth canal some and see if I can straighten the leg. It's not a big calf. I'd bet it's a heifer."

"Is it dead?"

"I can't tell, but regardless we've got to save the cow. I need some short ropes to hitch to the calf's legs when I get the troublemaker straightened. I'll need you to help pull, too."

"Me?"

"Yeah, you and Andy. Don't worry, you don't have to strip your shirt off if you don't want."

Her brow furrowed, and she gave him a glare that told him she did not find his remark funny before she headed into the barn to fetch some ropes.

In less than ten minutes, Jaye straightened the leg and soon the front hooves and nose were appearing at the vulva exit. He quickly anchored ropes to the legs, assigning Andy and Sheena each to one. "You pull when I tell you. I'll slicken things up as best I can and guide the head and legs."

After a few 'pulls and stops,' and the cow's straining and bawling, the calf shot through the opening and lay stretched out the ground. It moved a bit, and Jaye moved to clear the calf's mouth and pumped his hands on its diaphragm. Soon the calf raised its head. "We got us a little girl. And she's going to be fine," Jaye said. "You did a good job, Andy. If you hadn't seen that cow and recognized she was in trouble, she would have been dead by the end of the day."

Andy grinned. "I'll be keeping my eyes open. Between what you and Dad have taught me, I'm thinking I might be a cattleman myself someday—after I become a veterinary surgeon."

"Oh, Lord. Think carefully about that, Andy," his sister said. "That's not an easy life."

Jaye said, "It's not so hard, Sheena. Most things aren't if you love what you're doing. Now, to me it couldn't get much harder than teaching school."

She rolled her eyes. "I suppose you've got a point. Anyway, thanks for coming over."

"Glad I could help. Besides, under my arrangement with Morg, I've got a special interest in his herd now."

They talked for a spell, and before they left the pen the cow was up licking her newborn, and Jaye knew that soon the baby would be sucking at its mama's teat.

When he closed the gate to the pen, he noticed a dust cloud rolling rapidly down the trail that connected the two ranches. Somebody was in a hurry, and that generally was not good news.

"Did you have breakfast?" Sheena asked. "I did get some fresh biscuits made without much damage this morning, and I've got some bacon Susana shared with me, because she said it's hard to ruin bacon. And, of course, there is a pot of coffee. The least I can do is feed you after helping us out."

"As a matter of fact, I didn't have time for breakfast, and that sounds good."

"She's getting better," Andy said. "Bad thing is, though, she's making me do most of the cleanup." Dingo came beside him and looked up with sad eyes. "I know, girl. You're hungry, too, and you did a good job, too. I'd never got her in without you."

Jaye nodded toward the dust cloud. "Somebody's coming from my place. Maybe it's just a feller passing through, but I need to wait a few minutes and see."

Sheena said, "I'll go ahead and get the bacon frying. I'll look for you two shortly. If the rider is one of your cowhands, I'll be glad to feed him, too."

Jaye could make out the rider now as he approached. It was Avery Holland, and he almost never hurried about anything. Jaye stepped out to meet Holland as he rode up to the building site. Avery saw him and dismounted, leading his horse as he limped up to Jaye. The ashen-faced old man seemed nearly breathless as if he had carried his mount instead of vice-versa.

"Avery, are you alright? What is it?"

"Colt's dead. Somebody shot him in the back."

Jaye felt weak. That good, hard-working young man. He could not accept the notion that his new hand's life had been robbed from him. "You're sure he was dead?"

"I know dead when I see it. I've spent a lifetime seeing dead, too dang much of it. I ain't figured out why it ain't claimed me yet. Should have taken me and left Colt behind."

"How did it happen?"

"We was eating breakfast up at the house when we heard the critters making a terrible fuss down at the stable. Colt picked up his Winchester and headed down to the stable to check on the commotion. We figured some animal might have got in there and was getting them all excited, maybe a couple of dang coons or something. They got a knack for opening doors and such. They wouldn't take on a horse, but they could sure as hell get the critters all stirred up."

"So what happened after that?"

"Well, I heard a gunshot coming from the stable, but didn't think nothing of it. Figured it was Colt killing a coon. I finished my breakfast, figuring he'd be back soon to finish his. When he didn't show up, I headed down to the stable to see what was going on. I wasn't worried about him or nothing. Thought maybe he was skinning whatever creature he shot. He's never been one to waste a bullet. He'd try to find a use for a dead coon. I can tell you this, I wouldn't cook and eat one of the dang bandits. I did once, and I'll be starving before I do it again, and I ain't sure I'd do it then."

Jaye sighed. Avery would never answer in a few words when he could use a hundred. "Avery, just tell me what you saw."

"Well, the stable door was wide open, and I just walked in and there was poor Colt laying face down in the dirt, his shirt soaked with blood that was still leaking from his back. I looked around and didn't see nobody, but I was sure as hell wishing I'd brought a gun with me. Anyhow, I stooped down and didn't see no sign of life, but I rolled Colt over to be sure. Them eyes—I'll never forget them eyes—told me he was gone, but I checked for signs of breathing and such anyhow. He was dead. I got my horse from the stable, and after I had him saddled up, I closed the door behind me and headed over here. Dang, I really liked that kid."

Jaye turned to wide-eyed, sober Andy. "Tell your sis I won't make it to breakfast. I've got to head back to the ranch. I'll try to check back later today. And tell Dingo to keep an eye out for visitors. Don't go out to meet anybody unless you know them to be good friends. That includes anybody from the Tall T."

"I'll tell Sheena."

Chapter 27

JAYE AND AVERY stood over Colt Louden's still form in the stable passageway. Tears glazed Jaye's eyes and anger boiled within him. Death coming for the young always seemed unjust, but it was even worse when it was the result of the calculated murder of an innocent. It saddened him to think that this might never have occurred if he had not approached Colt about working for him, guilt he would likely carry the remainder of his days.

He understood now what Morg said once: "The burden of accumulated guilt can get dang heavy when you get to a certain age. You got to put down the load for a spell when you can." Morg had mentioned that sometimes he envied folks who didn't seem to be saddled with conscience.

"We'll bury him here in the little cemetery that was carved out when my two little brothers died. You're handy with the blades. Maybe you can fashion a marker of some sort when things settle down a bit."

"Sure, Jaye, I can do that," Holland said. "What about his family?"

"They live out in the Sandhills country someplace, but I don't know where. We'll check his papers when we collect his belongings, maybe find out more about his people there. I'm sure his mom and stepdad are still alive. They've got a passel of kids, and Colt said he sent half his monthly pay to them to help out. I'll track them somehow. I'll need to report this to the law when I get a chance, but the only counties with sheriffs in this part of the hills right now are Custer and Lincoln. That takes me all the way to either Broken Bow or North Platte. I'm hoping Morg will get back soon to provide some direction."

"You don't really think he's coming back, do you?"

Jaye shrugged. "I don't know. I just don't know." And there was Jim Hunter, another life he felt responsible for. He had roped Hunter in to helping with the exchange. What if he had been killed, too?

It was nearly one o'clock by the time the two men buried Colt Louden. When they walked back to the house to fix some lunch, Sheena and Andy with Dingo in the wagon box reined their mule team and buckboard into the ranch yard. Jaye noted that Andy was handling the reins.

Jaye walked over to the wagon and looked up at Sheena questioningly.

"I brought lunch," Sheena said, "if you haven't already eaten."

"The kitchen was our next stop, and we were just going to see what we could scratch up."

"I've got roasted beef sandwiches and an apple cake, if you are brave enough to try them."

"They're good," Andy attested. "Her cooking ain't half bad some days. Dingo loved the beef."

"Well, if Dingo approved, a fella can't go wrong. Come on in." He extended his hand to assist Sheena off the wagon. Dingo leaped over the wagon's tailgate and hit the ground before she did.

Sheena said, "Lunch is in the basket if you want to bring it."

Jaye said, "Andy, you know where the water pump and buckets are if you want to unhitch and water the team. Give them some hay and grain from the stable if you like."

"Sure, Jaye. Dingo and me will be up to the house after a bit."

As they walked up the limestone path that led to the front porch of the house, Sheena said, "You know, I've never been in your house before."

"I wish it were a happier occasion, but I'll show you around after lunch. Not much to it. Three bedrooms upstairs, the parlor and a study, and, of course, the kitchen downstairs. More than enough space for me, but who knows, I might need it someday." Especially if he could lure this stunning woman into marrying him in the future.

They avoided talking about Colt's death while the two men ate, and Jaye felt a bit self-conscious as Sheena watched silently. She took the coffee pot off the woodstove and poured their cups full.

She said, "I assumed you had coffee. It couldn't be worse than mine."

"Avery's coffee is pretty darn good brew."

Avery said, "Ma'am, those beef sandwiches don't come no better, and that apple cake would be worth fighting for."

"He's right, Sheena, I might come by and beg for a meal now and then," Jaye said.

"You'll have to settle for roasted beef and apple cake. That's the only thing I'm not burning up, but I'm working on it with some coaching and recipes from Susana."

"I'd say you've got a good coach."

"She's such a wonderful lady. I can't wait to start teaching school with Susana. I know I will learn a lot from her, but that isn't what I came over to talk about."

Avery said, "I've had my two pieces of cake and too much coffee. I think I'll go out and talk to the boy. He generally listens to my stories. Jaye ain't that good of listener."

Sheena said, "There's nothing secret about what I've got to say, Avery. You are welcome to stay, and by the way, I am leaving the rest of the cake behind."

"I take that kindly, ma'am, but Jaye will tell me what I need to know. And I look forward to finishing up that cake."

After Avery went out the door, Sheena said, "He's an astute man. He sensed I would prefer the talk to be between the two of us, and I hoped to keep Andy out of it."

"So what did you wish to talk about?"

"First, I wanted to tell you how sorry I am about Colt. I liked him, and he seemed like a good man. Do you know any more about what happened?"

"Not much. From powder burns, it's fair to say he was shot by somebody not more than a few feet away. I don't think Colt ever knew what happened. He was probably killed instantly. Somebody was waiting in the stable for whenever Colt showed up. If Avery had gone in first, he'd likely be dead but not by gunshot. The wait was for Colt."

"And it could have been you."

"This happened after I headed over to the Bar F. I think somebody was watching the place and saw me leave. They weren't after me—yet. I didn't see a horse, and neither did Avery. Whoever it was likely had a mount tied down by the river. After the shooting, he headed down that draw and out of sight. The hills hid him before he got too far."

"But why would anyone want to kill Colt?"

"They probably decided he knew too much, and it wouldn't have helped that he came here after he quit his job at the Tall T."

"You are saying Thomas Towne did it?"

"Not Towne personally, but who else? He was worried that Colt knew more than he did. Or maybe Colt saw something and didn't recognize what the significance of it was at the time. We will likely never know. Colt said he never told Towne that he was taking a job with me, and I suppose it took a few days for word to get back to him."

"Shouldn't you report this to the law?"

"I'm writing a letter to the U.S. Marshal's office in North Platte. I'm riding over to the Loup Trading Post this afternoon to send it special delivery at the post office there, but it could still take a week or more. Your father's the law. I hope he's back before anybody shows up from North Platte."

"Do you really think we're in danger?"

"I think we're all in danger if Towne is starting to panic. I'd just like to know how he fits in to all this and how many of the hands on the ranch are part of it. I don't think the cattle on the Tall T are bought with honest dollars, or the ranch and house, either. I'd bet serious money that Thomas Towne is connected to the man who wants Morg dead. He just might be the link Morg and the Marshal's Service are looking for to help break the case. I'd sure like to ride over to the Tall T and ask him a few questions."

"Why would you do that? He's not going to come out and make a confession. Most likely he will take care of you like he did Colt, and he would be more likely to come after all of us."

"I realize that. I'm just saying what I would like to do. I can't. Not yet. I wish I could convince you and Andy to stay over here. I've got two spare bedrooms. You can see them when I show you the rest of the house."

"I would like to see the house, but Andy and I are not staying over here, so get the idea out of your head. We're staying right where we are."

Jaye knew better than to argue with her about it. She had a stubborn streak that made itself known at times like this. "Stay here with Avery at least till I get back from the trading post."

Chapter 28

SHEENA, ANDY, AND Dingo visited Susana Mercer the morning following Colt Louden's murder, and Susana insisted they stay over for lunch so they could discuss plans for the school they were establishing. Andy and Dingo went fishing in the Dismal after promising to stay within sight of the house.

Sheena helped Susana prepare lunch, adding a few new skills to her repertoire. Susana appeared to enjoy teaching her young colleague new domestic skills, and Sheena was now finding herself eager to learn. At first, Sheena had been reluctant to spend time on such things, insisting that she was not going to spend her life trying to satisfy some glutinous male's appetite. But Susana reminded her she would not be truly independent if she could not provide meals for herself and, perhaps, Andy. Besides, if she boarded with Susana, she would be expected to carry her share of household chores, including cooking.

Sheena had been putting it off, but she finally told Susana about the killing at the J Bar B and her skirmish with Jaye over moving into his house temporarily. "I'm very fond of Jaye, but he is often overprotective, and it annoys me. I'm perfectly capable of taking care of myself."

Susana said, "Yes, you have survived a most difficult situation. But what would have happened if your father, Jaye, and Jim Hunter had not come to your assistance? There is strength in numbers, dear, and you do have a responsibility to protect Andy, too."

"You think I should have accepted Jaye's offer, don't you?"

"Now that you have asked for my opinion, yes, I believe so, but there is another option."

"What's that?"

"You and Andy move over here temporarily. When your father returns, you said you would do that anyway. I can handle a rifle, and that would provide one more gun."

"But you would be in danger."

"A widow living alone out here always runs a risk. Besides, you and Andy are very special to me. From what you say, I don't think it is likely that there is imminent danger anyway, but it seems to me that you are an innocent bird inviting the fox where you are. Your stepfather knows exactly where to find you now. It is unlikely that he would expect you to be here. I have never met the man, and I doubt he even knows I exist."

"I'll discuss it with Andy when he comes in."

Later, as they ate lunch, Sheena broached the subject with Andy.

"No, I have my stable chores, and I want to check out Dad's herd. I saved a cow and calf yesterday morning. You know that."

"You will do as I say."

"Under what authority? I've hardly seen you for years, and then you just show up and take over. I ain't going." He turned to Susana. "I ain't got anything against you, Missus Mercer. I just got responsibilities to tend to, and I don't want Sheena bossing me around anymore."

Susana said, "Would you stay with Jaye Boyden if Sheena approved? I'll bet he would ride over with you to do chores, and you could help him during the day."

He was silent for a moment. "Yes, I guess that would be alright."

Susana looked at Sheena and smiled. "What do you say, Sheena? You can still stay here, if you like. There would be two men at Jaye's place, and they are alerted to any dangers now."

Susana was allowing her to partially save face by allowing Andy to stay with Jaye but giving her the option to decline Jaye's offer to take them both in. "Yes, I guess I would go along with that."

"After lunch, why don't I ride over to Jaye Boyden's with you and Andy. On the way back, we can stop at your father's house and pick up what you might need for the next few days. I've only met Jaye a few times and would like to know him better. He sounds like an exceptional young man."

The trip to Jaye's and back to Susana's place took most of the afternoon. Sheena noted that Andy and Dingo were happy to be at Jaye's, and he was more than welcoming, not even hinting that he had won a partial victory. And he did not seem a bit disappointed that she was not staying. On the contrary, he seemed most pleased with the arrangement which annoyed her some.

After picking up a few clothing items at the Bar F house, the women rode on to Susana's at a near walk. Susana said, "Jaye is such a nice young man and so interesting to talk to."

Yes, Sheena thought, Susana and Jaye were so engaged in conversation that she barely got in a word. "Yes, he's been a good friend to Andy and me."

"And he's quite handsome. If I were thirty years younger, you might have some competition."

"There would be no competition. I have no real romantic interest in him."

"Really? The way he looks at you, he is certainly stricken by you."

Her mind flashed back to the image of Jaye stripped to his waist in the calving pen. So well-muscled, and, yes, handsome even when half-blood soaked. She had totally undressed him in her head. "Jaye is not an ugly man and has a few redeeming characteristics. I just do not wish to encourage him at all. I don't have time for a man right now and intend to keep him at a distance, certainly until I know where I am going with my life."

She scolded herself. She had not exactly kept her distance when she kissed him several days earlier and awakened feelings she thought were dead.

Susana said, "You and Jaye will be fun to watch. As for me, I will make time for the right man, but until recently none have interested me, and, of course, in this lonely country, it's slim pickings anyhow, especially for an old widow lady."

"Until recently?"

"Yes, but of course, it takes two."

Sheena was not going to ask, but she had a feeling that the potential second person was her estranged father.

Chapter 29

JAYE FOUND HIMSELF enjoying the company of Andy and Dingo who shared an upstairs bedroom in the house. At Jaye's insistence, Avery had temporarily moved into the other spare room. After Colt Louden's murder, he was not comfortable with a lone occupant in the bunkhouse. Avery was a reluctant guest, but Jaye promised he would find another hand and then the old-timer could return to his usual dwelling place.

He conceded that Avery's risk of meeting Colt's fate was miniscule if Jaye was on target about the primary suspect. Motives for Colt's killing could be pieced together, although Colt had not known enough about Thomas Towne's enterprises to constitute a threat to the man. Jaye assumed he was not immune from an attempt on his own life, and he worried that Sheena might be vulnerable because of her contact with the men who had abducted her.

Truth was that Jaye doubted he could just wait to see if Morg returned. How could they just hide out like frightened rabbits for days, maybe weeks? They might never hear a word about Morg or Jim Hunter. They could both be dead, and those odds increased by the day.

It was early afternoon, and Jaye and Andy, followed by Dingo, were walking across the yard to the stable to retrieve their mounts so they could ride over to the Bar F to collect the five horses and two mules there and bring them to the J Bar B. Jaye had decided it made more sense to move the critters to his place temporarily and remove the need to care for horses at Morg's.

They would be less susceptible to surprise by someone hiding out there to strike when they showed up at a predictable time. He figured they would also save time. They would still ride over that way for cattle checks at staggered times but stay clear of the building site. Dingo started barking behind, and Jaye and Andy both stopped and turned.

The dog's eyes were fixed on the trail leading to the county road north of the farmstead. "I don't see anything," Jaye said.

"We will," Andy said. "Dingo says somebody's coming."

Jaye's fingers instinctively moved to his holstered Colt and brushed the pistol grip. "I'll never figure out how that dog knows such things."

Andy bent over and gently patted the dog's head. "She's just smart, ain't you girl?"

"Do you think she hears those words?"

Andy shrugged. "She knows. Do you think he's coming to kill us?"

"Well, he's not going to if he's got that in mind, but I'm thinking any killer would more likely go after us by ambush."

"Dingo would warn us."

"Depends on how far away the shooter was. Even Dingo has her limits."

As the man neared, Jaye sized him up. He was not an ordinary cowhand. He wore a white Stetson hat that did not show much wear and a rust-brown suit with a string tie. The shiny boots looked free of any cow shit. This was a man who was loathe to dirty himself with common labor. He wore a holstered gun on his belt but did not appear threatening. Jaye gave the man a friendly wave, and the stranger reined in and dismounted.

The visitor was graceful in the saddle and no stranger to horses despite his city slicker looks. He was a young man, probably a few years younger than himself, straw-colored hair, clean shaven, tall and trim. Women would likely be drooling over this man. Jaye stepped forward and extended his hand, "I'm Jaye Boyden." He nodded toward Andy who was standing five paces off to one side. "And this is my friend, Andy Fraser."

The stranger returned a firm grip. "And my name is Charles Vaughn." He looked at Andy. "You've got to be Sheena's little brother."

Andy's eyes narrowed. "Yeah."

Jaye said. "You know Sheena?"

"Very well. We are old...friends. Very good friends."

Charles. This must be the old boyfriend from North Platte. The one headed for fancy law school. He instantly was struck by a little wave of jealousy. "I see."

"I traveled a long way to see Sheena. We corresponded with some frequency, but my last two letters were returned. I was worried, so when I returned to North Platte a week ago, I set out to find her. I knew she was teaching at the Willow School, and her mail was always sent in care of some folks named Markham who kept a boarding house nearby. I went to their place and spent last night there. They told me about Sheena being abducted and all. It must have been a terrible experience. Anyway, the Markhams told me that you would know where to find her."

"Yes, I do. I should warn you, though. She could still be in some danger. You'd better watch your back. Her father, the U.S. Marshal, still has not returned, and we don't know if he's dead or alive. You are here at a very difficult time for Sheena."

"All the more reason I should find her and be with her. I could offer Sheena and Andy a safer, more civilized refuge, and I am hoping they might come with me." He looked at Andy. "What would you think about that, Andy?"

"Thanks, but I'll be staying on here. My dad will be back soon."

"Well, we'll see what your sister says."

"She ain't in charge of me, sir."

Jaye said, "Andy and I were just headed over to the Bar F, the Fraser ranch is just down the road from my place. Give us a few minutes to get saddled up, and you can ride over with us. We hit the Dismal Trail there, and I can point you in the right direction. Sheena is staying with a teacher friend at the next house on the trail. You can't miss it."

"I'd take that kindly, Jaye."

"You can water your horse here and grain him at the stable if you like. Grass is plentiful now, but the critters won't turn down a grain snack."

Later, at the Fraser farmstead, Jaye and Andy watched as Charles Vaughn reined his mount onto the Dismal Trail and continued his journey to Susana Mercer's house. Jaye said, "Charles seems a nice enough fellow."

"I ain't going with him even if Sheena takes a notion to go. They can rope and tie me, but I'll get away."

"Andy, I don't think anybody's going to rope and tie you and drag you along to North Platte. Besides, your sister has agreed to teach school with Susana next fall. I don't think she'd back out on that promise."

At least he hoped not. But did he really know Sheena Fraser that well? Certainly, as they came to know each other better, she was turning out to be a different woman than he had conjured up in his mind. Still, this different Sheena only captivated him more, summoned him to solve all the mysteries surrounding this woman. Of course, Charles Vaughn could well put it all to an end.

Chapter 30

SHEENA SAT AT the desk in the office she now shared with Susana. The desk had previously been used by Susana's late husband who had occupied the office space with his schoolteacher spouse. The desk was an oak rolltop nearly identical to Susana's, and Sheena loved the fine piece that somehow made her feel at home. She was compiling a list of books and supplies she would require for the fall school term based upon Susana's enrollment projections. They had agreed to make a trip to North Platte by midsummer to purchase what was available and to order what was not.

From the window, she could see the Dismal River through a break in the trees, its water splashing over the rocks protruding from its bed on its journey eastward. It was a calming scene, and it occurred to her that she was increasingly appreciating such views. It was as if she were just beginning the past several weeks to see her sur-roundings with different eyes. Maybe this was what Jaye was talking about when he said that if he did not have work to get done, he could sit and watch cattle grazing the Sandhills dunes for hours. He claimed such times were almost religious moments for him.

Her momentary embrace of this vast, quiet land was interrupted by Susana, who had a rifle cradled in her arms. "Visitor," Susana said, before she wheeled and left.

Sheena grabbed the Winchester she kept next to the desk and followed. Susana was leaning against the wall, peering through the edge of a curtain when Sheena caught up with her and looked over her friend's shoulder. The man had his back to them as he hitched the horse to the rail in front of the house.

When he turned to walk up to the porch, Sheena whis-pered, "Oh, my God."

"Do you know him?"

"It's Charles."

"Charles? The old boyfriend you mentioned?"

"Yes. Why would he be here?"

"I doubt if he came to see me. But he is a very hand-some visitor. A bit gussied up for a visit to cattle country. Do you want me to answer the door?"

A surge of panic made Sheena want to run. "I can't. I'm wearing these ragged britches, and I'm swimming in your husband's old shirt. I must be a sight."

"You are beautiful, my dear. You can't hide it, but I will answer the door and give you a few moments to collect yourself. You go back to the office, and I will talk with the gentleman a bit and call you in, and you can act surprised."

Sheena returned to the office but did not sit down. She began pacing as she was inclined to do when worried or anxious. She froze when she heard rapping at the front door. Then she listened to the mumbling, trying to hear the conversation that seemed to go on forever, but picking up only a word here and there. She could make out bursts of laughter occasionally and wondered what they found so humorous. Charles was likely charming Susana. He could charm most women, including herself. She wondered how many he had charmed into bed since their last encounter well over a year ago. But why would he come here?

"Sheena, come out. You have a visitor. An old friend."

It was Susana calling from the parlor. Sheena took a deep breath, stepped out of the office and walked the short distance down the hallway to the parlor, where she saw Charles, displaying a big smile and Susana with mischievous twinkling eyes standing off to one side. He opened his arms, signaling that she was expected to come forward and embrace him. She accepted the invitation and gave him a chaste hug and offered her cheek. He kissed her but held her close, reminding her of their past and triggering hunger she thought she had long since buried.

She stepped back, slipping from his arms. "Charles, my heavens, this is a surprise. You are the last person I would have expected to see in the Sandhills. What are you doing here?"

"I came to see you, of course." He nodded at Susana. "And your gracious friend has been so kind to offer me supper and a room for the night so we can get reacquainted and catch up a bit."

This was getting too complicated. "Oh, that's nice."

"You don't sound enthused. I hope I'm not interrupting anything."

"No, not at all. It's just that I'm so surprised by your visit."

Susana started to leave the other two, giving Sheena a gentle squeeze on the shoulder as she brushed by. "I have some work I should be doing in the office. I'll leave the parlor to the two of you. Charles, Sheena can show you where to put your horse up, and, Sheena, don't you worry about supper. We've got apple pie left over from yesterday, and I'll prepare something simple, maybe stew and biscuits."

"Uh, okay. Thank you, Susana."

She turned back to Charles. "Would you like to put up your horse first?"

"Yeah, that would be good."

Charles followed her to the stable, leading the big sorrel gelding. After Charles unsaddled the mount, Sheena began brushing him down while Charles retrieved hay and a small can of grain from the far end of the stable. "There's a bucket near the haystack," Sheena hollered. "Pump's just outside the door. We walked past it."

When she finished brushing the horse, Sheena removed its bridle and turned the sorrel loose in the stall. No sooner had she hung the bridle on a wall peg than she felt strong arms enclose her and Charles's body push up against her backside. His lips pressed against the back of her neck and soon his fingers cupped her breasts, leaving her breathless.

He spoke softly in her ear. "Remember those times in my father's stable before and after we went horseback riding? That haystack?"

She firmly grabbed his wrists, removing his hands, and twisted away to face him. "Charles, you aren't suggesting..."

His arms were around her again, pulling her close, and this time his lips found hers. She felt his tongue seeking her mouth, and she surrendered to a deep kiss. Now she felt his hardness against her and swore she could feel the pulsating of his manhood, and she ached for him.

"I was more than suggesting, Sheena. I want you, and you want me. I know it. Let's celebrate old times in the haystack."

She pulled away from him again. "I do want you, Charles, but I can't let it happen. Not this way. We hardly know each other after this much time apart. I won't chance the possible disgust, and guilt and hurt."

"What disgust? What guilt? We've done this a hundred times."

She whirled and raced for the house.

"Oh, shit," he said. "Wait up. We'll go in and have that nice talk your friend proposed."

In the parlor, Sheena pointed to a stuffed chair, signaling that Charles should sit there, and she claimed a chair facing his that placed a tea table between them. She did not want to touch him now, not even accidentally, for fear she might reignite the fire. She studied him before she spoke, but then it occurred to her that he had always been unreadable and divulged little of himself. She had shared her life and her dreams, but she knew little about Charles, except that his father was a wealthy business-man and that the only son had never wanted for anything.

She even had given him everything he wanted. He was her first and only, and she had spread her thighs for him within two weeks after their first meeting. He had known all about her then, and she had known only the feel and touch of his naked body and the pleasure it had delivered. She had been a child then, naïve and foolish, and these past weeks she was learning she still had some growing up to do.

"Charles, I don't think you came all this way to find me. Don't tell me you haven't been pleasured by other women since our parting."

"I haven't ignored nature calling, and I daresay you haven't, either."

She did not respond. She was not going to tell him there had been no other. "You asked me to write. I wrote monthly for eight months to the address you gave me. I received no reply, so I quit. I even mailed my Willow School address to your parents at North Platte."

"I was busy with my studies. Law school is very de-manding, especially at Yale."

"From what you told me, you should have a full year remaining."

"I left after my first year. I didn't like it there. My father had connections with a law firm in Omaha, and I have been clerking there. I will take the bar examination this summer and should become a full-fledged lawyer then."

"You returned to Nebraska and never even wrote me about that, even after I finished high school and normal training and moved from North Platte. You had my mother's address. She would have passed a letter on to me." Sheena realized she could not say that with certainty.

"You are trying to put me on the defensive, and I won't have it. I am here now to make amends. That should mean something."

"How did you find me?"

"Well, I went to the Willow School and then to the boarding house where you stayed. Missus Markham told me that this Jaye Boyden would likely know where you would be. I stayed a night there and moved on down the road. I stopped at the Tall T and visited with your mother and Thomas a spell and they told me the location of the Boyden place. I suppose Boyden's the guy you're sleeping with these days."

"It's none of your damn business who I sleep with."

"You've turned into a feisty bitch since I last saw you. I recall you being gentle as a lamb."

"I don't like that you stopped to see my mother. Thomas Towne is an animal."

"Your mother always treated me very well. In fact, I was invited to spend the night at the ranch if I didn't make other arrangements."

"Just what is your connection with my stepfather?"

"I guess it doesn't hurt to tell you. The law firm I work for represents Thomas. I brought a bundle of papers for him to review and sign. I am to pick them up when I head back to Omaha."

"So you didn't make the trip just to see me?"

"Well, no, but I did want to see you. Your mother and stepfather wanted me to find you and see how you are doing also."

Charles was a spy. A damn spy. And he would let Towne know where she was at. Charles was likely not a part of any conspiracy. She was beginning to see that beneath his charm was a very shallow man of no more than average intelligence. He probably was booted out of law school because Yale did not grade on charm. Well, if this was a spy game, two could play.

"I assume you heard about my abduction."

"Yes, from both Missus Markham and your mother. Nobody has much in the way of details. Thomas was wondering if you had heard from your father."

"As a matter of fact, I have received a message by courier from North Platte, the U.S. Marshal's office there. He is well and should arrive home within another ten days. He has been asked to meet with a dozen deputy marshals who have been called in to pursue the parties responsible for all this. Whoever took me and forced the trade made a huge mistake when they went after a U.S. Marshal. The entire marshal service takes this personally."

"Really? Do you have any idea who might have been involved in this?"

"No. None at all. I saw the men who took me, of course, but they said nothing that would identify their leader." She decided that it was best not to mention Arthur and the Tall T connection.

Susana came in and began preparing supper in the kitchen. With no wall separating the rooms, she would be able to hear much of the conversation if she chose. Regardless, Charles began asking questions like she was on a courtroom witness stand, most of which she found irrelevant and juvenile. She answered mostly with a flurry of lies or "I don't remembers" and found herself halfway enjoying the dialogue.

Finally, he said, "So you have no idea who was behind your abduction?"

"I think I have said as much at least a half dozen times. Why are you so interested in this?"

"These people should be brought to justice, and Thomas wishes to see if he can help. He is outraged at what happened to you. You are fortunate to have such a caring stepfather."

Yes, she thought, the animal who molested me as a child and who does not want me or my brother living in his home.

"Supper's on the table," Susana called. "Maybe you two can catch up more later."

Susana did most of the talking as the three sat at the table, Charles at the head and Susana at his left with Sheena seated across from her. "Did you enjoy your time together?" Susana asked.

"Very much so," Charles said. "I have missed Sheena so much. Incidentally, the stew and biscuits are delicious. I can't thank you enough for taking me in for the night."

"My pleasure, Charles. I'm so glad you could stay a spell." She turned to Sheena, "And how has your afternoon been, dear?"

"Interesting. Very interesting. I hope you will join us in the parlor after we clean up the supper dishes. Maybe

Charles will be so kind as to check the horses in the stable and be sure they all have water and hay for the night." She did not want to be alone with him and was thankful now she had not given in to temptation when they were in the stable.

Later, as they were cleaning up and Charles was tending to the horses, Susana said, "You have not enjoyed a happy reunion, have you?"

Sheena shrugged. "It's been interesting. I will tell you about it after he leaves tomorrow, but I must talk to Jaye about a few things. It is strange how we view things with different eyes as we grow older, isn't it?"

"That will never change, Sheena. When I look back on my life, I ask myself all the time, what was I thinking about things I did and decisions I made thirty years ago, or even five, but especially in my teen years. You are escaping those now, but we all have things in our pasts that we must consider parts of our educations and somehow put aside for the sake of sanity."

"Charles has stood in my way for a long time and kept me from giving another man a chance."

Susana smiled, "Like Jaye?"

"Yes, like Jaye. I may be ready to get to know him better, hopefully see him through wiser eyes. But I will move very slowly and with great care."

The remainder of the evening, the three sat in the parlor. Susana again carried the female part of the conversation, asking Charles about his ambitions and plans. Charles was not shy about talking of the success he would have over the years ahead. He would soon be a senior law firm partner representing wealthy clients, and in no time at all would become a wealthy man. Sheena noted that he did not mention that he was the sole heir to a small fortune and that his father had bought his way to his present position. Once she had been impressed with his wealth. Now it meant nothing to her.

Eventually, Susana surrendered and stood up. "It is past my bedtime. I'm afraid you must excuse me."

Sheena did not wish to be alone with Charles, and when Susana reached the stairway, Sheena jumped up and said, "Mine, too. I'll be right back." She hurried into the office and returned with her Winchester.

"Do you sleep with that thing?" Charles asked.

"Sometimes it's more comforting than a man, and I do know how to use it, thanks to you. Remember?"

"Oh, I certainly do." His pale blue eyes fastened on hers, and he gave that little smirk she used to find seductive. "And I especially remember those moments on a blanket after practice sessions. You said that firing a gun made you horny, and you were like a cougar in heat. You wanted more and more. About wore me out."

She did remember, and she was embarrassed. She had been crazy then, believed she was in love with him, and he had awakened something in her that had been sleeping after the sick assaults by Thomas Towne. She would give Charles that much credit. "I guess I did some pretty stupid things then."

"No, the good life is meant for pleasure. You gave me great pleasure, and I obviously brought you some, too. You were an innocent little kitten, and I raised you into a cat. I daresay I was a good teacher."

She supposed he was in some respects. She had learned to enjoy the body she had once hated. She would give him credit for that. "Yes, I suppose you could say that."

"Tonight, we could have that again. Why don't you let me give you a good night kiss, and I will visit your room after we have given Susana some time to fall asleep?" He smiled. "But you must be quiet. You cannot scream and moan like you used to do."

"I'll pass on that. I will be sleeping with my gun tonight, and there is a bolt lock on my door that will be in place."

His lips tightened and she swore she could see sparks leaping from his angry eyes. She did an about face and rushed up the stairs.

The next morning, she rose shortly after sunrise to go downstairs and prepare breakfast. She cradled the rifle in her arms as she tiptoed down the stairs. She stopped when she heard pans clattering in the kitchen and then continued. She was not entirely surprised to find Susana in the kitchen. "It was my turn to fix breakfast," Sheena said.

"I thought you had a difficult day yesterday and that I would surprise you with a little celebration. Hot cakes, fried eggs, and sausage, and, of course, coffee."

"Celebration?"

"You didn't know? Your old friend Charles rode out of here half an hour ago. He didn't even stick around for a cup of coffee."

Chapter 31

WHEN HE EMERGED from the barn after doing morning chores, Jaye was surprised to see a rider crossing the ranch's rolling grasslands to the southwest. The horse and rider appeared to be moving at a good pace, so he assumed it was not somebody enjoying a casual ride on this sunny, balmy day. The bay horse and its rider disappeared for several minutes behind the dunes, but when they came into sight again, Jaye recognized Sheena wearing the low-crowned hat that nearly covered her eyes and a farmer's bib overalls of all things.

Why would she be heading to his place this morning? He had thought she would likely still be entertaining Charles Vaughn, but he was not disappointed she was not. Soon she rode into the ranch yard and dismounted. He walked over to her and said, "You look lovely this morning." He meant that but knew she would take it as sarcasm.

She lifted the brim of her hat and conveyed a bit of aggravation with her beautiful green eyes that glittered like jewels in the bright morning sun. "This is all I could find to wear. I laundered my only riding britches. A dress can be very uncomfortable riding astride, and I don't have much of a riding wardrobe. I pretty much gave up riding after high school."

"First, I meant it when I said you look lovely, but maybe you would join me on a trip to Broken Bow this summer to replenish that riding wardrobe. Since the railroad came, it's something of a boom town with shops for everything."

"That might be nice."

"But you didn't ride over to talk about shopping."

"I wanted to talk about Charles. I think you met him."

"Yeah, he stopped by here. Andy and I rode over to the Bar F with him and showed him how to get to Susana Mercer's. He seemed a nice enough feller."

"Things and people are not always what they appear to be."

"True enough." He thought it best to allow Sheena to lead the conversation.

"Did Charles tell you he had visited the Tall T before he stopped at your place?"

"Nope. He gave me the impression he had come here directly from the Markhams."

"He works for a law firm in Omaha that happens to represent Thomas Towne. His father in North Platte has connections of some sort with the office. Charles brought legal papers from Omaha for Thomas to sign, but I think his past relationship with me was no mere coincidence. Charles had visited the Tall T Ranch with me on two occasions, and my mother and Thomas both met him then. Anyhow, I'm sure Charles was sent to see me to find out just how much I know. I don't think he understood why. I doubt he is smart enough to figure out that he's being used."

"I see." And this man was her boyfriend and likely lover for two years?

"You're not saying it, but you are thinking it. You are asking why this young woman was with this man for all that time if she has so little respect for his intelligence. Well, I wasn't so smart myself, not much more than a child. I hope I'm growing up. I'm starting to see the world differently. I'll never know it all, but I intend to learn a lot more. I realize now that I haven't treated you well. I've been downright mean sometimes, and I apologize for that. Be patient with me, Jaye. I want to be your friend. Time will tell if we can be more."

"I am your friend, Sheena. I always will be even if we take separate trails through life. Now tell me more about what you learned from Charles."

She told him about Charles's questions and the lies she told him. Jaye suspected that their conversations went beyond that, but it was not his concern, especially since he was more than satisfied with the conclusion.

"You told some tall tales. You could be a dime novelist. My guess is that Thomas Towne is on the verge of panic. I don't think you said anything that puts you and Andy in more danger. To the contrary, I suspect Towne is not wanting to stir up more trouble here if he fears Morg is returning. Also, it seems to me that his sending Charles on a scouting mission indicates that Towne has no evidence of your father's death. If he is as deep in this as we suspect, he should have received confirmation by now. I'm looking for Morg to ride in here about any day now."

"You are truly an optimist."

"I've been told that before by your father."

"Should we be doing something?"

"Wait. We don't have much choice but to let the story tell itself as I see it. I sent the letter to the U.S. Marshal's office over ten days ago now. They surely have it, and I can't believe they won't send someone to investigate. We have no legal authority or backing to do anything, even if we could."

"You certainly would not be called a reckless man."

"Unless I'm forced to act, I guess I tend to ponder some before I go ahead with anything. I'd like to ride over to the Tall T and confront Thomas Towne, but he's likely got a few men handy to put a bullet in my back. There's also the fact that I would end up interfering with finding out what this has all been about. This was at first all about somebody avenging the death of a brother, but now it has turned into something bigger. Just curious, do you know if Thomas Towne had a brother?"

"I have no idea. There was never any discussion about his family in the house. Supposedly, they are all in Australia. I'll bet he's not even Australian."

"What makes you say that?"

"He only uses a foreign accent and Aussie expressions when visitors are around. I suspect the Australian cattle dogs are as much props as a desire to establish a new breed in this country. The dogs fear him, incidentally. He's by nature a cruel man."

"As Dingo learned."

"Otherwise, he sounds east coast American. He used to talk a lot about Boston when I was still living at the house. Wherever he's from, he's a filthy, sick man. I hate him. He ought to be put down like a rabid animal."

Jaye did not press, but he gathered that Sheena had suffered some kind of personal mistreatment from Towne. "Andy and Avery are having breakfast at the house, and I was heading up to join them. What about you? I'm sure there's plenty to eat, and I'd bet Andy would like to see you."

"I ate a huge breakfast already, but I could handle another cup of coffee. I'm not certain about Andy. We didn't have a very congenial parting the last time we were together."

"Kids have short memories over family fusses. You'll be fine."

When they walked into the house, Andy looked up from the table and grinned. "Hi, Sis. Wondered when I was going to see you again."

"Hi, Andy. I thought I'd stop by and see how you're doing."

"I'm good. Avery's got me milking the Holstein cow mornings now. We agreed that I'll do mornings, and he takes nights. The problem is we can't use all the milk. Her calf takes a fair amount, and the five cats help some, but we've still got to throw too much away. Jaye says we need a bunch of kids around here to drink the stuff."

"Susana lost her milk cow, and she likes to have milk for cooking and the school kids. Maybe you can work something out."

Jaye said, "When your dad gets back, maybe we can move the cow over to the Bar F. That would be closer to Susana's. If you can make a deal to sell the milk, the money is yours. We just want enough to satisfy our needs here."

"Darn, I like that idea. Let me figure it all out."

Jaye poured a cup of coffee for Sheena who took a chair at the table beside her brother. Jaye served himself two cinnamon biscuits from the Dutch oven on the wood-stove, shoveled a helping of scrambled eggs from the frying pan and set his plate on the table before retrieving his own coffee cup and sitting down next to Avery across from the two siblings. Jaye saw Sheena eyeing his plate and said, "We've got enough biscuits for another meal. Do you want to try one of Avery's cinnamon biscuits? He makes dang good biscuits. Don't judge him by the coffee."

Avery said, "I ain't seen you turning it down."

"No, but I don't think I've turned down a cup of coffee since I was five years old."

"I might try one biscuit," Sheena said.

Jaye got up, scooped one onto a plate and set it in front of her.

"Thank you," she said, "you make a good servant."

"Yes, ma'am, I try to be."

As they ate, Avery and Jaye talked about the day's work plans. Jaye said, "We'll start repairing the south fence along the Dismal Trail after breakfast. It'll take five or six days' work to get it in shape again. The cattle won't likely break free for as long as the grass is good, but if we get a serious dry spell this summer, we'll have some fence jumpers who will call the other herds to break through. And it won't be fun rounding them up and herding them back along the river, especially if some take a notion to cross. It's open range on the other side of the river."

He turned around when he heard Dingo scratching on the door. She was standing on her hind legs, front paws digging frantically on the scarred, oak door. He got up and moved over beside the dog, patting her on the head to get her attention. He raised his right-hand signaling stop, and she obeyed. However, when he opened the door partway to peer out, Dingo squeezed past him and darted out, racing out the door and heading for the entry road where a rider was just approaching the house.

"I'll be danged," Jaye said.

Chapter 32

SHEENA WATCHED AS Jaye flung the door open. "What is it?" she asked.

Jaye turned around, smiling broadly. "Sheena, Andy, your pa's home." Jaye disappeared outside.

Andy knocked over his chair in his hurry to catch up with Jaye. "I knew Dad would make it. I said so all along," he told his sister as he rushed past her.

She got up but hesitated at the doorway, her heart racing. She was both overjoyed and afraid, not knowing where she fit in this man's life. She stepped onto the porch and took in the scene. Her father held the reins of his bay gelding in one hand as he knelt on one knee with his other arm wrapped around Dingo, as she showered him with dog kisses. When he finally got to his feet, Morg and Andy embraced. She could tell that her brother had tears running down his cheeks and found herself surprised at the emotional reunion.

Jaye was shaking Morg's hand as she walked slowly toward her father. Jaye moved away and took the horse's reins from Morg's hand. "Sheena," Morg said. "I like this better than our last meeting."

He held out his arms and she fell into them and started sobbing and could not control it. He just held her until she finally got a grip on her pent-up emotions. She looked up at him and saw that his own eyes were tear-glazed. "Dad, I've been so wrong about you. I love you, and I just want you to know that."

"And I love you, Sheena. I always have, but I did a lousy job of showing it. I hope someday you can forgive me for that."

"It's already done. It happened at Mad Rock, but it took a while for me to realize it."

He released her and looked around. "Now, tell me, how do you all happen to be gathered here? Dingo coming out to greet me was a total surprise." He bent down and brushed the dog's head again. It was obvious to Sheena that her father held the first claim on the cattle dog's affection.

Jaye said, "She knew you were coming. She was crazed to get outside just before you showed up. Sometimes I wonder if this deaf business isn't just an act."

"Well, I was sure glad to see my sweetheart."

"We've got a lot to talk about, Morg. Why don't you come up to the house and sit down with us over coffee. Avery's got cinnamon biscuits if you haven't had breakfast."

"I slept off the trail last night and was too lazy to fix breakfast—of course, no food anyhow. I was hoping to get home before bedtime, but I got so sleepy, I about slid off my saddle. So, yeah, coffee and a biscuit or two sound good."

Jaye said, "This will take a spell. Maybe Andy would take your horse and put him up in the stable."

"I can do that," Andy said, taking the reins from Jaye. "He's a nice-looking critter. I like the white stripe down his nose. Is he yours?"

Morg hesitated. "Well, yeah, I guess he is. That's another story, though."

"What's his name?"

"He doesn't have one just yet. Maybe you can come up with one."

"Sure, I'll think of something."

Avery was waiting on the porch to welcome Morg back, and Sheena gathered the two were old friends. "Well," Avery said, "I always thought you had as many lives as a cat, but I'd be careful from here on. I'd guess you're getting near to using them up."

"I'll keep that in mind, Avery. You're probably right."

Inside, they took chairs in the parlor, Dingo lying beside Morg's stuffed chair. The dog had disregarded Andy's signal to join him while he took care of the horse. Sheena saw that her brother was a bit disappointed, but he did not push the dog. Dingo was probably not ready to let his rescuer out of her sight for a spell. She had heard about bonds between dogs and owners, and it was obvious that Dingo and her father had one.

When they were all settled and Morg had a steaming coffee cup and two biscuits on the thick walnut tea table in front of him, Jaye said, "You first, Morg. Where the blazes have you been?"

"I'll give you the short version for now." He told how he had been incarcerated in a town jail and Jim Hunter's breaking him out, his acquisition of the bay gelding and the pursuit by his captors into the Badlands. "I suppose the gunslingers' bones have been picked clean by now. I doubt if Four Fingers did enough burying to keep the coyotes and buzzards out for more than a day or two."

Sheena said, "But what took you so long to get back?"

"Well, we went on to Fort Robinson, deciding that was safest in case others were tracking us, and we didn't have more than just enough provisions to get us out of the Badlands and halfway to the fort. We stayed there two nights, and I sent a telegram to the U.S. Marshal's headquarters in North Platte, just giving him enough information to whet his appetite for more. I got a reply that I should report to headquarters immediately. Well, 'immediately' was four more days by the time we caught a train connection at Crawford, traveled across the state and back with our horses in cattle cars and changed trains four times before we got to North Platte."

Sheena said, "Dad, we've been worried sick. Why didn't you get word to us that you were alright?" She did not wish to start a fuss with him right off, but she was a little miffed.

"I should have found a way, but Broken Bow was the nearest town with a telegraph connection, and I'm not well acquainted with folks there. The sheriff likely would have taken days to deliver a message, and I had not figured on the long delay getting to North Platte. By that time, I figured I could get to Broken Bow in a day and head home from there. That would take us right past Jim Hunter's bunkhouse at the K Bar K. Well, it took two days with waiting for connections to get to Broken Bow, and another two for me to ride back here."

Andy came in now and took a place on the floor beside the sleeping Dingo. Jaye said, "I wrote to the U.S. Marshal at North Platte about the killing of a fine young man—Colt Louden—at the J Bar B. I don't suppose he had the letter yet when you were there."

"As a matter of fact, it arrived the day before I showed up. The acting U.S. Marshal there shared it with me. That's when I knew I had to get home as fast as I could, not that it changed my route. I gather you are convinced Thomas Towne is playing a major role in all this."

"Yes. And we've had further confirmation since I sent the letter." He turned to Sheena. "Why don't you tell him about your friend, Sheena."

"You never met Charles Vaughn. He was a boyfriend of mine during high school. He was a few years older and went back east to attend law school at Yale before I finished my own schooling. And for your information, I now know who paid for my high school and normal school education. I am grateful for that, Dad. It's made possible all the things I want to do."

Her father seemed embarrassed and gave a little shrug.

She continued telling her father, with some editing, about her conversations with Charles. "I lied to him a lot when I figured out what he was up to, and I think Thomas Towne is worried that a posse of marshals is going to show up and be looking into his affairs."

"It will be good for him to worry about that. But I'm the posse. The marshals' service is swamped, too few men and increased demand from the states and territories for help. I submitted my resignation effective July first, but I agreed to see this case through. It's my last case, and I don't have even two months to solve it."

Jaye said, "You do know that I will help where I can? I can at least be another gun."

"Me, too," said Andy.

"Count me in," Sheena said.

Morg furrowed his brow when Sheena spoke.

Jaye said, "I saw her kill a man, Morg. We haven't told you much about our journey back here after the exchange."

"I'll certainly want to hear about this. What I want to do now is go home and digest all this. I won't make a move without letting you know what I'm doing." He turned to Andy. "Son, I'd like to have you stay here with Jaye until we get things figured out. It won't be long, I promise."

"Sheena, from what you said, I gather you are staying at Susana Mercer's. I think that's good. My place may not be safe when Towne finds out I've returned. He may already know. I've got a hunch somebody's watching the J Bar B and Bar F these days."

"Yes, I'm staying with Susana. We're establishing a new school, and I will be living with her at least for the next year. We can talk about all this another time. If you are headed home, I'll ride with you as far as your house. Susana will want to know you are back. Don't be surprised if you have a visitor yet today or tomorrow."

"Oh, I doubt she'd be in a hurry to see me. I'll get over there as soon as I can."

"I don't doubt. You will have a visitor."

"Dad," Andy said, "I want Dingo to go with you, and I know she'd like to. If you are going to be staying at the house, she needs to be with you. She's better than having another gun in the house."

Chapter 33

MORG SAT ON the front porch, feet propped up on the railing and Dingo dozing on the tattered rug next to the chair, listening to the Dismal's water washing over the stones downslope from the house. After the turmoil of the past several weeks, he treasured these moments as he never had before. He missed having Andy with him, however. The boy had obviously matured immeasurably during their days apart.

He had read once that a person is never too old to be the person they might have been. When they got past the dangers lurking nearby, he hoped that there was yet time for him to be the father he might have been to Andy.

He was less certain about Sheena. The door to forming a relationship with her appeared to have been opened, but she was a grown woman now and his best guess was that he should proceed cautiously, allow her to determine the extent to which she wished him to be a part of her life.

It was midafternoon. He had no chores to tend to since Buckshot and the other critters were boarding at Jaye's stable temporarily. He would get back over to visit Buckshot tomorrow, maybe bring him and at least a few of the horses back home. His longtime mount should get acquainted with his new companion, "Stripe," the name Andy had assigned to the new bay in the stable.

Now what about supper? The cupboards were nearly bare. The fixings for biscuits and coffee were there. No meat or eggs, not even jerky, although he had a few sticks of deer jerky in his saddlebags. He supposed he would need to do some hunting tomorrow. He was not going to sacrifice one of his beeves to feed only himself and Dingo right now. He got up to go into the house and scavenge for supper when Dingo leapt to her feet, her ears stiffened, and she looked to the east in the direction of the Dismal Trail, whimpering softly.

Morg bent over and stroked the cattle dog's head. "What is it, girl?" Of course, she would not hear his voice, but as soon as they arrived at his house, he had quickly taken on the habit of talking to her, thinking it made more sense to talk to a deaf dog than chatting with himself as he was inclined to do.

Soon a horse and rider appeared on the trail, and he recognized Susana Mercer instantly despite her low-crowned hat and faded, denim britches. She was astride a bald-face sorrel mare. He waved and stepped off the porch to greet her. She waved back and rode into the yard and dismounted. He took her mount's reins and hitched her to the rail and almost fell backward when Susana came up and hugged him. His arms wrapped around her, and he chuckled. "Now that's a nice surprise."

She stepped back. "I nearly collapsed when Sheena told me you were back. I was worried sick about you, but I tried not to let on to her."

"I was never in that much danger," he lied.

"I learned enough about your situation from Sheena to know you're fibbing, but I'll excuse it this time. I'm just so glad you're home."

"Well, I appreciate you paying me a visit. I'm not sure you ought to be seen with me, though."

She ignored his admonition. "I brought the fixings for supper. I intend to stay a spell and have supper with you and Dingo, if you don't mind. My saddlebags are about to burst open. Let me take them in the house while you put April up in the stable if you don't mind."

When Morg returned to the house, he was struck first by the aroma of baking bread. He walked into the kitchen area where Susana was hovering over the woodstove. "I don't know if there's anything I like better than the smell of fresh, baked bread—well eating it, I suppose."

"I had the dough nearly ready for baking when Sheena came in. I left half for her. I was hoping you might have hot coals in your stove."

"Yeah, I don't know what I was going to cook. There's not much here, but I got a fire going earlier."

"Well, I have some leftover baked beans and beef roast to warm up, and a few slices of cherry pie. Dingo's already eating on some meat scraps I brought. Nothing fancy, but I figured you wouldn't have much to work with here. You are invited to my house for meals until you get resupplied. Regardless, I hope you and Andy will take your evening meal with us indefinitely. It will give you an opportunity to spend some time with Sheena. And I would enjoy seeing you, too."

Abruptly, Morg's sense of smell was taken over by his eyes. This was a dang attractive woman in his kitchen, a pretty thing for any age, and the snug shirt and britches she wore today revealed a womanly, yet petite, figure underneath. If he did not know better, he would think she was trying to seduce him or at least get his attention. Well, she had certainly done so, whether it was intentional or not. It had been so long since he had been with a woman, he doubted if he could read one very well, and he was not about to make any assumptions.

"I'm not helping much," Morg said. "I could make coffee, but mine always tastes like mud."

"I don't want you doing anything. Your presence is enough. I found your coffee, and I'll have it brewing soon. We'll eat in half an hour, a little early for suppertime, but I'm betting you are hungry enough to eat."

"Yep. Didn't eat at noon."

"Just sit down. We can talk while I finish up."

He took a chair at the table. "How are you getting along with my daughter over there?"

"It's been wonderful. She's so bright and has so many ideas about our school. She has a sense of humor and has brought so much life to my lonely house."

"As you are no doubt aware, I hardly know Sheena."

"That's going to change. She wants to know you. The time is right for the two of you to make peace."

He nodded. "I sensed that. We talked more this morning than we have in seven or eight years. She didn't seem hostile, standoffish sometimes, but friendlier than I have any reason to expect."

"Quit beating up on yourself. You had a job to do. We can all look back and try to redo things from our pasts, but what's done is done. We can only move on from now."

"You're quite the philosopher."

She smiled. "I suppose so. I must be careful sometimes. Maybe it comes from teaching school, I tend to give advice even when it's not welcome."

"I don't mind a little advice now and then. I've had some over the years, I guess always from other men, but I didn't always listen that well."

"For what it's worth, Sheena says that Jaye is always quoting your advice."

He thought about that. "Hmm. Maybe I'm better at giving it than taking it."

She laughed. "That's probably true of most of us. Do as I say, not as I do."

Before they ate, he waited as Susana gave a blessing, especially thanking God for Morg's survival and presence. They continued talking as they ate, Morg gradually finding himself captivated by Susana Mercer.

They cleaned up together in the kitchen. When that chore was done, Morg said, "You will be wanting to get home before dark. I can saddle our horses, and Dingo and I will see you home."

"Are you trying to get rid of me?"

He was taken aback. "Lord, no. If I had my way, you'd just stay for good."

She moved nearer to him and looked up into his eyes. Was there an invitation there? Only one way to find out. He took her in his arms and pressed his lips to hers. She accepted his kiss eagerly and pressed her lithe body against his. He felt her tongue on his lips and the nearly unendurable pressure in his trousers. Her fingers danced down his thigh, and he wanted her as he had never wanted a woman.

He looked down and saw Dingo looking up at him with those sad eyes that looked like she was worried.

Susana said, "Perhaps, we could retreat to your bedroom and shut Dingo out for a spell."

"Yes, the bedroom, but I will send Dingo outside."

Dingo did not resist the sign to go out onto the porch and appeared somewhat relieved. She would also stand guard against possible intruders, Morg reasoned.

Susana was already in the bedroom when he turned away from the front door. She had removed her boots and britches by the time he walked into the room, leaving no doubt as to her willingness. In a matter of a few minutes, they lay naked in bed together. She did not seem the least shy or reluctant and hurried him to their coupling like she shared his urgency. Her quivering and sighing confirmed his suspicion quickly. They lay spooned together silently for nearly a half hour, his hand resting on one of her small, firm breasts.

Then he felt her fingers tracing a path down the flesh on his abdomen. "Can you?" she said.

"I can," he replied.

This time, their lovemaking moved slowly like a drifting raft on a quiet river. It was well past sundown when they got dressed, and Morg lit a kerosene lamp in the parlor. He opened the door to allow Dingo in, but she was sleeping on her blanket on the porch and seemed to want nothing to do with him for the moment. She awakened when he went to the stable to retrieve and saddle the horses and followed him then.

As they rode along the Dismal Trail to Susana's house, Jaye said, "Sheena is likely worried about you."

"I told her I would be late. Of course, she admonished me to be back before dark."

"What is she going to think?"

"Whatever she wants. I am of age, you know. And be assured that I do not say a word to anyone about my experiences with my lovers. Of course, you are the first lover I've had since my husband died all those years ago. I thought that part of me had died until I met you, Morg. You set off a resurrection that became an obsession."

"I won't deny I wanted to bed you right off, but I couldn't imagine you being interested in a beat-up old codger like me."

"I'm not that much younger than you, and I sure don't see you as beat-up, and certainly not an old codger. I see you as a ruggedly handsome cuss who isn't full of himself like some such men, maybe even a bit on the shy side when it comes to the female sex."

"So what now? Do you want to be with this old man again? I mean the way we were tonight."

She giggled. "This evening you were a young stallion. And for now, we grab every chance we get. We don't need to hurry things or sort out other complications just now. I hope I don't have to rope and hogtie you to get my way next time."

"No, ma'am. I can guarantee that."

When they reached the ranch yard, they saw Sheena on the porch with a lantern in one hand and her Winchester cradled in the other arm. She came off the porch, "Where have you been, Susana? I've been worried sick."

"Oh, your father and I just got to talking, and the time got away." She turned back to Morg. "You and Dingo better head home, Morg. We can get April put up for the night." With her fingers, she furtively blew him a kiss. He winked and nodded.

Chapter 34

MORG FOUND HIMSELF distracted by re-
membrances of last evening's encounter
with Susana Mercer as he rode Stripe across
the grasslands to the J Bar B building site. The woman
had caught him by surprise. Within an hour after giving the blessing at the supper table, she had led him to
the bedroom. This morning, he could not help but think
that she had come to his house with that exact mission
in mind. She had as much as admitted that when he
thought about it.

He had liked the woman from their first meeting, and
she had wakened in him thoughts of a romance, but he
had taken on new challenges in his life and figured he
was a good year away from anything beyond a growing
friendship. Well, they had raced right past the growing
friendship and might need to back up some to get to

know each other better, but it appeared neither was in-clined to give up the intimacy they had shared.

He was already trying to come up with a strategy for future trysts. Susana would be under the watchful eye of his own daughter, and he would soon have Andy at his own house. Dingo did not appear to approve of this sepa-ration from her master. Good Lord, he felt like a teenage kid plotting evasion of his parents. These things could be complicated.

As he neared Jaye's house, he suspected he would soon be forced to deal with his young friend's objections to the course of action that he intended to take. But he, not Jaye, was the U.S. Marshal, and the burden was his to enforce the law and, in the process, bring some normalcy back to their lives.

Dingo raced ahead now, and shortly Morg saw why. Andy was in the yard just outside the stable astride Buck-shot, and the dog was obviously eager to greet the boy. By the time Morg reached Andy, his son had already dis-mounted and was on the ground with his canine friend, arms wrapped around the dog's neck as he received the animal's kisses. Morg swung out of the saddle and joined the two. "Palouse is going to get jealous with you taking Buckshot for a ride."

"Buckshot ain't had much work since we got back from Snake River country. I been riding Palouse every day, but Jaye's been making me stay close by unless he's with me."

"I'm glad to hear that. I'm going to be riding on a ways when I'm done here. How about us trading critters? I'll ride Buckshot, and maybe you can put Stripe up for me. I'll likely be gone till late afternoon. When I get back, we'll all go home. Might wait till morning to get the mule team."

"I'll have to see if Jaye wants me to take the milk cow and a few of the cats."

"Maybe that's a bit much for tonight. I'll bring you over here to milk in the morning and see what we can work out with Jaye. Where is Jaye, by the way? I'd like to talk to talk to him a few minutes."

"He's in the stable talking to a feller he's thinking about hiring as a new hand."

"Oh, that's good. Anybody I might know?"

"Doubt it. He's a colored feller from east of here. Homesteaders. He doesn't want to be a farmer. Says he's looking to be a cowman. He just showed up here yesterday afternoon looking for work. Name's Luke. I don't remember the last."

Morg did not want to interrupt, but he was impatient to be on his way. His impatience was resolved when Jaye and a rangy, young colored man walked out of the stable, chatting amiably. Jaye saw Morg, gave him a wave and nodded for the man to come with him as they turned toward Morg.

"Good morning, Morg. I'd like you to meet my new hired hand, Lucas Hackett. Luke, this is the friend I told you about. You'll spend a lot of time on Bar F land."

Morg extended his hand, and the young man stepped forward and exchanged a firm grip. "Most call me Luke."

"Well, Luke, you've got a first-rate boss here. He'll treat you right."

"I'm sure of that. He'll need some patience. I got a lot to learn about the cattle business, but I'm grateful for the chance."

"I'm sure you'll do fine." He turned to Jaye. "I've got to be moving on, Jaye, but I'd like a word with you first."

Jaye took the hint. "Andy, why don't you introduce Luke to all the stabled horses, tell him about their quirks and such. Let him try a mount or two. His gray gelding is a fine critter but has no experience working with cattle. He'll need to use another horse till he gets his trained."

Morg removed his saddlebags and rifle scabbard from Stripe and moved them to Buckshot, and then Andy led the bay away with Lucas Hackett walking beside him. "So you're taking on a greenhorn of sorts?"

"In some respects. Luke knows hard work, though, growing up as the eldest of eight kids. His folks have a quarter-section of farm ground forty miles east of here and when he wasn't busy on that, he was hiring out to neighbors. He's been around cattle in small numbers, loves animals. I can teach him to do things the way I like, just like some U.S. Marshal did for me."

"You told him about what happened to the last hand you hired?"

"I sure did. It didn't faze him. He can use a rifle. He'd been hunting the family's meat since he was ten-years old—he's nineteen now. He's got a six-gun, too. He's well spoken, got eight years of schooling and likes to read. My promise to share some books sealed the deal, I think."

"He'd be welcome to any of mine, too, but that's not what I stopped by to talk about. I just wanted you to know I'm headed over to Thomas Towne's."

Jaye just stared at him for a minute. "You're insane. Are you looking to commit suicide?"

"I'm hoping to confront the man about some things, keep him nervous about his future. I'll let him know right away that others are aware of my visit. He's not going to kill me on his place, and I intend to give him good cause to leave me and mine alone."

"I don't like it. Let me go with you."

"Nope. You're to look after Andy and Sheena in the unlikely case things don't work out. I wanted you to know that when I was in North Platte I stopped to see my lawyer, Audra Scott Adams, to update my will and other legal papers. She has the documents in the firm's safe. I'll need to get rid of the will you've been holding. You go to Audra just in case."

"I don't like the way you're talking."

"I'll be fine. I've got lots of reasons to live these days. I got no intention of dying anytime soon."

"Nobody does."

"Dingo went to the stable with Andy. I don't want her following me. Tell Andy to tie her up if necessary." He stepped into the stirrup and lifted himself into the saddle. "Let's go, Buckshot."

Chapter 35

"WHAT IN THE hell are you doing here?"

"Good afternoon, May," Morg said. He stood on the veranda just outside the front door of the Tall T mansion. His former wife had not stepped out of the entryway and held the door ajar.

"You're not welcome at the Tall T, Morg. You should know that by now."

"This isn't a social visit. I am here in my capacity as a U.S. Marshal. I want to see your husband."

"He's not here."

"When do you expect him back?"

"When it suits him. He has many business interests. Sometimes he's gone for several weeks."

"When did he leave?"

"That would be none of your business."

"May, if I'm not going to receive any cooperation, you give me no choice but to send a message to the North Platte office to have a warrant issued for his arrest. That will result in every marshal in the territory looking to track him down. It won't take long before he's in custody, I assure you."

"Custody? Why on earth would you do that?"

"Murder. Attempted murder and kidnapping for a start."

"You are accusing Thomas of those things? That is beyond ridiculous."

"Would you like to tell me why?"

"I...I'm just confused about what is going on. Perhaps it is time for me to find out. Why don't you come in. We'll talk."

Just before he stepped inside the house, out of the corner of his eye he caught sight of a man at the near corner of the stable leaning near the wall nearly thirty yards to the south. He could not see the man well enough to identify him, but he could see that the man's interest was clearly focused on the front of the house, and he was more than casually interested in what was taking place there. Morg would take it as a warning to take care when he stepped outside again.

Inside the house, which he had never entered previously, he was nearly overwhelmed by the tall ceilings and railed staircase that wound its way to the second floor. May gestured toward the giant parlor off to his left. "Find a chair. I'll have Helga bring us tea."

He had at least a dozen seating choices but claimed a firm, cowhide-covered chair adjacent to a lamp table where he might place his cup. Soon May returned and seated herself in an identical chair facing him some ten feet distant. Shortly, a buxom, blonde young woman came in with a silver teapot and porcelain cups on a tray. She poured them each a cup of tea and left the pot on Morg's table.

"*Danke*," Morg said.

The young woman returned a warm smile. "Bitte Sehr." She turned away and left the room.

May rolled her eyes and looked at him with disgust. "Still charming the young ladies, I see. She does speak English, you know, with a thick German accent. Helga is a good worker. She's been here almost a year now."

"I never saw myself as a charmer. She is quite obviously German with her name and appearance. They're flooding this part of the country. Industrious, intelligent folks. They are a great asset to the country."

"I don't know about that, but I do remember you were a charmer of young ladies. You charmed me before I had good sense."

Time to change the subject. "You allowed me in the front door to discuss your husband. I will give you the benefit of the doubt and assume you really don't know what he is involved in. But I am told that Charles Vaughn, our daughter's former boyfriend, visited here while I was gone and that he stopped here, also. Didn't you speak to him?"

"Well, yes, just briefly. We exchanged pleasantries. I inquired about his parents, that sort of thing, but he spent most of his time with Thomas. My husband's companies use the law firm Charles is associated with. I had hoped Charles and Sheena might decide to renew their friendship. I think Thomas would have welcomed that, but I gather things did not go well."

"Are you personally acquainted with Charles's parents?"

"I have met George and Helen at social events in Omaha and Denver and stayed with them in North Platte on occasion. George Vaughn is a close business associate of Thomas's."

"Just what kind of businesses are they engaged in?"

"Besides the ranch, I have no idea. Thomas does not think a woman's place is to engage in business, and I have no interest in such things. He provides me with more than I need in the necessaries and luxuries of life, and he makes time for me and our two sons. He often insists I join him on his travels."

He took her remark as a reminder of his own failings. He doubted if she would have enjoyed traveling with him by horseback in pursuit of outlaws. He had a feeling, however, that she was speaking truthfully and was either clueless regarding her husband's illegal activities or consciously blinding herself to his actions.

"What if I told you that Thomas ordered Sheena's kidnapping in order to capture and hang me?"

"I would say that you are a liar."

"A man was murdered at Jaye Boyden's. He was a former ranch hand at the Tall T. His name was Colt Louden. Did you know him?"

"I saw him around the ranch on occasion, spoke to him a few times, but I can't say I really knew him."

"Your husband is suspected of having him killed."

"That makes no sense. Why would he do that?"

"Because he was afraid Colt might know something about your husband's illegal activities. For instance, he verified that a man named Arthur previously worked or stayed at the ranch for a short time. Arthur and another man tried to kill our son and daughter after the exchange was made. Fortunately, Arthur is the one who ended up dead."

She said nothing, which told him that she was aware of Arthur's presence on the ranch.

Morg continued. "I believe Arthur was hired by Thomas to kill Sheena after the exchange. He could not risk her learning something that might incriminate him."

Her face flushed scarlet. "That's ridiculous." She stood up, tipping over her tea and yelled, "Helga, get in here and clean up this mess." She glared at Morg. "And you get out of here now. I'm sorry I ever met you. You've brought nothing but unhappiness to my life."

He assumed that the unhappiness did not include the children they shared, but he held back any retort. Helga appeared, saw the scattered porcelain pieces and the pool of tea drifting toward a bearskin rug. She hurried in and snatched up the rug to remove it from the tea's path before she turned and hurried away. "I will get rags and a bucket," she said, almost bumping into Morg as he started for the door.

"*Auf wiedersehen*, Helga," Morg said.

She smiled and rolled her eyes, signaling that she was accustomed to May's tantrums. "*Auf wiedersehen, Herr* Fraser."

He tossed a look into the parlor where May still stood and said, "And, May, ask Thomas if he sometimes works with Monte Oxford."

"Get out before I call some hands to remove you. I don't want to hear from you again, and you will henceforth be treated as a trespasser at the Tall T."

"Remember this, the U.S. Marshal's office in North Platte is prepared to send an army of deputies if anything happens to me or any of my friends or family. Tell your husband, and I suggest you inform the so-called cowhands here."

When he stepped onto the veranda, he surveyed the yard and dirt road in front of the mansion. He saw no sign of the man who had been watching him earlier, so he stepped off the porch and walked toward the rail where Buckshot was hitched, still wary despite the man's disappearance.

Suddenly, the sound of a dog barking and growling from the side of the house froze him, and instinctively his fingers closed on his pistol grip. In the same instant as he heard the crack of a pistol, he felt the sting between the right side of his neck and shoulder. His Colt was in his hand when the gunman stumbled out from behind the house, kicking at the Australian cattle dog latched onto his leg, trying to get his aim fixed on Dingo without shooting himself.

Morg charged the would-be ambusher. "Drop your gun now!" he yelled.

The man swung toward Morg, getting off a wild shot before Morg sent two slugs boring into his chest. He tumbled backward, landing faceup in the yard. Morg hollered, "Dingo, stop!" before he remembered the dog could not hear. He hurried to where she now guarded the prone form beside her, signaling her to halt when he knelt beside the man. The gunman was dead, which was unfortunate because Morg would have welcomed a chance to question him, perhaps leverage information.

The dead man's legs, through shredded britches, were generating more blood than the chest wounds. Dingo had been tearing the flesh to the bone with her unrelenting attack. The cattle dog whined and seemed to be looking at Morg worriedly. Only then did he notice the blood dripping off his shoulder and saturating his shirt. It had felt like no more than a bee sting when the slug hit him, but now it could have been a knife twisting between the neck and shoulder.

"Marshal Fraser."

He started and looked up. "Helga, I might need a bit of help here."

"Yes, and I can help you if I do not attempt to take you into the house. Missus Towne was adamant about that. Sit down. Stay where you are for now and let me look at your wound. I see you have a small skinning knife sheathed on your belt. May I borrow it, *bitte?*"

"Of course. And I must warn you that I have now exhausted my German vocabulary."

"I suspected as much." She began slicing and ripping the shirt away from his shoulder. He flinched when he felt her fingers probing the tender flesh about the wound. "You have a cut between your neck and shoulder like a knife slice. The slug passed through. Some other places the blood would not flow so badly. At least that cleans the wound. I am going to make a compress from some of the cloth of your shirt. Can you hold it there while I run into the house and find something to bind the wound with and get clean water to wash around the cut?"

"Yes, I can do that. But, first, do you know the man who tried to kill me just now?"

"No, he arrived a few days before Mister Towne left on his business trip. I have seen him slinking around the ranch but have never spoken to him." She moved toward the house. "Do not try to get up till I bind the wound."

"Yes, ma'am."

Helga returned soon with a pillowcase and kettle of water. She cleaned the wound, applied a salve that eased the pain some, before cutting a bulky compress and making a crisscrossing bandage that went below both underarms to secure it.

"You're not a secret doctor by chance, are you?" Morg said.

"Seven brothers and sisters lived in our home along with my parents and grandparents—my father's parents. I started with animals but became the family doctor before I left home. I felt like I was abandoning the family but feared I would never have a life beyond the farm if I did not leave. I still send money to the family to help."

"May gave me the idea that you spoke with an accent and could barely understand English."

Helga laughed. "I do that for her. It makes her feel superior, and it is useful sometimes not to understand things. I was born in America, and my parents allowed me to attend school through eighth grade. High school was thirty miles away, and the family had no funds for a boarding school." She finished tying the bandage. "Now, how far must you ride to reach friends or family?"

"An hour, maybe an hour and a half at a slow pace."

"Do you think you can stay mounted on your horse that long?"

"Yes. I've ridden much longer with worse wounds. And my horse, Buckshot, and I have been together a lot of years. He will see that I get there." He nodded at Dingo who sat next to him. "And Dingo will look after me. She wasn't supposed to follow me today, but if she hadn't been here, I likely wouldn't be alive right now."

"I remember this dog. The dark patch that surrounds her right eye and ear. I cried when I heard Mister Towne brag to his wife that he had shot the dog. And then Andy was broken-hearted about her disappearance."

"Well, they're together again, but Dingo seems to think she's got to look after me first. Now, you might need to help me get to my feet."

"I am taking what's left of the pillowcase to your horse. Wrapped up inside is one of Mister Towne's shirts. It will be large for you, but it will keep you warm if it turns cool and will help keep the dust from your wound. Missus Towne would not be pleased if she knew I had stolen her husband's shirt, but he has twenty or more and will not miss it."

Helga was a strong young woman and had no difficulty helping Morg stand. He leaned on her shoulder while they walked slowly to his horse.

"You are dizzy, aren't you?" Helga said as they walked.

"Some, but once I get mounted, I'll be fine."

"Missus Towne is leaving the day after tomorrow."

"She is? Where is she going?"

"She has not said. I will look after the boys as usual. She said she might be away for several weeks. Wait an extra day, and then I will talk with you."

"I take it you know some things that might be helpful to me."

"I cannot promise that, but I am willing to share any information I have."

He mounted Buckshot without any problem. "I won't have any difficulty making it to Jaye Boyden's. Thanks for all you've done for me. I don't think I dare meet with you here again. It might put your life in danger. I wouldn't risk that." The thought of this young woman meeting Colt Louden's fate sickened him. "Are guards posted here at night?"

"Yes, for two or three weeks now."

"I will think on this and get word to you somehow. I'd better move on now. May will start getting suspicious."

She nodded and headed back to the house.

Chapter 36

SO YOU WERE going to confront Thomas Towne at his home? Where in blazes did that notion come from? And you nearly got yourself killed for it. It upsets me that you didn't get word to me right away. You've been home a day, and I would not have learned you were shot if Jaye Boyden hadn't dropped over to tell Sheena this morning," Susana said. "I would at least have kept you and Andy fed." She knew that she was sounding like a shrew, but she was more than annoyed at him.

"Well, the food basket you brought over this afternoon should feed us for a spell."

"Sheena will be coming over to have supper with you. She's bringing a cake and cookies. She is turning into an excellent cook. After some successes, I think she's starting to enjoy it. But I didn't come to talk about cooking."

"Well, I'm more than able, but I don't think I'd better try to pleasure you with Andy and Dingo close by."

She furrowed her brow, feigning disgust, but it was nearly impossible to be truly angry at this man. If the boy wasn't around, she might make Morg prove his ability. "Morg, I do care, and I just had to satisfy myself you are alright. Do you need the dressing on the wound changed? I brought gauze and tape with me and a jar of honey to help with healing."

"You just want to see me half naked."

"Not that half, thank you."

"Ah, go ahead. The dressing hasn't been changed, and I suppose it should be. The young lady cinched me up like a roped calf to stop the bleeding."

"Take off your shirt." She lifted her saddlebags on the kitchen table where they had been talking over coffee. He obeyed, and she began digging her medical supplies from the leather bags. "I'll leave these here and stop by and change the dressing every afternoon." Carefully, she removed the pillowcase harness that anchored the cloth pad Helga had fashioned.

Morg said, "How does it look? Infection?"

"Swollen, but it's not bleeding, draining a little bit, but the flesh looks healthy. I could stitch it some, and it won't scar so much. The slug dug a groove of about three inches but doesn't appear to have burrowed far beneath the skin."

"No stitches. The scar can complement the others."

"I thought you would turn down stitches." She spread a spoonful of honey over the wound itself and then fashioned a gauze compress and taped it over the wound. "That should do for now. We should keep it bandaged for a week, but that will likely be enough." She placed a hand on his forehead for a bit. "I don't feel any signs of fever. Let's keep it that way."

"Thank you, Sue. It appears Helga patched me up okay."

"Tell me about this Helga."

"Pretty girl, not yet twenty I'd say. Comes from a German family. She's invited me over to talk to her as a matter of fact."

She knew he was teasing her, but he had piqued her curiosity. "Alright, I know you saw your ex-wife, and now there is a young German girl in the picture. Why don't you just give me a rundown about what happened. Jaye told me about your reason for going to the house, but Towne wasn't there. How did you end up getting yourself shot?"

Morg gave her a summary of his Tall T visit. "I had never seen the fella who shot me before. He had the look of a professional gunslinger, guns holstered on both hips. Duded up like a professional gambler, expensive clothes, cleanshaven face with a thin mustache. The kind described in a dime novel. Ironic that he should be put out of business by a deaf cattle dog."

"I'm glad Helga was there to help you, too. I suspect that, left to her, May would have watched you bleed to death. But you said Helga invited you to come visit."

"I think she is willing to share information about Thomas Towne. She might not be helpful. She doesn't have any idea what I am seeking, but she is very aware that I represent the law, and that someone tried to kill me. She told me that May is going to join her husband someplace and that they will be gone for several weeks."

"So you would have an opportunity to speak with her while they are both away from the ranch."

"She seems to be a cooperative witness. My challenge is first to ask the right questions. The biggest problem is how to do this without risking her life. I don't see how I can go back to the Tall T. Someone at the ranch would likely report to Towne that I visited. That could be a death sentence for Helga. I can't chance that."

"Couldn't you have arranged to meet her someplace?"

"We didn't have time to talk about arrangements, but it would be almost impossible for her to leave unnoticed for any time. School isn't in session now, and Abraham and Simon would be home all the time. She is evidently responsible for their care and would not dare delegate this to someone else without explanation. I think there is a household cook, who probably does other chores as well, but who is to say she would not also report Helga's absence?"

Susana said, "You are making this too complicated."

"And why do you say that?"

"I will go talk to Helga. I can ask the questions. We just need to go over what I need to find out first."

"No, I can't allow you to do that. It could be dangerous for both of you."

"Just hear me out. I will come back tomorrow afternoon, and we will discuss the questions you wish me to ask and give me more background about this case so I know what evidence you are trying to gather. It will probably take most of the afternoon. Will Andy be here tomorrow?"

"Yes. He is living here now. When he found out I was wounded, he insisted on coming back as we'd planned. He likes Jaye, but for some reason he wanted to be with me. He pointed out that there were a hundred ways he could get hurt at Jaye's just helping on the ranch. He said that with Dingo here, we wouldn't be surprised by anybody. How could I argue with that?"

"I will ask Andy to spend the afternoon at my Keystone Ranch with his sister tomorrow afternoon. I can be persuasive with kids, perhaps, offer a dollar for stable cleaning that is seriously needed. I will explain to Sheena why we need privacy."

"You really can be a devious woman. Are you certain we are just going to plot strategy for your meeting with Helga?"

"It depends on how you are feeling. We might want to take a break or two."

"Just for coffee? Are you going to tell Sheena why you are really seeking privacy?"

"I don't know what you are talking about."

"I'm convinced that you can gather information from Helga. You are a woman who clearly has a knack for getting what she wants, but that doesn't eliminate the danger of your going to the Tall T."

"I will be going as a missionary of sorts for the Dismal River Methodist Church. I will travel in my one-horse buggy, and I will wear a very matronly dress—black, of course. I have several boxes of Bibles at home, and I will take a few to leave at the Box T house, so Helga has something to prove the purpose of my visit if she should ever be asked. My hair suggests I could be quite ancient. I will take a cane and hobble to the front door. I can look quite harmless."

"So can a sleeping grizzly. Tell me, is there such a place as the Dismal River Methodist Church? I've never seen or heard of it."

"At my home. Methodists congregate there whenever the circuit rider preacher comes this way, usually every month or two. When he schedules a service, usually, but not always on Sundays, he sends letters to members informing them when he will be at my home, and I set up my house for the service. We usually have fourteen or fifteen in attendance. Since we only receive mail weekly out in the hills, he must schedule several weeks in advance, of course. We should be holding another service soon. Maybe you would like to join us."

"I've never been much of a church goer."

"I will never push, but you are always welcome."

"Anyway, your idea makes a certain sense. I don't like the notion of you going to the Tall T alone, though."

"There is no choice. Towne is obviously behind all this chaos that has surrounded the lives of you and your family and friends. We won't have normal lives in this part of the Sandhills till this is behind us. I have a stake in this, too. I will have a Winchester in my buggy and a Derringer in my shoulder bag, and I know how to use them if forced to, but I see that as highly unlikely."

"I'll be crazed with worry till you get back."

"We'll have time to talk about this tomorrow afternoon. I will talk to Andy about visiting his sister as I leave." She slid her chair away from the table and stood. "I hope you enjoy supper, and don't forget that Sheena will be over with dessert."

He got up to escort her to the door, and she turned to receive his embrace. She tilted her head upward and their lips met, setting her on fire again. Tomorrow was so far away. "I hope your shoulder will be up for an afternoon break or two."

"I just need to move a bit carefully, that's all. We can't do much wrestling in bed, I'm afraid, but it's not my shoulder that needs to be up to it anyhow."

She placed her fingers softly on his cheek. "Tomorrow, you will just lie back and relax. I will keep you awake, of course."

Chapter 37

SUSANA REINED IN the gray buggy horse in front of the Towne mansion. It was an impressive structure, she thought, having previously viewed it from the east-west county road that passed by several hundred feet to the north. It reminded her of the North Carolina childhood home that the Yankees had burned to the ground during the War of the Rebellion. Her parents had died that day, and she had already lost her two brothers fighting for a cause that none of them had a stake in from her viewpoint.

Her father had been a physician, and they resided on the outskirts of Charlotte, North Carolina. They had no slaves, and her father had utilized part of the house for his offices and a small hospital. The fighting had bypassed Charlotte for the most part going into 1864, and she had been married to John Mercer, who farmed and raised cattle on the three hundred acres that surrounded the house. John had lost his lower left forearm during the fighting early in the war, but had adapted, and she had been grateful that the injury had likely saved his life when he was discharged and sent home.

After her parents died trying to rescue patients from a burning house, she and John had moved north as far away from the war as possible and ended up in the Nebraska Sandhills, which offered prime pasture for grazing cattle and the isolation they both welcomed. The children had all been born and later buried here. Ten years ago, John had joined them in the Keystone Ranch cemetery. She set those memories aside now. They had nothing to do with her mission. It was strange how her romance with Morg was tugging back memories of another time. They had nothing to do with him. Or did they?

She climbed out of the buggy, trying to appear as decrepit as possible. Establishing her footing on the ground, she reached into the buggy and grabbed her shoulder bag and the beautifully carved cedarwood cane that was one of the few keepsakes she had from her father, Doctor Mason Parker. Then she picked up two Bibles, tucking them under her free arm, and commenced hobbling up the stone pathway to the veranda.

She had almost reached her objective when she saw a stocky man walking her way from one of the ranch buildings.

He called to her in an unexpectedly high-pitched voice. "Hold up there, lady."

She stopped and waited. As he approached, she saw a middle-aged man of a slovenly sort with a scraggly black beard who likely had not bathed in months, perhaps years. The low-crowned planter's hat might have been white when he bought it, but now it was different shades of dirty grays and browns, tattered on the edges of the brim. His belly looked like he could be carrying a child.

The man walked up to her. "What's your business here, lady?"

"I am a missionary for the Dismal River Methodist Church. My business is the word of God."

"The owners ain't home, won't be for a spell."

"I don't need to speak to the owners. I will deliver the word to anyone who will listen. Surely there are women in the house who would be interested. Why don't you join me. I will give you a Bible if you promise to read daily." She would bet her horse that he could not read or write his own name.

"I ain't inclined to reading, least of all a Bible."

The mansion door opened, and a young, blonde woman stepped out onto the veranda. This had to be Helga. Dressed in a conservative light blue, gingham dress, the tall woman could not hide a shapely figure. Sparkling blue eyes complemented her attire and were welcoming. She said, "Good afternoon, I am Helga Gerhardt. Is there a problem here, Moe?"

"Woman's selling religion. I told her the owners wasn't home."

Susana looked up at Helga, fastening her eyes on the young woman's own and hoping she might convey the importance of their talking. "I am Susana Mercer. I live on the Keystone Ranch, one of the small ranches along the Dismal River. I am representing the Dismal River Methodist Church and am delivering free Bibles to folks in the area with invitations to visit our church. I was hoping someone here might take the time to hear my message. I won't take more than an hour of your time."

"Well, why don't you come in, and we can have tea, and I'll hear what you have to say. I rarely see any of the neighbors in our area, so I would enjoy getting acquainted, I'm sure." She looked at the man who greeted Susana. "Moe, would you care to join us?"

Moe frowned. "Some of us got real work to do around this place. I'll be getting back to it."

Helga turned back to Susana. "Come in the house. Can I help you up the steps?"

"No, thank you. I'll be just fine." As soon as they were inside, Susana spoke barely above a whisper when she said, "Morgan Fraser sent me. We must speak privately."

Helga said, "I knew he would think of something. We can talk freely. There are no others in the house. The boys are not here, and the cook will be gone for two weeks. Follow me to the kitchen, and we can talk over tea as I suggested, or I can brew coffee if you prefer."

"Tea would be nice." Susana straightened and, carrying the cane and Bibles, followed Helga to the kitchen, taking in the magnificent home as they walked to their destination at the opposite end. "The home is breathtaking," Susana said.

"Yes, I suppose I am accustomed to it now and don't give it much thought. I prefer, however, the small home I came from with three children sharing a bedroom, a home filled with love and caring."

When they reached the kitchen, Susana noted the spaciousness of the room with endless cupboards, an enormous sink with its water pump and two coal cook stoves. Coal was becoming commonplace in most towns now, but it would have been cost prohibitive for most ranchers to arrange for hauling so many miles from a railroad city. She assumed the house was heated by a coal furnace when weather turned cold.

When they were seated at the table and steaming tea poured into the cups in front of them, Helga smiled and said, "I notice you dropped many years in age when you entered the house and that the cane is no longer necessary."

"I wanted to look as harmless as possible in case questions ever come up about my visit." She handed Helga one of the Bibles. "And you may keep this as proof of my mission."

"Thank you. I have no Bible since I left home, and I will enjoy reading it. I come from a devout Lutheran family, but I gladly accept a Methodist Bible."

"The translations may differ some, but they all take us to the same place. Now, I guess we should get down to the immediate business. Morgan said I would need to separate you from the boys and the cook somehow, but you indicated they are not here."

"No. Missus Towne took the boys with her when they left with Carl Winters, the mule skinner on the old Conestoga wagon that was stored in the barn. Packer Osborne, the ranch manager rode alongside. She took an unbelievable amount of luggage for the boys and herself and said they would return in about two weeks. I'm not sure."

"You suspect it may be longer?"

"I just don't know. A rider showed up the day after Marshal Fraser visited with a message of some sort. He rode with them, also, when they left the Tall T. Anyhow, that's when she told me the boys were going with her, but she wanted me to remain and tend to the house. There is not much to do but feed myself. I keep the doors locked, and I keep one of Mister Towne's rifles and a handful of cartridges in my room in case I am forced to deal with a randy cowhand who's had too much to drink while the boss and his family are away. I can handle a rifle just fine."

"Where were they headed?"

"Missus Towne told me they were going to Omaha and would make train connections at Broken Bow, but I heard the mule skinner explaining to her the trail they would be taking goes to North Platte. I don't know why she would feel a need to lie to me about that. Whether she is going to Omaha by way of North Platte or Broken Bow makes no difference to me. Broken Bow would involve somewhat less wagon time, I think, but an extra train transfer is required. North Platte is farther west of Omaha, but I don't suppose there is a lot of time difference in the end."

"Unless they were not going to Omaha. Do you have thoughts on another destination?"

"They frequently went to Denver. Missus Towne loved Denver."

"Did her husband do business there?"

"Yes. That is what I thought the marshal might be interested in. When I cleaned his office, I sometimes saw envelopes addressed to 'Oxford and Company' in Denver on his desk. Smaller ones were sometimes sent by mail service, large ones were taken by horseback someplace by Packer Osborne. I think he might have delivered them to North Platte considering the time he was gone."

"Are you aware of any connections Towne has in North Platte?"

"Oh, yes. Mister George Vaughn. His son Charles visited here several weeks ago. But I don't know anything else about him. The father made personal visits here on occasion, and he and Mister Towne would meet in the office for long spells. Sometimes he would stay several days. I assumed they had business dealings of some sort."

"What can you tell me about Packer Osborne?"

"Well, he is called the ranch manager, which I gather outranks the foreman, but he's more than that. He doesn't do any of the cowhand dirty work, but he must know something about ranching because he gives the orders to the foreman. I don't know if Mister Towne knows the difference between a heifer and a steer to be honest.

As I mentioned, Packer Osborne sometimes acts as Mister Towne's personal messenger, and there is no question he is what some call the 'right hand' man. He has most of the direct contact with the gunmen that show up at the ranch. That's what I call them, anyhow."

"Gunmen? What do you mean?"

"Well, that's what I call them. They are men who come here but never do any ranch work. They strut around like roosters with holstered guns hanging low on their hips. Some might have one on each hip. They are guards of some kind, I guess, but I never understood what they were guarding. Like the man who tried to kill the marshal several days back, he must have been told to kill the marshal and somehow scouted him out, or how could he have known it was the marshal making a visit?"

Susana plucked her tablet and pencil from her bag and began to write. Names might be useful. "Do you know that man's name?"

"He had been here less than a week. Missus Towne referred to him as 'Weasel,' but I'm sure that wasn't his name. There were always one or two of these men around but usually for short spells and then they moved on."

"Do you remember a man named Arthur?"

"Oh, yes. He was here longer than most. Arthur Prather. He, more than the others, almost always talked directly with Mister Towne. I only spoke with him when I was helping with meal serving in the dining room. He dined with the family. Of course, staff ate in the kitchen. I heard Missus Towne address him as 'Mister Prather' on occasion."

Susana said, "Do you have any of these so-called gunmen on the ranch right now?"

"Oh, yes. At least two. There have always been no less than two. Only four men make up the working crew that tends to the cow herds, horses and such. The bunkhouse is partitioned off with separate entrances, so the gunmen and cowhands don't intermingle much. I think the gunmen are supposed to be guards or something, but I don't know what they are guarding against. It's not like we are having Indian troubles or anything anymore. Sometimes it is like Mister Towne is hiding out here."

They talked for another half hour without Susana learning anything useful. Then she remembered that Morgan had some questions about his ex-wife. "Tell me. How much do you think May Towne knows about her husband's businesses?"

Helga giggled. "I'm sorry. Missus Towne is a strange woman, and her 'servants' as she calls us must learn to dance around her moods and whims. But I would never be persuaded that she knows anything about her husband's business affairs. I heard her ask him once why the ranch always had the men around who appeared to do no ranch work. He just told her it was none of her concern, that her job was to tend to the house and children—his children, not hers. He hated his stepchildren. He could be quite cruel to Andy, and I heard him insist several times that the boy be turned over to his father. Sheena, of course, had moved out by the time I arrived at the Tall T, but I overheard him refer to Sheena as the snotty bitch sometimes. I think something happened between them."

"Like what? Do you suspect he made inappropriate advances of some kind?"

Helga shrugged. "I can't say. I shouldn't even have suggested it, but something between them wasn't right, and I wonder if Missus Towne knows. She's like a puppet in his hands, always trying to please him, like she is afraid of him but does not want to risk losing him. No man will ever own me that way. I would gladly live my life out alone first, but things between them were very strange."

"What do you mean?"

"They had separate bedrooms."

"That would not be strange necessarily."

"No, but I tended to the two little boys down the hall at nights and could not help noticing a few things. I shouldn't be saying this since it is their private business, but Missus Towne shared the room some nights with Packer Osborne. Oh, he would not be there at sunrise, but I don't see how Mister Towne could help but know. Still, there was no sign of hostility between the two men."

"Yes, I agree. That is beyond strange."

"I cannot deal with the situation here much longer, and I do not wish to move back to the farm with my parents, but I will not stay here after the family returns. I may depart earlier. I have funds that would allow me to live several months in a boarding house someplace if I can figure out how to get there."

"What would you like to do with your life after you leave here?"

"I would like to be a nurse, or even a medical doctor, but my formal education stopped at the eighth grade."

"Hold on to your dreams, Helga. I am a schoolteacher. Perhaps, I can offer some ideas about such things. When things have settled down some, we will talk again."

Chapter 38

ORG GAVE A sigh of relief when Susana's buggy trailing the horse rolled up in front of the house. He had been pacing back and forth in the parlor, out the door and down to the riverside before returning to the porch for the past hour or more. Thankfully, Andy and Dingo were at Susana's house with Jaye and Sheena where they were all going upriver to fish along the Dismal. He had worried himself into something of a state about her safety, but her wave and smile told him that his stress had been wasted and unnecessary.

After she reined in the horse and braked the buggy, he extended his hand and helped her to the ground. "Thank God, you're back."

"What is the matter with you? I wasn't running away with another man. Nobody else would have me."

Susana was the sassiest dang woman he had ever dealt with. On the bossy side, too. She was a pretty thing and a tigress in bed, but there was much more than that. From their first meeting she had cast a spell over him, and it was suddenly like they had been friends for years. He had never been so hogtied by a woman, but how long would it be before she tired of him like May had? "Are you going to tell me what you found out at the Tall T?"

"Oh, I might. Do you have any whiskey in the house?"

"Uh...yeah. I'm not much of a drinker, but I think there's a bottle hidden in the cupboard."

"I would like to sit down and have a shot of whiskey to perk me up."

He took her hand, and they walked to the house. Inside she sat down at the kitchen table, while he found the nearly full whiskey bottle in the cupboard and two small whiskey glasses. He placed the glasses and bottle on the table. "The glasses might be a little dusty. I don't remember when they were last used."

"I've been eating dust all day."

Morg sat down and poured each a small glass of whiskey. "I thought Methodists were big supporters of the temperance movement."

"Oh, yes, but some are bigger supporters than others. I'm not on board that train." She tasted the whiskey, nodded approvingly, and pushed the glass toward Morg. "One more and then I'll tell you the story."

He complied. "I am listening."

She told him about her conversation with Helga Gerhardt. He was surprised to find Susana had even taken notes. He listened to every word without interrupting, spellbound by her narrative.

"Questions?" Susana said.

"Are you sure you never worked for the Pinkerton Detective Agency? You gathered a basketful of valuable information on your visit, and Helga deserves a medal for her helpfulness."

"I think I got most of what you wanted, but I have no idea what you can do with it. What now?"

"I am riding to North Platte. I'll talk to the U.S. Marshal there and bring him up to date, see if I can sic him onto this George Vaughn and find out how he fits into this puzzle. Then I will send a telegram to the U.S. Marshal in Denver and tell him to expect me and to place a watch on the Oxford and Company offices but not to contact anyone there till I arrive."

"I assume you will go to that office, but what will you do there?"

"If Monte Oxford is there, I hope to visit with him. If he is not, I will find out where he is at, or I will go to his home and wait."

"You know where Oxford lives?"

"Yep, pretty sure I do anyhow."

"Where?"

"The Tall T. I think Thomas Towne is also known as Monte Oxford, or vice versa."

"Are you serious?"

"He has been too much a part of the vendetta. Andy mentioned him losing a brother. I gave that a passing thought at the time. Lots of people lose brothers, but I've been like a wound festering on his neck, living nearby and his being married to my ex-wife. On top of that, he was forced to see my son every day at the ranch. He wanted me dead, but after one failed attempt on the Dismal Trail, he decided to put some distance between the two of us, and that's why he arranged Sheena's kidnapping. The Monte Oxford of Denver would not have known of the relationship."

"Towne could have informed him and then Oxford given the orders."

"I agree that's possible, but I just don't see it. Too many things have happened too fast for Towne to be waiting for orders from Denver. But the only way I can know for sure is to confront Monte Oxford in Denver."

"You do remember that you have a son you are responsible for?"

"I know, but none of my family will be safe until Monte Oxford is put out of business, and neither will you and Jaye, possibly Helga. I am hoping that you and Sheena will take Andy in while I'm gone, or maybe Jaye. Andy and Dingo have already spent a lot of time at the J Bar B."

"I plan on going with you."

"I can't go hunting a killer with a woman tagging along."

"I could take offense at that but will give you a pass this time. I will be well armed, I assure you. I will be your wife when we stay at hotels. We can pretend we are on a honeymoon."

"Sue, this will be no honeymoon. We will be sleeping on the ground at least one night on the trail. And we will have serious business to tend to."

"I don't mind camping. Sounds fun. I haven't done that for years. Are you suggesting I haven't been helpful with your case?"

Damn, that woman was clever. He felt like a cornered rabbit. Which way to jump? "Of course not. You have been extremely helpful. I just don't want to put you in danger."

"Shouldn't that be my choice?"

"But you are not a marshal."

"I'll bet you can get me appointed a special deputy or something when we are in North Platte. Think about it. I have never met Thomas Towne, and I am quite good with disguises. Your ex-wife met me ten or more years ago when I tried to pay a neighborly call at your house, but she ran me off like I was stray cat she didn't want around. I promise she will not recognize me in the unlikely event we should encounter each other."

Against his better judgment, he surrendered. "You are headed home, and Sheena and Jaye are over at your place. I'll saddle up Buckshot and ride over with you. You can go ahead, and I'll catch up. But you must give Sheena the news you are going with me."

Chapter 39

S HEENA HAD RESISTED the notion of fishing when Jaye showed up with poles that he and Luke had fashioned from tree branches and announced that they were going to go fishing. She remembered fishing with her father when she was small and failing to catch a fish, being bored to death and hating it. She had enjoyed this afternoon of fishing, pulling in three catfish from the Dismal, which Jaye said would likely average over a pound each and would be eating size. Andy had pulled out two trout, and Jaye had yanked in nothing but wormless hooks.

She was ready to fish again soon. Strange how success and victory changed a person's outlook. She and Jaye sat on the rocky bank now, listening to the soothing music of the water splashing over the rocks and continuing its journey east and watching Dingo and Andy wade in the shallows downstream. It was nice when Jaye slipped his hand over hers and held it gently.

Jaye broke the spell, however, when he said, "You do know how to clean fish, don't you, Sheena?"

"What are you talking about?"

"You don't catch fish and throw them away. You cook and eat them."

"Well, yes, I guess so."

"That means you must cut off their heads and get them skinned and degutted and prepared for cooking. That's what most call cleaning."

She nearly gagged at the thought. "I don't know how. Would you do it?"

"The fisherman's code is 'you catch it, you clean it,' but I'll show you this time. We should have just about enough time to fry some for supper before Susana gets home. We could fry some potatoes, too, if you've got some."

She sighed, "Alright, I'll learn how to clean fish, but it doesn't sound like fun. I can slice and fry potatoes, though, and we've got leftover cake for dessert. With Andy's trout, we should have plenty of fish. Will you stay for supper?"

"If you like."

"I like. Besides, if you're cooking, you are required to eat what you cook. Incentive to do well."

"Andy's having a good time. We can clean his fish, too, this time and give you more cleaning practice."

"This time I'll let him off but not next." Besides, she rather enjoyed sharing time with Jaye today.

They had just finished cleaning the fish, and Jaye was preparing them for the pan, when Sheena heard the buggy roll up in front of the house and Dingo barking a greeting. She pulled the kitchen curtain aside and peered out the window. "It's Susana, and my dad, too."

Jaye said, "Go on out and greet them. Invite Morg for supper, too. You've got the potatoes ready, so I can go ahead with frying if you don't get back."

Jaye was handy in the kitchen. With his help she had started some biscuits baking in the Dutch oven, so there would be plenty to eat. She was no longer helpless when it came to meal preparation, but she still had a lot to learn. She stepped outside onto the porch and waved as her father dismounted and hurried to assist Susana from the buggy. Sheena knew Susana could easily get out of the buggy without assistance, but she appeared to enjoy a gentleman's hand—this gentleman anyhow. There was something going on between those two, and she was uncertain how she felt about it.

Morg gave Sheena a quick wave, "Go on in, Sue. I'll put the buggy away and tend to the horse. I see Andy coming. Maybe I can recruit him to help."

"Dad, Jaye and I are fixing supper. We caught some fish today. Why don't you stay to eat?"

"I'll just do that. I'm not one to pass on a free meal. I'll put Buckshot up in the stable, too."

Andy had already taken Buckshot's reins, and father, son and dog headed toward the stable. Susana joined Sheena on the porch and shared a quick hug. Sheena stepped back. "You seem in a good mood. Your mission must have been a success."

"Yes, your father seems happy with the results."

"You're not going to tell me anything else, are you?"

"Morgan is the marshal. That's his place. We agreed that if Jaye was still here that we would have a meeting of sorts to discuss plans with all of you. We will need your help."

Sheena decided not to press for now, but Susana had whetted her curiosity.

Following supper, they all sat at the table, the adults drinking coffee and Andy nursing a sarsaparilla that Susana had hidden away. Dingo lay on the floor chewing a bone. They had learned this evening that Dingo did not like fish. She had simply gone off to the corner to pout after sniffing the offering, and Susana, taking pity, had found something more agreeable.

Morg did not disclose his suspicions about Thomas Towne. "Andy, Sheena, from the information Helga gave us I am convinced that your stepfather is in Denver and that your mother and brothers are there with him. You are already aware that we believe he is somehow involved in all the trouble we have been having. I want this case solved before I leave the marshal service, and I only have a few weeks to accomplish this. I think the answers are in Denver, and I am going to go there and find them."

Sheena said, "Dad, do you think Mother is somehow involved in this?"

"Everything Susana learned from Helga indicates that she is not. She appears to know next to nothing about Thomas's business dealings. I suspect we may be doing her and the boys a favor by getting this resolved, although she might doubt this at first."

"This is making me very uneasy. Will you have help in Denver?"

"I am stopping at the U.S. Marshal's office in North Platte to see if he has a deputy or two available. Regardless, we will wire Denver and request assistance." He nodded at Susana.

Susana said, "I am going with him to Denver."

Sheena's eyes widened and she stared at Susana in disbelief. "Why?"

"Morgan and I agreed that I might be helpful."

"What in heaven's name will you do in Denver?"

"That will be decided after we get there."

"That could be dangerous. You need to think about this, Susana." She realized she was speaking out of turn when she got the annoyed glare from her friend. She quickly added, "But it's your decision to make, not mine."

"I'm glad you understand that, dear."

Morg interrupted. "I don't think there is great risk of attacks on my family right now. There would just be no point. I suspect that for the moment I am low priority to these people, but Andy, I want you staying with Jaye while I'm gone, if that's agreeable with you, Jaye."

"You know it is. I would also go with you if you want, and Susana could stay here."

"Thanks, Jaye, but that's been decided."

Jaye turned to Sheena. "Why don't you stay at my place while your dad and Susana are gone?"

"I'll be fine here, thank you, and I have morning and evening chores to do."

"Well, Andy will have chores at the Bar F. We can swing over here and do chores mornings and evenings."

"No, I'll be fine."

"Andy and I could stay here nights."

She was on the verge of losing her temper over this nonsense. "No."

Morg said, "Well, Andy and I better be heading back. You riding with us, Jaye?"

"Might as well."

Susana said, "Wait, Morgan. I should have said something before, but I've been worrying about something ever since we left your house."

"What's that?"

"I keep thinking of that man who stopped me at the Tall T—Moe, I think Helga called him. She's the only woman on the place right now with all those men, some of them outlaws. I should have insisted she come with me. I think we could hire her for the house and school help. She's a bright young woman."

"So what do you want to do? We really need to get started for North Platte, but I'll hold off a day if you think we have cause to be concerned."

Jaye said, "You go on Morg. I'll check on her."

"I don't know, Jaye. I don't like the risk."

"I'll go with you," Sheena said. "Helga may be fearful of a man showing up to see her. She saw me once when Andy and I tried to pick up the few things we had there. We didn't formally meet, but she will likely recognize me.

If not, she would still be more comfortable talking to another woman."

"I'm not sure," Morg said. "I'll be worrying about this. And what about Andy?"

"He will be with my two hands. They think the world of him. You are making too much of this, Morg. Sheena and I have been through a lot together. Remember? This will be a picnic. You can't do everything yourself. This will probably amount to nothing. We will just check on Helga and offer to take her with us. If she's fine and wants to stay, we will be on our way."

"I will be at the J Bar B by noon tomorrow, Jaye," Sheena said.

Morg said, "Alright, Jaye, you win. But be careful. Don't take any foolish chances."

"Said the man who spent a career doing just that," Susana said.

After the others had ridden away on the Dismal Trail, Sheena started boiling a kettle of hot water on the cookstove for cleanup. Susana still had not returned to the house. She and her father had slipped away someplace to talk before he left. She wondered if he kissed her. The image disgusted her.

Susana walked into the house just as the water was ready for washing the dinner dishes and cookware. "I'll help with that, Sheena. It's the least I can do for the delicious meal you and Jaye prepared."

There was an uneasiness between them as they washed and dried dishes, but finally Sheena summoned the courage to commence the conversation she needed to have. "You didn't say when you and my father are leaving for Denver."

"That's what I was talking to him about when we disappeared in the stable for a bit. He will come by midmorning tomorrow. We'll have one night on the trail, and he thinks by the next night we can stay in North Platte. There will be some hard riding to do this, though, and we'll stop if it's too much. We're each going to take an extra mount. I'll have to work on packing tonight and putting a bedroll together. It's been some years since I've slept on the trail."

"It seems like you and my father have become rather friendly lately."

"Good friends, I'd say. I liked Morgan from the moment I first met him."

"It's none of my business, but I'm going to ask anyway. Are you and my father having a...a romantic friendship?"

"Oh, Sheena. That's what you have been so edgy about. I'll say this much and that's all. Yes, and I like what you called it, a romantic friendship. You will need to get comfortable with the notion, my dear. I think Morgan Fraser and I will be friends for a long time."

"I feel better with confirmation. My feelings about my father change from hour to hour. I don't hate him like I used to. Sometimes, I look back, and I am angry. There have been moments when I love him like a daughter should. I never had those for some years."

"That's progress, dear. Just remember, I am your friend, too, and we can talk in confidence privately like we always have. I will not repeat anything to your father about your thoughts. Those are yours to do when the time is right."

"There is something about my stepfather I never told anyone but my mother, and she did not believe me, but I feel a need to share it."

"I told you that you may speak confidentially to me, but you are also free not to speak at all."

"He came to my bedroom when I was a child and touched and felt me in places a man should not."

"Oh, my Lord. I can't imagine."

"And then finally, one night he tried to rape me and would have if my mother had not heard me screaming. Of course, he said it was all my imagination, but things were never the same between my mother and me after that. I was so thankful when I won the scholarship to attend high school in North Platte. I only learned recently from Jaye that the so-called scholarship and room and board were funded by my father."

"I am not surprised by that."

"I do hate Thomas Towne. All the time."

Chapter 40

ORG AND SUSANA camped the first night along a stream about thirty miles south of Susana's house. Now, as dusk was starting to cast its shadow over the grass-cloaked dunes that surrounded them, they sat across from each other at a small crackling fire eating a plate of beans, bacon, and some of the previous night's biscuits.

Morg's eyes wandered to Susana as they ate. A day of dust and sweat had made her no less attractive to him. This lady was tough as a boot, and earlier in her life she had apparently spent plenty of time outdoors. She talked about helping her husband with branding and cattle drives when they started their small ranching operation, and her endurance on this journey made it obvious that her words were not idle talk.

He guessed they would be sharing a bedroll tonight, because she had taken it upon herself to combine their blankets into a single bed sheltered by some of the cottonwood and willow trees that lined the stream. His initial thought was that they would just drop onto their blankets and sleep, which would suit him just fine. His second thought told him that they likely would not. This lady had an appetite stored up, and it appeared to be far from being satisfied yet, not that he objected to being the beneficiary.

Susana interrupted his musing when she spoke. "You've sure been watching me. I'm not going anywhere for sure. I'm lost out here. Ready for coffee?" She leaped to her feet, graceful as a cat, slipped on a glove and took the coffee pot off the coals next to the dying fire.

He did not have time to answer before she placed a steaming cup of coffee in his hand. He guessed she had not expected an answer. Of course, he wanted his coffee.

This time she sat down beside him. "Over these past years, you've sat at a lot of these fires alone, haven't you?"

"Yeah. Too many. A lot of them have been cold camps with no fire and no coffee, worrying that some outlaw who knew I was on his tail might double back, find my campsite and try to solve his problem with a bullet or two."

"A lonely life. A dangerous life."

"To some, I suppose. But you get used to it. Lots of folks have dangerous jobs. Being a cattleman can be more dangerous than a lawman. You've got to be careful not to turn your back on a mean bull or be dang careful if you're breaking a wild horse. As to lonely, I suppose lots of fellers have called me a loner. True in a way. I don't mind my own company. I was never much for spending evenings in saloons and such. I never played poker more than a couple times in my life, not the card kind anyhow. I like the music of the outdoors like we've got tonight. The coyotes barking in the distance, the hooting of the owls, the flow of the stream, and the rustle of leaves in the breeze."

"You are the strangest man I've ever encountered. I want to know everything about you, but you probably won't surrender half of what I'd like to learn."

He chuckled. "I got a few secrets I'll carry to the grave." He wrapped his free arm gently around her shoulders.

Susana said, "You like your own company. Does that make me an intruder?"

"I said I 'don't mind' my own company. That doesn't mean I don't welcome others from time to time. And you are not an intruder, Sue. You never will be. I sort of like you right here beside me." And in his mind that was an understatement. The notion scared him some, but he was falling in love with this ornery female, and he could not help himself.

"What happens tomorrow?"

"Well, we should ride into North Platte before suppertime if we keep up today's pace. We'll find us a hotel room and then dig up a meal someplace. After we eat, I suggest a good night's sleep before we meet with the U.S. Marshal the first thing in the morning. That's when we firm up a strategy."

"Am I still going to be your wife?"

"If you're willing."

"I don't suppose that's a proposal."

He wondered what her response would be if he said it was. No, not the time to head down that road. "It would be less complicated all the way around if you play the role of wife on this trip. It puts forth a more respectable image, causes fewer questions. I don't like dodging the truth with the marshal's office, but if you're not my wife, they'll resist your involvement at all in the case. I'd like to get you deputized."

"I'll be a good wife. But I was thinking that I am very tired, and I wonder if we might head to bed early."

"Yeah, I want to leave at sunrise, and we do need a good night's sleep."

"Well, that too."

Chapter 41

MORG AND SUSANA ate in the hotel dining room the morning following their arrival in North Platte, and he was enjoying a plate of syrupy hotcakes, fried eggs, and bacon. He had selected the new Heaven's Inn that included a bathroom with hot water for bathing for premium main floor rooms, a rare accommodation in small towns. He figured the fact that North Platte was becoming a major railroad town could be thanked for the luxury.

After putting the horses up at the livery when they rode into town, Morg had decided to rent a room that was a bit pricey for his budget, and after a quick supper, they had returned to the room where Susana bathed, crawled naked into bed, and collapsed. By the time he finished bathing and shaving several days' growth of whiskers, she was sleeping so deeply, he had to watch her for a minute to confirm she was breathing. He had slipped under the blankets, snuggled up beside her, and fallen instantly to sleep.

Susana had selected biscuits and gravy from the menu, eaten every crumb like a hungry cowhand, and now nursed a cup of coffee. "I could live in this luxury for a spell," she said.

"We might have one more night here depending upon the outcome of my meeting with the marshal and train schedules for Denver, but we won't be living quite so high on the hog after we leave North Platte." He looked at her and smiled. "That dress becomes you, incidentally. The blue matches your eyes. Of course, I have yet to see you in anything that is not becoming, even faded denims."

"Flattery will get you everywhere, but we don't have time for a poke. You had your chance this morning, but you got out of bed and dressed before I could attack."

"You were sleeping, and I could not bring myself to wake you."

"Always the gentleman, dang it."

Later, Morg was not pleased to find that his old friend, Bert Kennedy, the supervising marshal at the North Platte office was on furlough in Virginia because of his mother's death. The deputy in charge, a pudgy, fair-haired young man of no more than twenty-five years, suffered from smart-mouth disease. His name was Harlan Fitzwater, and immediately after introducing Susana as his wife, the deputy had said, "Gotta bring mama along to help, huh?" It was not a good start.

The young man had not yet bothered to get to his feet from behind the marshal's desk. Morg outranked him, being a senior U.S. Marshal, but he was looking for help, not war. "Did Marshal Kennedy tell you I might be stopping here about a case?"

"Yeah, something about some feller that's been trying to kill you and kidnapped your daughter. You got her back, Bert said, and you look more alive than dead to me."

"I have concluded, and Bert agreed, that the folks who wish to kill me and members of my family are part of an organization headed by someone who goes by the name of Monte Oxford. This organization has been responsible for many killings, robberies, and countless fraudulent enterprises throughout the western and central United States, and it's time to stop this outfit. Bert Kennedy agreed and promised to help any way possible."

"Well, I ain't Bert Kennedy, and I am in charge here till he gets back."

"And I promise you will be out of a job when Bert returns. I outrank you and am your superior right now.

There is a lady present. Now get off your fat ass and stand up and take off your hat."

Fitzwater's face turned scarlet, and he slid the chair back and stood, removing his hat as he rose. The man was angry, but Morg already doubted he was going to be much help. "Now, I've been on the road during my past years of service, but I've headquartered out of North Platte the past ten years, and I've spent some time in this office and at that desk on occasion. Second drawer down on your right side of the desk, you should find some deputy badges. Pluck one out and give it to me."

The deputy obeyed and tossed a badge on the desk. "I don't know what the hell you're up to, but you can't just pin them things on anybody."

"As a matter of fact, I can and will. I can see you won't be any more help than tits on a boar hog."

"Well, what in the hell do you want me to do?"

"We can start by you answering a few questions. Do you know George Vaughn?"

"I know who he is. Seems he's got his fingers in a lot of things around here. Rumor I just heard in one of the saloons is that he ships liquor north and west to sell just off the Indian reservations."

"Now we're getting someplace. Maybe we can get a fresh start yet. You didn't happen to be with some marshals and deputies that were going to investigate a town in Dakota Territory called Badlands City? I don't even know if there has been a follow-up yet."

"Oh, yeah, Bert sent me with four others that gathered here—he's always putting me on the road."

Morg could see why. It would be hard to have this guy around the office. "So what did you find out there?"

"Not a damn thing. No people. The place was deserted, two of the buildings burnt down. Jailhouse was still up but no lawman."

Morg supposed the operators of the so-called city knew that the law or the Army would be checking out the situation there. He and Jim Hunter, after looking over reservation maps at Fort Robinson, had already concluded the town was likely on reservation land. "Does Vaughn still live out north of Bill Cody's place?"

"Yep. I never done more than ride by it, though. From the road, it makes Cody's look like a poor man's shack."

"Does he still keep an office near the Union Pacific Railroad station?"

"Yeah. He's there most of the time days. Him and two suited fellers work out of the place, but lately there's been a few gunslinger-looking fellers not far from the door like they're keeping an eye on the office. I could never understand the need for that, but they ain't caused no trouble, so it's not our concern."

"Well, I'll look over the set-up when we stop by the railroad depot to see about tickets to Denver. Is the telegraph office still over there?"

"So you're headed for Denver?"

"Yes, hopefully early tomorrow. I may need some handcuffs. Can you come up with three or four sets?"

"Well, yeah, I guess so. You ain't bringing in some prisoners are you?"

"I don't know. I just might. You might want to tidy up your cells some just in case."

"I don't really like the idea of taking on prisoners when the marshal ain't here."

"We don't get to do much on a schedule in this business. It might be time you learned that."

Fitzwater collected some handcuffs, put them in a burlap bag and handed it to Morg. "There's four of them in there, but there's no way I can deal with that many prisoners here."

"You've got three cells by my count, two cots in each. Just double up."

"That ain't the problem. I gotta feed these men, get them out to the privy, and things."

"Get some slop buckets to put in the cells. I'm sure Bert has arrangements with a restaurant for meals that are billed to this office."

"I've never emptied slop buckets before with shit and piss and the like and then washed the dang buckets out at the pump. The notion makes me sick."

"Goes with the marshal business. Think of it as training. Now, we've got to get moving. We'll be checking back later this afternoon."

Morg and Susana stepped outside to climb into the one-horse buggy that Morg had decided would be more convenient for Susana wearing a dress and might give them more of a look of respectability as they made their stops in the town. As he was getting ready to assist Susana into the buggy, he caught sight of a man with shaggy red hair sticking out below the brim of his hat standing in an alleyway across the street. He froze.

"Wait here," he told Susana and turned away and ran toward the alley where he had spotted the observer. The alley was empty by the time he reached it. The man had disappeared. He returned to Susana and grumbled, "I move like a snail anymore."

"What was that all about?"

"I recognized that man who was watching us from over by the alley, and he knew me for sure. His name is Goober, and he was my jailer up in Badlands City."

Chapter 42

JAYE AND SHEENA, sharing a buckboard seat, bounced down the road to the Tall T behind a mule team. Jaye's saddled, strawberry-roan gelding followed on a leather lead-strap anchored to the wagon's rear. They had agreed that the wagon might be necessary if Helga wished to vacate the house with her belongings. It was also useful for hiding a double-barreled shotgun and a few rifles under a blanket behind the seat.

Sheena was the muleskinner today, a skill she had mastered under Susana's tutelage, and the mules and wagon had come with her from Susana's barn. As they neared the Tall T entry road, she said, "Have you thought about how we're going to handle this?"

"Yeah. If it suits you, I thought I might just stay outside near the wagon till you say you need me to help carry something. That way if anybody tries to interfere with our visit, we won't all be trapped inside. I can fire a shot if there's trouble outside. From there, we'll just have to play this by ear. I just don't know what to expect. Maybe Helga won't even let you in the house."

"I don't know why she wouldn't. I wore a dress today, so I wouldn't look like a grungy cowhand, the style I've adopted most days since we got back from Mad Rock."

"Nobody's going to take you for a grungy cowhand, Sheena, no matter what you're wearing."

"I guess that's meant as a compliment, but if I had my way, I'd get rid of this dress."

"Fine by me."

He felt her elbow dig into his ribs. "I mean, I don't care if you wear britches all the time."

"That is not what you meant, but I know you were just displaying your tasteless sense of humor. Well, as a teacher, I need to wear a dress to have my students take me seriously in these times, but next chance I get, I'm getting more riding clothes for my meager wardrobe."

"You almost sound like you are becoming a Sandhills girl."

"It could be. I just don't know yet, but I do like the fishing here. I admit I'm starting to look at this country differently than I used to." She guided the mule team off the county road and onto the wagon trail that led to the Tall T mansion. "My stomach's getting queasy."

"I'm plenty nervous myself, but we've got to see it through now. When we get to the house, I'd suggest you rein the mules around so they're facing the road in case we're forced to get out of here fast."

"That makes sense." When they reached the mansion, she followed Jaye's suggestion before she reined the mules in and braked the wagon. Jaye dropped down from the wagon seat and walked around to the other side of the wagon to help Sheena down from her seat. "Take my hand," he said.

She accepted his assistance but caught her heel on the wagon's edge coming down hard, landing almost in Jaye's arms. He would have kissed her were it not for potential audiences nearby.

Sheena stepped away, her red cheeks suggesting a bit of embarrassment. "I could have done this on my own if it hadn't been for the dang dress and shoe heels."

"I know that, and I would have stayed out of your way."

"You're not arguing with me so much lately."

"You're getting me trained, just like a dog."

"I doubt that you are trainable. You're just learning to pick your fights."

Jaye just smiled. "We're being watched by two men down by the corrals. They may just be curious about the visitors, but maybe you had better head up to the house."

Chapter 43

SHEENA RAPPED SOFTLY on the door, and it opened immediately, suggesting that the mansion's occupant had already seen her when the wagon stopped in front of the house. The pretty blonde woman who greeted her could be no one other than the woman she came to visit. "Good afternoon," Sheena said, "you must be Helga. I am Sheena Fraser, Marshal Fraser's daughter. May Towne is my mother."

"I have heard your name, and I saw you when you were here with Andy. I am Helga Gerhardt. Why don't you come in?" She opened the door just enough to allow Sheena to enter, nodding toward Jaye who was leaning against the wagon, looking in the direction of the corrals. "The man?"

"Jaye Boyden, a dear friend of mine."

"We can sit down in the parlor, but if you stay too long, there could be a problem."

Sheena noticed the Winchester propped against the wall just inside the front door as she stepped into the parlor. "That's why we are here—to help you if there is a problem. I live with Susana Mercer who has been worried about you since her visit. We are here to take you away if you do not wish to stay here. You may come with me to Susana's house. She will offer you an opportunity to work there and help with our school if you wish."

"I do not wish to be here. I am afraid. Moe, the man Missus Mercer encountered when she visited, has informed me that I am not to leave under any circumstances until Missus Towne returns. He came to the house and tried to force his way in. I fired a shot with my rifle, and he left. You will see where the door is splintered at the top. There are three others of his kind here. The other hands stay away from them, and I fear they would be unable to help me even if they tried. They are not killers."

"Have they threatened you?"

"Not with their words, but they stalk the house like lions circling for an attack. They come up and peer in the windows sometimes, and I see their eyes from where I am hiding. I know what they want. For now, they are moving cautiously, but they can break in through a window or batter down a door whenever they choose. I have stuffed my few items of clothing in a gunnysack and personal things in my carpetbag. I planned to sneak away one night—soon, if not tonight, tomorrow. I will have my rifle. If they follow, I will fight, and I will kill myself before these animals take me."

"Come with us, now. Let me help with your bags. We will walk out of the house and directly to the wagon out front. You will leave this place."

"Thank God. You are my angel. My prayers have been answered. Come with me, my bags are in a hallway closet."

Helga handed the stuffed carpetbag to Sheena and claimed the heavier gunnysack for herself and raced for the door, pausing to snatch up her rifle. Just as Sheena reached for the brass doorknob, two gunshots cracked outside and then a third that seemed more distant. She opened the door enough to view the scene beyond the house and was surprised to find that Jaye was mounted, his Colt drawn and aimed in the direction of the outbuildings.

She did not hesitate. "Helga, follow me. Run for the buckboard. Climb onto the wagon seat but stay low. If the gunfire comes too close, drop back into the wagon box."

They rushed out onto the veranda and down the stairsteps before they hit the ground and raced for the wagon. Now she caught sight of three men, one of them, Moe, taking cover behind a hay wagon stacked with hay near the stable. For the moment, there appeared to be a stalemate with everyone holding their fire. Her guess was that Towne's men did not have their rifles, and that the distance was such that their sidearms would not be effective. That was confirmed when she caught a glimpse of Jaye holstering his pistol and pulling his Winchester from its scabbard.

As Sheena and Helga scrambled onto the wagon and Sheena clutched the mule team's reins, Jaye fired several rifle rounds at the gunslingers, she supposed, with the thought of keeping them hunkered down as long as possible. She released the wagon brake, cracked her whip above the mules and hollered, and the team lurched forward with a force that almost tipped the two women backwards off their seat.

Sheena heard gunfire behind her and tossed a look over her shoulder. Jaye had not budged yet, obviously trying to give her a good head start. There was no chance that the mule-drawn wagon could outpace men on horseback once they were saddled and giving chase. But she was sick at the thought of the risk Jaye was taking. She was going to give him hell for that when they made it to the J Bar B where Avery and Luke were on alert.

For the first time since they boarded the wagon, Helga spoke. "I will get into the back of the wagon. I can be more help with my rifle from there."

"My Winchester and a shotgun are under the blanket back there, both loaded if you need them." She hoped it didn't come to that but did not see how it could be avoided. Jaye would have to catch up soon. He couldn't help them if those scum took him down.

They were not quite halfway to Jaye's place when Helga yelled from the wagon box. "I can see him now—your friend. At first, I saw only dust, but now I can make out the roan he is riding."

Jaye caught up with the wagon five minutes later and reined his mount up even with Sheena who did not slow the wagon. "We're not going to outrun them with the wagon," he hollered. "Just keep going, I'll slow them up some more."

"No, Jaye," she yelled. "No. We'll make a stand together."

Helga screamed, and her gun fired. Jaye wheeled his horse around. Helga said, "I didn't hit him, but he turned away for a minute, waiting for the others, I think."

Jaye was behind the wagon again when gunfire exploded from the dust.

Helga said, "His horse is going down, but I think Jaye got his rifle. No, the horse has pinned him down, but he is firing the rifle yet, I think. I cannot see. The dust is too much."

"I'm sorry. I won't go on without him." She reined in the mules, braked the wagon and grabbed her shotgun from the back. "If you are coming with me, bring my Winchester." Guns were still firing as Sheena closed the gap. She could see Jaye now, his leg beneath the horse, but his rifle still firing. The horse was offering him some cover, and the poor critter had to be dead by now, she thought. Two riderless horses swept past her. Jaye tossed his rifle aside and struggled to get his pistol free from its holster, but now a big man stood over him with his pistol aimed at Jaye's head. She stopped, now not more than twenty feet from the man who had not seen her. She took hasty aim with the shotgun, praying she was high enough to spare Jaye any of the buckshot and squeezed the trigger. The blast took half of the gunman's head, and he toppled over beside his would-be victim.

Jaye looked up at Sheena in disbelief. "I thought it was over for me," he said, but then panic appeared in his eyes.

"But there is one more. There were four. I'm sure I took down two, but there's another."

Sheena swung her shotgun around, seeking another target just as a rifle fired, and she heard a man grunt and the clatter of metal against stone. "This was Lester," Helga said, nodding to a body sprawled in a roadside ditch. "He will not lust for me again."

Sheena went to Jaye's side and knelt beside him. "Are you hurt?"

"I'm alive. That's all that matters. Thanks to an angel who appeared from nowhere." Then tears glistened in his eyes. "But poor Runner wasn't so lucky. He was a good horse. Likely took a lot of lead slugs meant for me."

"But now we've got to get him off your leg."

"Yeah, and that could be a problem. I think my leg's broken."

She looked up at Helga. "I don't think we can move the horse without doing more damage. We've got plenty of extra horses grazing nearby. They seem tame enough, like they're not inclined to move to the wild. I'm going to catch one and ride to the J Bar B and bring help. Can you stay with Jaye?"

"Of course. I can do that."

An hour and a half later, Sheena returned with Luke, Avery, Andy, and Dingo. Within fifteen minutes they had

Jaye free of the dead horse and loaded on the wagon with Runner's saddle and tack. Jaye said, "I can't leave Runner here for the scavengers."

Luke said, "We've got plenty of rope. I can cinch his hind legs and use the horses to drag him back to the ranch. You've got gulleys not far from the stables that need filling. We can put him in one and see that he's covered good."

"I'll let you figure that out, Luke. We'll take all the horses back to my place till we figure out what to do with them. Collect the bodies of the men and cover them with what blankets we have. Tomorrow morning, I'd like you and Avery to drop them off at the entry to the Tall T."

Sheena could see that Jaye was in agony and it struck her for the first time that Jaye Boyden was a leader, a man that took charge of getting a task done, and he did it in ways that made men willing, even eager, to follow. "Now, about your leg," she said.

"As you can see, while we've been talking, Helga took my knife and cut my left trouser leg off and looked at the problem. What do you think, Helga?"

Helga said, "It is swollen between the knee and ankle, but the bone does not protrude. With Luke's help and some whiskey maybe, I think I can set and splint it when we get to the ranch. I have seen and done such things, and you are at least two days from a doctor."

Jaye said, "Take me home, so this lady can get to work. I'm not much of a drinking man, but whiskey doesn't sound so bad right now, and I know Avery's got some stashed in the bunkhouse if we need extra."

Chapter 44

AFTER SEEING GOOBER across the street from the marshal's office, Morg decided to defer sending a telegram to the Denver U.S. Marshal. Something strange was going on, and this had to be approached carefully. "Sue, I want to stop by the railroad depot and ask the agent a few questions before we do anything else."

"Whatever you want, Morg. You are the boss—for now."

At the agent's window he was met by a balding, gray-haired man with thick-lensed, wire-rimmed spectacles. A droopy mustache and heavy jowls gave him a walrus look. He eyed Morg suspiciously and did not appear to be a congenial sort. Morg remembered that his badge had been pinned on his shirt pocket this morning and was covered by the buckskin jacket he wore. He had not wished to attract attention as he moved about the town, but it all seemed pointless now. He pulled his coat back to reveal the badge.

"I'm U.S. Marshal Morgan Fraser, and your name, sir?"

"Frederick Colmes."

"I gather you handle ticket sales for the Union Pacific. Do you maintain a list of folks who buy tickets here?"

"Yeah, I keep it for three weeks. I dump the sheets that are older than that."

"I'm looking for someone who purchased tickets to Denver, likely under the name of Thomas Towne. Could you check your lists and see if he bought tickets recently, possibly four or five?"

"No need. He bought five tickets just short of a week ago to be used three days later. He came in with the tickets the day his train was to pull out and said he wasn't going and wanted his money back. He raised quite a fuss when I told him he was too late for a refund. Pompous bastard."

"Yeah, that would have been Thomas Towne. Do you know where he was staying?"

"Nope. Never said and not required for ticket sales."

"And he didn't take a train to somewhere else?"

"Nah. Couldn't do that without me knowing."

"Very well. Thank you for your cooperation."

The agent nodded and turned away from the window. Morg sighed and looked at Susana who had been standing back a short distance. "You heard?"

"I guess I don't get a trip to Denver."

"Appears not. I need to ponder this. Let's go back to the hotel and have an early lunch."

When they arrived at the hotel, they were met in the lobby by Deputy U.S. Marshal Harlan Fitzwater. "Figured you'd show up here around lunchtime," Fitzwater said. "I got a telegram from the Denver office. It's directed to Marshal Bert Kennedy, but when he's gone, we don't just let this stuff pile up. It might be something important that needs doing."

"I understand," Morg said, as Fitzwater handed him the telegram. He read it quickly. It was short but pertinent to his mission. "Well, Sue. I don't know what's going on, but we for sure won't be going to Denver. The Oxford Company's offices are no longer there."

"They have closed them?"

"The whole darn office building has been blown up. Dynamited, I guess."

"Good heavens. They must have somebody after them besides the law."

"More likely done by their own people. If they didn't have time to move all their files and records out, what better way to destroy any evidence. It would also be a good distraction while the law dogs are trying to sort it all out." He turned to the deputy. "Harlan, we got off to a rocky start, but if you can help me with this, I will give you a glowing recommendation to your boss."

"I'll do my best, Marshal. You just tell me what you want done."

"Do you have any men around here who can handle a gun and follow orders that we might deputize?"

"I hail from southwestern Kansas. I ain't been here long enough to know that many. I got a friend, Homer Levis, that breaks horses for ranchers when there's a job for him and works at the stable part time. I saw him this morning, so I know he's in town right now. He's better than good with any gun."

"See if he can get away for ten bucks a day—I assume the marshal's got a contingency fund?"

"Yep. And that's twice what Homer gets at the stable. They got others over there. He'll talk his way into a day or two off."

"Hire him. I'll swear him in. Is Flint Capper still county sheriff?"

"Yeah. He's not going to run again when election comes up next year, but he's still on the job. Good man for his age."

Morg didn't tell Fitzwater that Sheriff Capper was two years younger than himself. "I've known Flint for years. Tell him I need his help along with whatever deputies he can spare. I want everybody to meet at the marshal's office at two o'clock. What I've got in mind will likely take the rest of today and most of tomorrow. I'll explain everything when everybody's there."

"I'll see to it, Marshal. I'll head over to the stable and talk to Homer now."

"Thanks, Harlan. We'll catch up with you at two."

"Most call me, 'Fitz,' Marshal."

"And you can call me 'Morg' if it suits you."

After the deputy left, Susana said, "Well, it's nice to see you boys have made peace."

"I have to remind myself sometimes of what an arrogant, hot-headed ass I was when I was at his age. As you have seen, the temper still flares sometimes, but not so often now. It was sort of nice in those days, to be so certain you knew everything. Somedays now, I think I know nothing for certain."

She smiled and gave him a quick hug. "I think they call that maturity. Some never get there. Now, let's eat."

"I'm not so hungry now. When the action starts, I sort of lose my appetite."

"Well, I never lose mine, so I hope you will take a lady to lunch. You can tell me how I fit into this party that is coming up."

Chapter 45

MORG SAT IN the corner of the hotel room, watching as Susana stood in front of the mirror mounted above the dresser and tied her shoulder-length, white hair into a ponytail. She was a stunning creature, and he could not imagine what she saw in a scarred-up and battered old marshal.

She sat on the bed and lifted her skirt to expose her long shapely leg while she anchored the holster of her short-barreled, .38 caliber Smith & Wesson to her thigh with a strip of cloth. The woman did not have a speck of modesty, when it came to him anyhow. He wondered if she was deliberately trying to stir his lust right now. If so, it was working, but they had business to tend to, and he would not be delayed. She stood and looked at him with that close-mouthed little smile that always teased him.

"I felt you watching me," she said.

"Not much else going on in here."

"We could change that real fast."

"I've got to get over to the marshal's office early."

"You get too serious when you are tending to the marshaling business. I'd still rather be wearing boots and britches if we're going to end up on horseback."

"You can slip back here and change if that happens. We'll both want to pick up my Winchester and your shotgun." He plucked a deputy marshal's badge from his coat pocket and handed it to her. "Consider yourself sworn. For now pin it on the inside of your collar where it can't be seen but so you can pull it out if you need to prove your authority."

She took the badge, studied it a moment, and pinned it on as instructed. "I hope I'm not wearing this long."

A few minutes later, they passed through the hotel lobby and exited through the entryway's double doors. When they stepped out onto the boardwalk and turned to walk to the marshal's office some three blocks distant, out of the corner of his eye, Morg caught a flash of light across the street. He shoved Susana off the boardwalk and sent her sprawling in the dusty street. He crouched and drew his Colt just as the cracking of two pistol shots cracked simultaneously with the shattering of the window behind him.

He saw the shooter now and returned two shots, charging across the street like an angry bull. The man panicked and got off another wild shot before he turned to run. He stumbled and, by the time he righted himself, Morg rammed into his back, toppling him forward and sending him crashing onto the boardwalk. The would-be killer's gun clattered out of reach.

Morg had the chunky shooter down with his knee pressed into his back, and he holstered his own weapon, clutched the man's head with both hands and began hammering it against the hard wood, his captive squealing like a pig. Finally, he stopped and got to his feet. "Have you had enough, Goober?"

Goober struggled to sit up. His forehead and face were covered with blood, and Morg thought his former jailer's nose might be broken. "I don't take kindly to folks trying to kill me and my lady friend."

"Wasn't after the woman," Goober said.

"But she was in the line of fire. She'd likely have gone down with me."

Then Morg realized he had not even checked on Susana. He tossed a look over his shoulder and saw she was on her feet, walking across the street and coming his way. Not far behind her, riding at a casual pace was a man he recognized, Sheriff Flint Capper. He turned back to his prisoner who just sat there seemingly dumbfounded by it all. "Well, Goober, I thought I'd seen the last of you up in Dakota Territory."

"Ain't got nothing to say to you."

Susana stepped up onto the boardwalk. "Morgan Fraser, you sent me flying back there, and the landing wasn't any too soft."

"Sorry, Sue, but I didn't have time to pick you up and set you down careful-like. It doesn't appear you broke anything."

"No, but you scared me so much it's a wonder I didn't dribble my panties."

"Well, Morg, I should've knowed it was you stirring up a racket. Thought I was going to meet you at the marshal's office in a half hour. And who is this pretty young lady you got with you, your daughter maybe?"

"Flint, I'd like you to meet my wife, Susana. If you hadn't guessed, Sue, the giant with the star is Sheriff Flint Capper."

Capper was six and a half feet tall, and his high-crowned Stetson added another three or four inches. He doffed his hat and bowed. "My pleasure, ma'am. Darn, I can't believe that old feller got to you first. You would have had a lot of choices."

Susana laughed, "Well, he does have some redeeming characteristics that some don't see."

"I won't ask what." He turned back to Morg. "What have we got here?"

"It's a long story. I've met this fella, and I'll tell you about it later. He tried to ambush me coming out of the hotel. You can see the manager looking at the broken window across the street. I got lucky and caught sight of the sun glinting off his Colt, and we got out of the way just in time."

"The old Morg I always knowed would have killed the son-of-a-bitch and saved us all some trouble."

"This guy's part of what I'm wanting to meet with you about. He's not the brightest candle, but he might know a thing or two that could be helpful to us later."

Capper said, "So what do you want to do with him? Federal jail or county?"

"I'd like to put him in the county jail for now. We don't need to have him listening in to our meeting. I'll stop by and chat with him later."

"I see one of my deputies coming this way. We'll let him take this no-good to the jail, and I'll walk you and the missus over to the marshal's office for the little get-together."

When the deputy rode up on his bay gelding, he dismounted. The sheriff made introductions and proceeded to give the young man instructions. His name was Ned

Carey, a reddish-haired young man of average height, who was dwarfed by the tall sheriff. Sinewy with dark blue eyes. Morg thought the kid would have the young ladies swooning when he got a little older. He seemed confident and serious about his job, and Capper appeared to have no hesitance about leaving him with the prisoner.

The sheriff turned back to Morg and Susana and stepped over and offered his arm to Susana, who smiled and took it. Morg trailed along behind the two, knowing that Capper, the ornery cuss, was just needling him a bit. "Hey, Flint," Morg said. "Are you hiring schoolkids for deputies these days?"

"If you are talking about Ned Carry, he's twenty-five years old and got a wife and two kids with another on the way. He's likely going to be my successor after the next election. He's got the Republican nomination pretty well sewed up, and you got to look under every rock to find a Democrat in Lincoln County. Every baby born out here gets an 'R' branded on his butt at his first birthday."

"He looks like a baby himself."

"Well, he ain't. At your age, most that are younger than you look like babies."

"You're just two years younger than me."

"But I'm still in my fifties."

Chapter 46

SIX MEN AND Susana gathered at the marshal's office. Besides Morg and Deputy Marshal Fitzwater there were Homer Levis, now a special deputy marshal, Sheriff Capper, his deputy Ned Carey, and another sheriff's deputy, a quiet middle-aged man named Paul O'Keefe. The participants were scattered about the room with some of the chairs pulled from jail cells.

First, Morg gave a quick summary of the Oxford organization and the vendetta Monte Oxford had against him personally. He related the story of Sheena's abduction, the exchange and his escape. Finally, he shared his opinion that Monte Oxford and Thomas Towne were one and the same person. "As near as I can determine, George Vaughn, who has lived in North Platte for the past fifteen years, works very closely with the man I will continue to call Towne for now. Flint, you and your men know more about him than I do, and I'm hoping you can help prove the connection between the two."

Capper said, "Nobody knows much about Vaughn except he must have a gold mine out to his place. He owns lots of land north of town and lives with his wife in the biggest house in the county. His son went back east to one of them fancy schools, but I heard he's in Omaha now. Vaughn has an office a block off Main Street, but I don't know what the devil folks do there. Usually, you just see strangers going in and out. Vaughn goes into the office regular-like, I think."

"Interesting. I may visit that office. Anyway, I am here to arrest both Vaughn and Towne. I think Towne has panicked, and I'm not certain he will even return to his ranch. I worry that he has the ability to leave here and just disappear. Would any of you recognize him if you saw him?"

Nobody responded.

"Well, as I mentioned, he is married to my former wife, and I know him. I've just got to find him. Flint, could you have one your deputies check the hotels and boarding houses to see if Towne is lodged there? You're looking for someone with a wife and two small boys. He could be going under another name. I've already spoken to the clerk at Heaven's Inn where we're staying. They're not there."

"Me and my deputies would know Vaughn, if that helps any," Capper said. "As to Towne, there's only two other hotels, maybe three boarding houses."

Ned Carey said, "I can handle that chore, Flint."

"It's yours."

"When I'm finished here, I want to talk to my old friend Goober at your jail. I would like to have a man posted near Vaughn's office to try to keep track of the comings and goings there and identify any folks he might recognize. I'll be by later for a report. We don't have enough men for a twenty-four-hour watch, so just leave when the office closes and check back here if I haven't got there first."

Capper said, "Paul, would you do that? You've been around these parts a long time. You would know any locals."

O'Keefe said, "Yeah, I'll take care of it."

Morg said, "Fitz, I want you and Homer to keep an eye on Vaughn's house. You'll need a telescope of some kind and some distance. I don't want them to figure out they're being watched. I would like to know who is staying there and how many men have the look of gunslingers. There are probably cowhands there that won't be interested in fighting the law. Can you find a spot to set up?"

Homer Levis said, "I know the place. I've been out there to break horses the past two years. Fanciest setup in the area, I'll tell you that. I generally deal with the foreman, only seen Vaughn hisself a few times when he peered through the fence to see what was going on. I can't imagine the foreman being any kind of an outlaw, but there's always been a few hanging around that didn't seem to have nothing to do. Anyhow, there's hills all around the place. Won't be hard to come in from the west and find a spot across the road."

Capper said, "You're looking for a gunfight at the Vaughn place?"

"I hope not, but we may be making arrests there tomorrow morning. It depends on what we turn up today. Now, I'll let you get about your business. Flint, I'll be over at your office shortly to see what I can learn from Goober."

The others departed to tend to their assignments, and Morg and Susana were alone in the office. "Morgan, I've been trying to think of something I might do to help out."

"You help by just being with me, and I'm not just saying that to make you feel good. I truly mean that Sue. I like life with you at my side."

"The feeling is mutual, Morgan, but there is something I want to do with your permission."

"And what is that?"

"I would like to visit the Vaughn office while you are at the jail."

"Why on earth would you do that?"

"I can find out how many are there and what sort of men are involved. I could meet George Vaughn and get a sense of what type of person he is. I wouldn't claim your last name, of course. I will be from Ogallala just fifty or so miles west, and I will be looking for May Towne, an old friend who wrote and said she was coming to North Platte and invited me to visit. She said I should check at the Vaughn office to see where she was staying."

Morg thought Susana's suggestion was not outlandish and that it might trigger an interesting reaction, certainly add to the confusion if word of her visit got back to Thomas Towne. He worried about potential risks, but she had already said that was part of what she signed up for.

As if reading his mind, Susana said, "Paul O'Keefe will be nearby, and I will try to speak with him before I go in. You will likely be there before I come out. They would not be stupid enough to shoot a woman in their office. It is an opportunity to stir the stew some."

"Alright. You heard Fitz give me directions to the Vaughn office."

"Yes, and I will locate Deputy O'Keefe before I go in."

"While you are at it, why don't you just invite Vaughn back to the jail with you? I would sure like to get him cut off from the herd."

They shared a kiss and embrace before they separated. As Morg walked to the sheriff's office, he had difficulty taking his mind off Susana, not just because of his concern for her safety. The darn woman had slipped into his life and caught him unaware, and now he was troubled at the notion she might somehow sneak right out again. She didn't show signs of it yet, but he was probably blinded by what he felt for her. He had never lived easily with undecided issues.

Hundreds of decisions had been forced upon him during his life, and he had made his share of bad ones. Still, he did not live comfortably within the realm of limbo and indecision. An old man had told him once, "A man's got to choose between the white horse and the black horse. You ain't going no place if you don't pick one. Either will likely get you where you want. One might just be a tougher ride." He had to know soon just where he and Susana were headed. Two decisions would be required for that, his and hers.

When Morg entered the sheriff's office, Flint Capper was leaning back in the chair at his desk, long legs stretched out so the boot heels protruded from the front edge of the desktop. Another kid deputy looked like he was getting ready to leave. He was another fair-complected kid who didn't look like a razor had ever needed to touch his face, taller than Ned Carey by several inches and had sort of a hungry look.

Capper said, "Morg Fraser, this here is Deputy Arnie Goode. He was watching the jail till I got back. I'm sending him over to keep an eye on the office with Paul. Figured an extra man wouldn't hurt."

"I'm glad to hear that. Susana is going to make a visit to the office."

Capper's shaggy eyebrows lifted. "I see. But I don't." He nodded at the deputy. "You can go, Arnie."

Morg explained what Susana proposed to do. "She's fearless, and she was set on doing it. It might not help, but I don't think it will hurt."

Capper shrugged. "She's your wife. Of course, it might be nice if you would get her a wedding band."

Why had he not thought of that? Everybody was probably thinking Susana was his whore. Why hadn't she said something? His mind was slipping. He was getting out of the marshaling business none too soon. His eyes just met Capper's evenly, but Morg could see from the twinkle in the sheriff's eyes that he was having fun. "I'd like to talk to Goober now."

Capper nodded toward a door to his left. "Cells are down the hall. Your friend is in the first cell." He tossed Morg a ring of keys. "The biggest one. He's not up to fighting anybody after you beat the hell out of him, so go on in if you like. He's stretched out on the bunk and there's a single chair in his cell. By the way, his real name is Floyd Baily. There's paper on him. Wanted for two bank robberies and rape of fourteen-year-old girl, all in Kansas. Reward of five hundred dollars. Of course, I know the U.S. Marshals don't claim reward money."

"You can put in a claim if you like."

"Lincoln County thanks you."

Morg opened the door and stepped into the cell block where he saw four cells, two on each side of the short hallway. Goober was stretched out on one of two bunks in the narrow cell to his left. He took the key and opened the barred door. "Good afternoon, Mister Baily."

The prisoner looked up through eyes that were half swollen shut. His face and forehead were swollen and turning red and purple from the beating he had taken. "Not you," Goober said.

"We're going to talk."

"Don't want to."

"You're nailed for attempted murder in Nebraska. Add that you tried to kill a lawman, and you've earned a life sentence in the penitentiary. And then you've got the bank robberies and rape in Kansas."

"Sheriff didn't say they had paper on me."

"Well, they do. If you can help me out, I'll recommend they drop any Nebraska charges, and I won't be interested in any federal charges you earned for kidnapping and imprisoning a federal officer. You might escape hanging."

"I guess I got nothing to lose. Ask your questions."

"Who is your big boss?"

"Somebody named Oxford. Never met him. Almost did. He was supposed to come to Badlands City to watch you hang. I worked for him when I was with the gang that robbed them banks in Kansas. Oxford & Company pretty much owned Badlands City, too."

"But you never saw the man?"

"Nope. I worked with his brother Joe. Heard you chased him down and kilt him over in Missouri someplace. He was a mean bastard. He kilt little kids without blinking if they was in his way."

"You just raped them."

"That gal was full growed and a slut to boot. I didn't hurt her much."

Morg was tempted to beat the man's head against the jail bars, but he continued. "Who did you get your instructions from?"

"Usually somebody different whenever we had a job, but we got called to North Platte, and Vaughn talked to Fincher about taking your daughter and making the trade. That's what Fincher said, anyhow. He had a few too many drinks. He wasn't supposed to say that. And then I got sent down here to be part of Vaughn's crew, and he was the one that ordered me to kill you. I didn't want to. I ain't a killer, but he'd of had me kilt if I didn't. I think they was keeping an eye on me anyhow. I wouldn't have dared talked if I got the job done."

"Will you testify to these things in court?"

"I don't suppose I got no choice."

Morg stood and looked around the cell block. Each cell had a window, apparently for air circulation only, since the sill was a good six feet high. An occupant would not be vulnerable to man with a gun. But a stick of dynamite or some other explosive? Vaughn had to know Goober was in custody and was no doubt worrying plenty about it. Flint Capper might be obnoxious, but he was far from stupid, so he would not take it kindly if Morg pointed out the need to protect the witness.

When Morg left the cell block, Capper said, "Did the feller know anything that will help you?"

"Yeah, he can be a big link in the chain."

"I hired some ex-Army fellers. Besides somebody on duty inside, we'll have two guards circling the building till this is all settled."

"We'll talk more later, but there's one man I want to take alive."

"Who's that?"

"George Vaughn."

Chapter 47

THE VAUGHN OFFICES were located on a side street, but Susana had no difficulty locating the single-story structure set on a spacious lot that would have allowed for an additional building on each side. It was not a pretentious building, a rectangular affair constructed of native limestone and identified by a small painted black-on-white sign above the door as "Vaughn Properties," sufficiently vague to cover any number of enterprises.

She saw a man sitting on a bench next to the front door, arms folded, low crowned hat pulled down on his forehead and chin dug into his chest like he might be sleeping. She found that unlikely. A half block down the street on the opposite side she recognized Deputy Sheriff Paul O'Keefe with his wide-brimmed Plainsman hat sitting on a bench in an almost identical pose. She wondered if the two men were surreptitiously watching each other. She dared not approach O'Keefe with him in plain sight of the other man.

There were three horses tied at the hitching posts out front, indicating there were three riders who did not intend to be there very long. She supposed a few could have been recently fetched from the stable since it was closing in on the end of a typical workday. There was also a buckboard nearly filled with crates and several file cabinets behind a team of horses just outside the door. Somebody moving? She stepped into the street and started walking toward the Vaughn offices. A glance down the street told her that O'Keefe had raised his head and was watching her now. She had the undivided attention of the man in front of Vaughn Properties.

"Good afternoon," Susana said as she approached the door to enter.

"Hold up, lady," the apparent sentry said. "Where do you think you are going?"

"And who is asking?"

"Hobbes, not that it is your concern."

He was an ugly man with a growly voice that matched his bear-like appearance. He had a scraggly, black beard and a thick scar that angled down his forehead, skipped his eye, and continued over his cheek, leaving a gulley in his beard. "I am here to see Mister Vaughn."

She reached for the door handle, and the man stood, towering over her now. "He ain't seeing nobody today."

She opened the door, walked into what appeared to be a receiving area of sorts and closed the door, leaving the unpleasant Hobbes outside. There were two men loading boxes and crates with file folders and what appeared to be ledger books, and they both looked up at her and then at each other. Susana judged them too young to be George Vaughn. The holstered pistols on their gun belts told her the men were not usually engaged as office workers.

"I must see George Vaughn immediately," she said. A short, trim man wearing a gray suit and string tie stepped out of a room adjacent to the reception area. He was a darker man than she expected, his skin lightly bronzed like he might have some Spanish ancestry. A thin mustache adorned his upper lip. She guessed him about her age and thought him quite handsome if one's tastes ran to the prissy type.

"Oh, George," she said, rushing to him, wrapping her arms about his neck and planting a kiss on his cheek. "It's been so long—too long."

"Uh, why don't we step into my office?" He pulled away and nodded toward the doorway. She walked into the room which she noted was essentially bare except for a nice oak desk and a crate full of its contents.

Vaughn said, "Am I supposed to know you?"

"I'm hurt. I would never forget you. I am Mary from Ogallala. We shared a very special night together."

She could see him thinking now, trying to recall. Obviously, he had shared special nights with women other than his wife.

"I am starting to remember you now. It's been how long?"

"It will soon be fifteen years."

"It seems like yesterday now. I must be having an old age spasm."

"I know I probably seem old to you, but I still can provide more mature men a special night. I'm almost embarrassed to say that's why I am here in North Platte."

"But why did you come to see me?"

"A friend of yours asked me to come here and give you a message."

"A friend?"

"A friend I have known for many years. He sent me a telegram in care of the hotel where I live. He said I should come to North Platte and rent a room at the Heaven's Inn, and that he would find me there and make it worth my while. He did, and I made it worth his, I assure you."

"And what is my friend's name?"

"He always registers at hotels where we meet with different names. But I know him as Monte Oxford."

Vaughn froze and stared at her in disbelief. "He had a message. He said that some man named Hobbes is working with the U.S. Marshal's office and that there will be an army of deputies here in three days. He wants to find out what Hobbes knows and then 'put him to bed' was the way he put it. I have to catch a train back to Ogallala in less than an hour, but I said I would give you the message. He wants you to get Hobbes and take him someplace—I'm trying to remember the name—and he will meet you there."

"The Flying V?"

"Yes, I knew it was the flying something."

"Wait here." He went out in the front room and closed the door behind him. She crept up to the door and listened. Part of what she heard was mumbled, but he was telling the men to direct Hobbes to drive the wagon and to get him to the Flying V immediately. After he tended to some business, he would follow.

But what was the business? Would he demand a poke? Not likely. He was seriously shaken. It occurred to her suddenly that Vaughn would have concluded he could not allow her to live. She knew the connection between

Vaughn and the man named Oxford. She lifted her skirt and drew the short-barreled Smith & Wesson from its holster. She was not as clever as she thought. She would never tell Morgan Fraser what happened here.

When Vaughn returned, he was carrying a hammer. That made sense. He would not want the sound of gunfire coming from his business place. He intended to club her to death. She raised her gun, easing her finger onto the trigger, steadying her wrist with her left hand. She would not miss, but Morgan needed this man alive. He stopped when he saw her gun and stared at the weapon.

"George Vaughn, I am a deputy U.S. Marshal. You are under arrest. Drop that hammer or I will be forced to place a lead slug between your eyes."

He took a step toward her, raising the hammer. "You wouldn't."

"Go ahead. I'll prove I would."

At that instant, she heard hammering against the outside door. He must have locked it. Then, the shattering of glass and Morgan's voice. "Sue. Sue, are you alright? We're coming."

Vaughn dropped the hammer and tears began to stream from his eyes.

Susana yelled, "I'm okay, Morgan. Take your time."

When Morg stepped into the room, he looked first at Susana, his brow furrowed, she hoped with confusion. She nodded at the man sitting in the corner bawling like a baby. "Meet Mister George Vaughn," she said. "I've placed him under arrest. I think Towne and anyone else you are interested in will be found at the Flying V unless one of the deputies has turned up something else."

Chapter 48

MORG AND SUSANA returned to their room so Susana could change into her riding clothes. As she stripped down to her essentials and slipped into a cotton shirt and riding britches, Morg tried to learn more about what transpired in the Vaughn offices. "You're not telling me everything," he said. "You didn't just walk in that office and say you had a message from Monte Oxford and that all the men were to head out to the Flying V to meet up with him."

"I told you that I said Oxford told me that Hobbes was working with the U.S. Marshal's office, and they should get him to the Flying V."

"But why would Vaughn believe you had a connection to Monte Oxford in the first place?"

"I just made-up stories as I went along. I do that for my school children all the time, and I even act them out. My mama always said I could have been a stage actress."

"That I believe."

"Anyway, I'll tell you all about it some night when we are a sitting at a campfire."

"Since you admit to making up stories, how will I know you are telling the truth, this religious lady who seems to be a natural born liar?"

She pulled on her boots and pressed her hat onto her head and said, "I guess you're going to need to work on that, Morgan, but know this: I always tell the truth about things that count. So when I tell you that I love you, Morgan Fraser, and I hope to spend the rest of my life proving it, you had better believe me."

Her words left him dumbfounded for a moment. "Did I hear you right?"

She started buckling on her gun belt. "I love you. Now do I have to tell you what you are supposed to say?"

"I love you, Sue Mercer. I just didn't know for sure that you felt the same. I guess I'm on the slow side when it comes to dealing with women."

She stepped over gave him a quick kiss on the lips, snatched up her shotgun and said, "We've got work to do.

I suppose we go to the livery and saddle up the critters first?"

Sheriff Flint Capper and his deputy, Ned Carey, along with Fitzwater, were already at the marshal's office when Morg and Susana arrived. Capper said, "We are to pick up O'Keefe and Arnie Goode at the county jailhouse on the way out."

Fitzwater said, "Homer's still keeping an eye on the Flying V homeplace, I'll bring him down from the hills when we get there, and he can give us an update. This going out at night is kind of scary business to me, and I ain't talking about ghosts."

Morg said, "They likely wouldn't be looking for anyone to strike at night, but most important, we're getting too close to risk Towne pulling out before we show up. He's got to be crazed with Vaughn not showing up. Did you and Homer get a count on how many guns might be there?"

"We figure maybe eight to ten. Can't say for sure with folks going in and out of the buildings and such. And then there's cowhands that wouldn't be looking for a fight, certainly not with the law. Need to keep them out of this. Near as I can tell, they got two bunkhouses out there. One on the north lodges the gunslingers and the south one sleeps the working hands. Of course, I'm guessing that the outlaws take watch shifts maybe two or three at a time during the night. If we could take them out, looks like we could trap the others in their bunkhouse. There's one man that sticks like glue to the feller that struts around like the head rooster on the place. Tall, lanky feller."

"That's likely Packer Osborne, the Tall T foreman. He seems to be the man Thomas Towne trusts most. Travels with him a lot I am told."

Capper finally spoke. "So, Morg, are you going to tell us what you want done tonight?"

"Priority is to arrest Thomas Towne, also known as Monte Oxford, and lock him up here. The man I know as 'Goober,' as well as George Vaughn, I want to keep in the county jail. I'd like to take Osborne into custody, too, and keep him separated from Towne. We'll arrest anybody else who resists us, but if they run, we're not going to try to chase them down. We just can't risk Towne escaping because we've spread ourselves too thin. I wish we could do this without firing a shot, but we're not likely to be that lucky. We'll talk more about this on the way and when we get near enough to get the lay of the building site."

It was nearly midnight when the posse members reined in their mounts a half mile from the Flying V headquarters, which was only several miles north of town.

Cloud cover was heavy this night, blocking any moon or starlight, and in the near blackness the men and horses were reduced to mere shadows. Morg had sent Deputy Fitzwater ahead to retrieve Homer Levis from his post in the hills above the ranch buildings, and he could make out two dark forms winding through the gap between the hills and moving their way like apparitions in the darkness.

When the riders approached, Morg nudged Buckshot out to meet them. "Well, Homer, what can you tell us about what we'll be dealing with when we move onto this place?"

"Well, after talking to Fitz, I understand better what's going on down there. Seems like a lot of confusion. Earlier, men kept coming out and looking down the road from town. Now, I understand they must have been looking for Vaughn to show up. They got four men outside playing sentries tonight, one by the main door to the house and another next to the back door. The other two just circle the house and pass by each other. They're all armed with rifles, of course."

"How many men in the house?"

"Three counting the head honcho. There's one of the regular crew that I'd call a gunslinger and then some tall feller that never gets more than twenty feet away from the boss it seems. There's a lamp burning in a room I'd guess is an office downstairs. I never see anybody pass by the curtains. Probably somebody in there that's got sense enough to stay away from the windows."

"Women and children?"

"Two little boys. Two women. Both were out with the kids this afternoon. An older woman and then a younger one, probably the mama. From the lamplights earlier, I would guess the bedrooms are upstairs, and it's a fair bet the women and kids are in bed."

"What about the bunkhouses?"

"Four hands in the south bunkhouse. The ones that don't seem to have work to do are in the north. Think I counted three go in there tonight."

"How close can we get before we're seen?"

"Head off a mile east and there's a cut through the hills that will take us up to the lots behind the stable. We can stake the horses when we get near the buildings, then go through the horse lots, into the stable and out the front. That's when it gets trickier."

Morg said, "Flint, I'd like you to go to the south bunk-house. The hands would probably recognize you. Just tell them to stay put and they'll be fine, then join the rest of us where you see the need. Fitz and Paul to the north bunkhouse. Keep those men out of the fight if you can. Declare they are arrested. Arnie, how are you with a rifle?"

"Better than most."

"I want you perched in the stable hayloft, ready to cut off anybody who makes a break for a horse. Homer, you know the layout better than the rest of us. I want you to come with me and Susana to take the house. Ned, you, too."

Later, when the posse reached the stable, Homer led the party single file through the maze of fenced lots into the rear entrance of the stable, a twenty-stall building with stalls almost fully occupied. Homer pointed to the ladder for Arnie to scale to position himself in the loft. He said, "For those headed out to the bunkhouses, go back to where we came in and follow the fence north. You're not likely to be seen behind the fence in the dark tonight. That will bring you up not far from the bunkhouses' rear doors. There's a privy back there they share, so the guards likely won't be spooked if they see somebody back there. I'd just move across the open one at a time."

Morg took over now. "Homer, can we see the front of the house from the stable?"

"Yeah, when you step outside. If you stay tight against the building, guards ain't likely to see you. Them in the back won't for sure."

"I'm going to go have a talk with the fella at the front door. The guy in back will likely stay put, but it's the moving guards that could show up anytime. I'd like to have the rest of you fan out ten or twelve paces behind me. If anybody raises a rifle, take them down before they squeeze the trigger. From here on, we just play the game however it unfolds."

They waited a short time to give the others time to secure the bunkhouse and then stepped out of the stable. Morg surveyed the front of the two-story house, which he guessed would be thirty or more yards distant. He could make out a black lump on the veranda that he assumed was a man. He hoped that the bunkhouses were secure by now and was pleased that no shots had been fired yet. "Let's get it done," he said, and started walking casually toward the house, his rifle cradled in his arm like he had no immediate purpose for the weapon. He noted that Susana, who had been silent most of the night, was off to his left with the shotgun ready to be raised at a moment's notice. At this distance, it would not do much good, but the night was not over.

As they neared the house, the lump on the veranda moved and formed into something resembling a man. Morg yelled, "Hi there. Need to talk to you, friend."

The man readied his rifle and moved to the edge of the porch. "Who the hell are you?" Then he saw the others, and hollered, "Help at the front!" raising his rifle to fire in the same instant Susana's shotgun roared. He tumbled off the porch.

A rifle fired to Morg's right and he saw another man go down at the side of the house. He turned to seek out Susana. She was shoving another shell into the shotgun as she hurried to his side. "The door," he said. "We've got to get in there." They rushed onto the porch, and he turned the doorknob. Locked.

"Stand aside," Susana yelled.

He stepped back, and the shotgun blast left a splintered hole where the knob and a chunk of the door had been. He kicked open what still hung onto the hinges and stepped in. A pistol cracked off to his left boring into the wall above his head. He squeezed the trigger on his Winchester. Nothing. Jammed. "Stay back!" he yelled at Susana as he drew his Colt and went to his knees an instant before another of the gunman's slugs passed through the air he had just vacated. He aimed, fired twice. The shooter's weapon clattered on the floor, and he appeared to take a step toward Morg before he crumpled and collapsed.

The shotgun roared again, stinging Morg's ears as it echoed through the room. He turned and saw Susana calmly pressing in a shell again. There was still intermittent gunfire outside, but it seemed distant. He got to his feet and looked around for the location of the moaning and spotted the big man in the lighted doorway. He stepped nearer and recognized the wounded man as Packer Osborne. His shoulder and side were blood-soaked, but he was alive.

He heard a desk drawer slam shut in the lighted room behind Osborne and readied his Colt again. "Towne, are you in there? Raise your hands and step out where I can see you." He sensed Susana behind him. "I want this one alive," he said. "Towne!" he yelled.

The unmistakable sound of a gun exploded from the room where he thought he had Towne cornered, then the crash of furniture falling and a loud thump. Morg stepped over the moaning Packer Osborne and into the room where he found Townes' twisted body next to a fallen office chair and handgun, what was left of his head draining blood from the entry throat wound and the ragged exit hole at the top of his skull. He would not be taking Monte Oxford and Thomas Towne alive.

Chapter 49

THE GUNFIRE HAD ceased outside, and the house was consumed by silence until the shrieking started. He turned and saw May on the floor cradling Packer Osborne's head in her arms. The ever-practical Susana was tearing off his shirt and ministering to the wounds that appeared to be primarily on the shoulder and ribcage. The shotgun blast had not centered on Osborne's body, and he knew that buckshot because of the spread often made wounds look more serious than they were.

May looked up at him, eyes spitting hate and fire. "You son-of-a-bitch. If you killed him, I'll get you and finish what Thomas tried to do."

Strange, she had seen Towne on the floor and offered only a glance. Packer Osborne was the object of her concern.

"I shot him," Susana said. "He was going to shoot Morgan. I had no choice, and I am not sorry."

"Just who are you anyway?"

"I am Susana Fraser, Deputy U.S. Marshal. It appears to me that Mister Packer Osborne will live if he gets a doctor's attention soon. I will get most of the bleeding stopped, but the shoulder's going to be left a mess, I imagine. And I hear children crying upstairs. Morg, I will help the lady here if you want to see how things are outside. A buckboard for this man would be mighty helpful, and maybe you could find one of your men who knows some doctoring to help here, so Missus Towne and I can tend to her boys."

"Yes, ma'am. That sounds like an excellent idea." He slipped back through the doorway and stumbled over furniture to locate the man he had taken down in the parlor and knelt and confirmed the man's death. When he went outside, he was met by Sheriff Capper who was just stepping onto the veranda.

"I was getting worried, Morg. Awful quiet in there except for some kids' crying. Everything alright?"

"Could be worse. Could be better. I was hoping to take Towne or Oxford or whatever his name is alive. I did not."

"Had to kill him?"

"Did it himself."

"I'll be danged. So the feller we were going to hang with all these witnesses is dead?"

"Yeah. How are our people doing?"

"Nothing too serious. Your deputy Fitz got his ear nicked, and Arnie's got a bandana wrapped around his head and ear till Doc can stitch it. I told him they might have to amputate, and he didn't find it funny. More serious, O'Keefe took a slug in his right thigh. Arnie got a tourniquet on it to stop the bleeding."

"That kid Arnie know something about doctoring?"

"That so-called kid did a stint in the Army and was trained for the Ambulance Corps, worked in Army hospitals and such for three years."

"I'll be danged. Send him into the house, will you? Susana's got an outlaw in there that needs some help. So how did the outside do?"

"Four dead, four prisoners."

"Add two more dead in the house and one wounded. We'll need a buckboard for the wounded man."

"Already getting one ready for O'Keefe. We can crowd in two. Fellers are bringing up our horses and saddling some for the prisoners. We'll get the dead all drug to a shed over by the stable. I'll send the undertaker out in the morning. He'll see pictures get took, so we can find out if there's paper out on any of the dead ones. Of course, we'll check all the prisoners, too. You may have given us a gold mine, Morg."

"How about tracking Arnie down first. Susana could use some help in the house."

"Oh, yeah, I'll tend to that." The sheriff turned away and headed toward the stable.

Morg walked about the ranch yard talking to the men and thanking them for their good work. He found Deputy Fitzwater with Homer Levis leaning against a huge cottonwood tree in the yard smoking cigarettes. Fitz had his free hand pressed against his right ear.

"How are you doing, Fitz?"

"Guess I won't die. Not sure I even need a doc. I'll see how the ear looks in the morning. A few more inches the wrong way and I wouldn't be standing here. What am I going to do with all the prisoners?"

"Sheriff plans to claim the reward money. Let him keep all but Vaughn and Packer Osborne—he's wounded and will be hauled to the doctor. I don't think there will be federal charges on any of the others, but I'd wire the marshal's service in Denver and ask them to send somebody here to review the case. Maybe they got something we don't know about."

"You sound like you're about to wash your hands of this."

"Yep, I'll be in town a couple days and will check in. Before I leave town, I'll drop off that deputy's badge and a dented and tarnished U.S. Marshal's badge. On second thought, I think they'll be lost. Kennedy already has my signed resignation. Are you okay with that?"

"I don't know nothing about any badges."

He returned to the house and found Capper again, helping himself to a shot of whiskey in the kitchen. "Want a snort?" he asked.

"No thanks. Stomach doesn't handle whiskey too well at night."

"Yeah, I hear that happens to some old people. The bodies have been drug to the shed and that Osborne feller is on his way to the doctor's. That tough lady you call your wife is upstairs if you were wondering, helping settle the woman and her kids. I talked to Missus Vaughn. She's kind of one of them recluses. Stays away from people. She won't come down till everybody's gone unless you've got to see her."

"Nope, I'm declaring myself off the case. I'd like to have you hold all the prisoners except Vaughn and Osborne until the marshal's office says they're done. You can afford to."

"Yeah, I suppose. Well, I guess I'll be heading out with what's left of my outfit. Can you and the lady find your way back to the hotel without an escort? By the way, if the pretty lady that puts up with you ever wants to get acquainted with a real man, you tell her to get word to old Flint."

"The last I knew, old Flint was a married man."

"Dang, I near forgot, and it's been going on thirty-five years now."

"It's been good seeing you, Flint. Take care of yourself."

"You too, pard."

Morg paced the floor another half hour before Susana came down the stairs. She looked as tired and drawn as he had ever seen her. She came up and wrapped her arms around him, holding him tight. He did not know what to say, so he joined the embrace and kissed the top of her head. She stepped back and looked up at him with sad eyes. "We can go now, if you are ready."

"Everybody has gone, but Homer said he would leave our horses saddled and tied to the hitching rail out front."

When they got to town, Morg suggested Susana dismount in front of the hotel and go to their room while he took the horses to the livery. When he returned, he found her asleep on the bed. She didn't even wake up when he pulled her boots off and with no small effort tucked her under the covers. Shortly he joined her.

It was midmorning when he woke, and still wearing the previous night's clothing, Susana was sitting on the side of the bed looking at him. "I have ordered hot water for the tub. You can join me for a bath if you like. I thought we could forego breakfast and go directly to lunch."

"Excellent idea. We didn't get to talk last night. I might not be with you in the hotel this morning if you had not backed me up at the Flying V. You sure impressed Flint."

"There's only one man I want to impress."

"If it's me, you did."

They shared the cramped but deep claw-footed bath-tub, but Morg could barely walk when he finally lifted himself out of the tub. Susana had more than a bath in mind when she suggested they bathe together, once again adding to the new experiences he was tallying with this woman. After he shaved, they dressed and strolled to the hotel dining room. As they ate steak and baked pota-toes, Susana initiated a conversation concerning a sub-ject he had to admit he was curious about.

"You haven't asked about my time with your former wife."

"I figured you'd tell me if there was anything I needed to know."

"I didn't press her for information, but it was obvious she was worried about the ranch foreman Packer Osborne. She asked if I knew any lawyers in North Platte that might help both she and Osborne. I recommended my lawyer, Audra Adams. She's in partnership with her husband here."

"Audra handles my legal business, too. She and her husband Ari are building quite a following."

"It appears that May will not suffer financially from her husband's death regardless of any arrangement her late husband made. She said the ranch is already titled in her name. That was a condition for her marrying him, but she insists she will never return there. She also has stashed away money over the years, but she claims to know nothing about Thomas Towne's other investments except they are seemingly endless."

Morg said, "The illegal enterprises will likely close down on their own, but there will probably be legal claims against others. A law firm in Omaha evidently handled his legal matters. She and the boys will likely end up with anything that's left. Anyway, May appears to be looking after herself."

"She did ask that I inquire whether Jaye Boyden would consider leasing the ranch and buying the cow herd. She wanted him to do something with the dogs, too."

"Towne knew about her relationship with Osborne, didn't he?"

"I find that very likely."

"Towne wasn't the kind of man to tolerate that unless he didn't care or even approved. If females were not his preference, marriage would at least have made him more respectable in business circles."

Susana said, "Or if he liked little girls..." She stopped abruptly. "Anyway, he's dead, and it's no longer our concern."

Morg suspected that Susana knew more than she was revealing, but he shrugged it off. "I think the man was crazy at the end."

"May said it started with an obsession over the death of his brother. She didn't know the details and had never met the brother. They lived a very strange life together. I turned my attention to explaining to the boys that their father was gone and comforting them as best I could. They were devastated for a short time but rebounded more quickly than I would have expected. They were very concerned about Osborne."

"I'd be willing to bet that he is their real father, even if they don't know. I suspect Osborne was the man who swept May off her feet before Towne entered the picture. There was a deal of some sort. But it's nothing to me. Other folks can sort out all these messes. I think the marshals are going to be busy for a long time unscrambling

Monte Oxford's businesses and that lawyers are going to be making a lot of money."

"You really are stepping away from this, aren't you?"

"Yep, I think it's time for us to turn to some deal-making of our own."

Chapter 50

JAYE AND SHEENA sat on the leather couch at the J Bar B ranch house. Sheena had brought lunch over from Susana's and fed the whole crew. Thankfully, Sheena thought, Luke had persuaded Andy to ride with him to check the herd in the east pasture. She wanted time alone with Jaye, and that had been hard to come by the past week.

"The food was scrumptious," Jaye said, leaning back with his splinted leg stretched in front of him and resting on a coffee table.

"You know as well as I do that Helga prepared most of it, but she is teaching me. I'll be a cook yet. There is so much to learn, but I'm a teacher, and I'm supposed to love learning."

"I'm just glad you make the time to come over, and I'll never forget you spent the first three nights here after I broke the dang leg."

"I wanted to be here, and it's so good to see you getting around on the crutches now."

"Yeah, thanks to the crutches Luke carved out with an axe and knife, I've got solid support."

"They look like the Tall T brand."

"I guess they do at that. Anyhow, I'll be fine, but I'm going crazy with no word from your dad or Susana."

"They have no way to reach us here so far from telegraph service. We don't even know where they're at. It's likely Denver. Jaye, I'm going to change the subject. I'd like to talk about us." She could see she had caught him unprepared.

"Well, I'm glad to do that. I've tried for several years, but you always cut the topic short. You know how I feel about you."

"And I'm guilty of keeping you off balance. Just hear me out. Jaye, I no longer have dreams of leaving the Sandhills. This is where I belong, but I don't want to get married for another year. I want to complete a school year teaching at Susana's. I still need to get my head all straightened out about things, but I'm getting there."

"I'm listening."

"I was thinking that you could court me if you wanted."

"Court you? I don't know exactly how to do that, but I'll try if it's a way to get you to marry me."

"I wouldn't be living with you, of course, but we would carve out alone time somehow. We could go fishing together, take a blanket and lunch. Who knows what might happen while we're waiting for fish to bite?" She just could not pretend anymore. She had been with another man. She wanted Jaye now, and she knew it was love she felt for him.

"Are you suggesting what I think you are?"

"But if I get with child, you will marry me promptly."

"You've got a standing proposal, and I will start the courting this minute if you like."

She scooted nearer, their lips touched, and she placed a teasing hand on his thigh.

"As soon as you can get around well enough to take me fishing." She kissed him again, this time deeply. Then Dingo started barking outside. She pulled away and got up from the couch. "Somebody's here. I'll see who it is. Strange, though, I thought Dingo was with Andy and Luke."

She opened the door and saw an empty buckboard before she caught sight of the man on his knees accepting kisses from the Australian cattle dog that had crawled upon his chest and had paws pressed upon his shoulders. Then she saw Susana walking her way.

She hurried out and embraced her friend. "Susana, we've been so worried."

"We stopped by the house, and Helga said you were here. We loaded some of my things, dropped them off at Morgan's and headed over here."

"I don't understand. Why did you take some of your things to Dad's house?" Susana held up her left hand, and Sheena immediately saw the gold band on the ring finger. "Oh, my Lord, you didn't?"

"We did. We went to the county courthouse in North Platte and did the paperwork and then I got your father into the Methodist Church there and we were married by the preacher, Reverand Locke, an old friend of mine from his days on the circuit. I'm your stepmother now, but I promise not to be like Cinderella's."

Sheena was stunned but happily so, and when her father came up beside Susana, she threw herself into his arms. "Oh, Dad, I'm so glad you're back safely—you and Susana, and I couldn't be happier for you. I love you so much, both of you."

She stepped back. "I see Andy riding like the wind this way. He must have seen you on the road, and Dingo took off ahead of him."

Susana said, "And now we've got to tell him his schoolteacher is moving into the house."

"When you are finished with Andy come on into the house and see Jaye."

"I'm right here, but come on in."

She started and turned to see Jaye standing behind her propped on his crutches. Morg said, "Helga filled us in on the broken leg. We'll come in for a spell, but I've got a feeling it will take some days to cover all we've got to talk about, and there's work to be done along the Dismal Trail."

About the Author

Ron Schwab is the author of several popular Western series, including *The Blood Hounds*, *Lockwood*, *The Coyote Saga*, and *The Lockes*. His novels *Grit* and *Old Dogs* were both awarded the Western Fictioneers Peacemaker Award for Best Western Novel, and Cut Nose was a finalist for the Western Writers of America Best Western Historical Novel.

Ron and his wife, Bev, divide their time between their home in Fairbury, Nebraska and their cabin in the Kansas Flint Hills.

For more information about Ron Schwab and his books, you may visit the author's website at www.Ron-SchwabBooks.com.

Made in United States
Troutdale, OR
04/20/2025